MONUMENT TO THE DEAD

Sheila Connolly

BERKLEY PRIME CRIME, NEW YORK

THE BERKLEY PUBLISHING GROUP
Published by the Penguin Group
Penguin Group (USA) Inc.
375 Hudson Street, New York, New York 10014, USA

USA | Canada | UK | Ireland | Australia | New Zealand | India | South Africa | China

Penguin Books Ltd., Registered Offices: 80 Strand, London WC2R 0RL, England
For more information about the Penguin Group, visit penguin.com.

MONUMENT TO THE DEAD

A Berkley Prime Crime Book / published by arrangement with the author

Berkley Prime Crime Books are published by The Berkley Publishing Group.
BERKLEY® PRIME CRIME and the PRIME CRIME logo are
trademarks of Penguin Group (USA) Inc.

For information, address: The Berkley Publishing Group,
a division of Penguin Group (USA) Inc.,
375 Hudson Street, New York, New York 10014.

ISBN: 978-0-425-25712-8

PUBLISHING HISTORY
Berkley Prime Crime mass-market edition / June 2013

PRINTED IN THE UNITED STATES OF AMERICA

10 9 8 7 6 5 4 3

Cover illustration by Ross Jones.
Cover design by Rita Frangie.
Interior text design by Laura K. Corless.

ALWAYS LEARNING   **PEARSON**

continued . . .

"*National Treasure* meets *The Philadelphia Story* in this clever, charming, and sophisticated caper. When murder and mayhem become the main attractions at a prestigious museum, its feisty fundraiser goes undercover to prove it's not just the museum's pricey collection that's concealing a hidden history. Secrets, lies, and a delightful revenge conspiracy make this a real page-turner!"

—Hank Phillippi Ryan, Agatha, Anthony, and Macavity award–winning author of *The Other Woman*

"Sheila Connolly's wonderful new series is a witty, engaging blend of history and mystery with a smart sleuth who already feels like a good friend. Like all of Ms. Connolly's books, *Fundraising the Dead* is hard to put down. Her stories always keep me turning pages—often well past my bedtime."

—Julie Hyzy, *New York Times* bestselling author of the White House Chef Mysteries

Praise for the Orchard Mysteries

"Sheila Connolly's Orchard Mysteries are some of the most satisfying cozy mysteries I've read . . . Warm and entertaining from the first paragraph to the last. Fans will look forward to the next Orchard Mystery."

—*Lesa's Book Critiques*

"An enjoyable and well-written book with some excellent apple recipes at the end." —*Cozy Library*

"The mystery is intelligent and has an interesting twist . . . *Rotten to the Core* is a fun, quick read with an enjoyable heroine." —*The Mystery Reader* (four stars)

"Delightful . . . [A] fascinating whodunit filled with surprises." —*The Mystery Gazette*

"[A] delightful new series." —*Gumshoe Review*

Berkley Prime Crime titles by Sheila Connolly

Orchard Mysteries

ONE BAD APPLE
ROTTEN TO THE CORE
RED DELICIOUS DEATH
A KILLER CROP
BITTER HARVEST
SOUR APPLES
GOLDEN MALICIOUS
PICKED TO DIE

Museum Mysteries

FUNDRAISING THE DEAD
LET'S PLAY DEAD
FIRE ENGINE DEAD
MONUMENT TO THE DEAD
RAZING THE DEAD

County Cork Mysteries

BURIED IN A BOG
SCANDAL IN SKIBBEREEN

Specials

DEAD LETTERS
AN OPEN BOOK

ACKNOWLEDGMENTS

While this is a fictional story, Edwin Forrest was quite real: he was the first great American-born stage star, and he was born and died in Philadelphia. The majority of the historic detail I've included in the book is accurate. Forrest as a person was a marvelous character, and long after death his legacy to both Philadelphia and the American stage lives on—I couldn't write about historic Philadelphia and not include him.

For several years I worked at The Historical Society of Pennsylvania, where much of Forrest's memorabilia could be found, including the imposing statue of Forrest in one of his favorite stage roles, Shakespeare's *Coriolanus*. The statue has found a new home at the Walnut Street Theater in Philadelphia, where Forrest made his formal stage debut in 1820.

The Forrest Trust and the Edwin Forrest Home for Retired Actors also existed, though no more. The Forrest Home now houses the Freedom Theater in Philadelphia. To the best of my knowledge, none of the members of the Trust died under suspicious circumstances.

I am grateful to the Historical Society for providing such a wealth of information. I also can't let another book go by without acknowledging Sandra Cadwalader, former HSP board member and, I hope, friend, who has finally figured out who she is in the series.

As always, thanks go to my agent, Jessica Faust of Book-Ends Ltd., and my tireless editor, Shannon Jamieson Vazquez of Berkley Prime Crime. Thanks also to Sisters in Crime and the amazing Guppies, the best cheerleaders a mystery writer could have!

The actor's popularity is evanescent; applauded today, forgotten tomorrow.

—Edwin Forrest

CHAPTER 1

Adeline Harrison was dead.

I couldn't remember when I first started reading the obituaries in the paper, but now I did it daily, and that's how I saw the news.

I had unfurled my morning paper as my commuter train rumbled out of the Bryn Mawr station. It seemed almost a shame to spend the ride reading when the June weather outside was so perfect. It seemed a shame to be inside at all, but I had a demanding job, and there was no way I could take a "nice weather" day, not when I was president of the Pennsylvania Antiquarian Society. I had to set a good example for the rest of my staff, and we'd already had a "spring fever" party of sorts, on the outdoor balcony adjacent to the staff room. I made a bargain with myself: I'd read the paper until we came close to the city of Philadelphia, then I would allow myself to enjoy the view of the Schuylkill River where the train tracks ran alongside it, before the tracks plunged into and then under the city itself.

I scanned the front page for new crises, then turned to the Local section. As a member of the cultural community of the greater Philadelphia area, I had to keep my eye on cultural and other events that might affect the Society, not to mention opportunities to take advantage of new trends and new funding. We had a meager endowment and received little funding from the city itself, so I always had to be ready to sic my development staff on any opportunity that presented itself. And I had begun to read the obituaries—not out of ghoulishness, but because our board, our donors, and most of our members are well past the half-century mark. I regret the passing of each one, though selfishly, I always hope that the Society would be remembered in their wills. Of course, that remembrance could take the form of family heirlooms (possible treasure, but equally possible of only sentimental value), or it could be a financial bequest (much more welcome).

Today yielded only one such notice: former board member Adeline Harrison. She had left the board not long after I had first joined the Society as director of development a few years ago, but I remembered her for her alertness, her surprising grasp of our collections, and her kindness to everyone. I was surprised to see that she had been eighty-six years old; I would have thought her at least a decade younger. The obituary was long and glowing; she had been a member of many local institutions over the past few decades. I made a mental note to send some sort of condolence, or at least delegate Shelby Carver to handle it. Shelby had taken over my position as director of development when I was bumped upstairs (down the hall, more accurately) to Society president. With her well-bred southern background, Shelby was very good at following up on such social niceties.

I looked up to find the train skirting the Schuylkill River, so I put aside my paper. There were a few scullers out on the water, catching the cool of the morning. The Dad Vail Regatta was a few weeks past; then the river had been crowded with competing sculls. Now it was peaceful, and as always, it reminded me of Philadelphia artist Thomas Eakins's sculling pictures. If you stood in just the right place on the banks, it didn't look much changed from Eakins's day.

The train stopped at 30th Street Station, and then we went underground. I got out at Suburban Station and climbed the stairs out into the fresh air of City Hall Plaza. Well, as fresh as Center City air could be, but this early in the day it was still fairly clean. I set off, glad for the walk to the Society. I stopped for a cappuccino before I mounted the stone steps and pulled open the heavy metal door. Front Desk Bob, a former policeman but quiet about it, was already in place behind the reception desk, getting ready for a new day, and we nodded at each other as I headed for the elevator to the third floor where the administrative offices were. While I waited for our lone, elderly elevator to make its stately way to the ground floor, I saluted the monumental statue of Edwin Forrest, which stood guard over the hallway. Edwin had been a superstar in his day, a larger-than-life actor who had risen from the slums of Philadelphia to command adoring audiences all over the United States and even Europe, scattering scandals in his wake. The statue was also larger than life (the sculptor had kindly added a couple of inches to Edwin's actual physical stature), and the actor appeared dressed in Roman garb as Coriolanus, one of his favorite Shakespearean roles. It had been occupying its rather dreary location since before I began working at the Society, but I had become increasingly fond of him since I had taken over running the Society. At least he didn't complain or demand something from me, the way some of my employees did.

It was still barely past eight thirty, but I liked to allow myself some quiet time to prepare for whatever my day might hold, to check my never-ending to-do list and to look through any messages that had come in after I left. Eric, my assistant, wasn't at his desk yet, but since his jacket was draped over his chair, I assumed he must be down the hall in the staff room. He liked to control the coffee-making process, and since I enjoyed the results, I wasn't about to stop him. Eric and I had worked out a deal when he had started working for me: whoever arrived first would start the coffee. I didn't want to stick him into an antiquated administrative assistant role, but I had to say that the quality was greatly improved now that he was making it at least part of the time. In any case, he usually beat me to it.

"Hey, lady!" Shelby said, dropping into the eighteenth-century damask-covered settee on the wall opposite my desk.

"Hi, Shelby. You're in early. Any particular reason?"

Shelby grinned. "Probably the same as you; I wanted a little quiet time. Besides, it was such a pretty day that I couldn't stand staying inside a minute longer, so I walked over."

I knew that Shelby lived on the other side of Independence Hall, and sometimes I envied her that walk, so rich with history. Okay, I had the giant wedding cake that was City Hall to admire, but otherwise my walk led me past prosaic stores and restaurants. "I hear you! I felt the same way myself." I took a long drink of my cappuccino and sighed. "Anything we need to worry about?"

"No, ma'am," Shelby replied promptly. "Oh, did you hear about Adeline Harrison?"

"I saw the obituary in the paper this morning. Did you know her?"

"Not from the Society, but we'd crossed paths now and then at other events. She was always very kind and remembered me from one time to the next, which I can't say about many of the older people I meet around here. Should I send flowers?"

"I think the family asked for contributions to one of her pet causes in lieu of flowers, and I don't think we're in any position to send money. But do see that we send a nice card. I'll sign it."

"Of course. See you later."

Shelby left, but the early morning spell was broken. Another week had begun . . . following a memorable weekend. I hadn't done much, but what I had done had been in the company of Special Agent James Morrison of the FBI, so I really hadn't cared what we did. James and I had been seeing each other seriously for a couple of months now, but neither of us was hurrying the relationship. We both led busy lives, with schedules that resulted in as many canceled dates as not, on both sides. But neither of us was in the first flush of youth, so we weren't impatient. And I was loving every minute of it.

James was . . . something special. Neither of us had said the *L* word yet. We were so cautious, so careful. He had never been married, even though he was past forty; I'd been married once before, in what seemed like another lifetime. When that had ended, without acrimony, I'd never looked for another long-term relationship. I'd been close to a few other men, but generally we had understood and respected each other's boundaries. But with James, I was finding I had to take another look at those boundaries. Especially since we didn't have any more professional conflicts to deal with at the moment. We'd first come together when a significant theft at the Society had been discovered, and been thrown together over various crimes within the cultural community since then. After the most recent problem, James and I had mutually decided that it was silly to keep waiting for external events to do the work for us, and started "dating." The pace felt almost old-fashioned, but hey, I work in a history museum, and he works for the government, so slow and stately suited us both.

Looking over today's agenda, I saw no official meetings, although plenty of official business to attend to—signing solicitation letters, reviewing grant proposals that Shelby prepared, looking over the list of prospective donors and/or board members to see who needed a personal touch again. And then there was the kindergarten.

Well, that was what I called the area where three of our youngest hires worked together in the third-floor workroom. Only a few months earlier, I had hired a new registrar, Nicholas Naylor, and taken on a new intern, Alice Price, at the same time. Their simultaneous arrival had coincided with the arrival of an extraordinary number of historic documents, artifacts, and who knows what—all courtesy of the FBI, which had seized the various items throughout the course of several investigations, dumped them in the Society's lap, and asked us to figure out what they had. We had taken the path of least resistance and put the bountiful collections together in the Society's largest processing space along with the new hires and turned them loose. I stopped in periodically to check on the progress they were making and to make sure they were on track. Collections weren't my area of expertise—that role belonged to our vice president of collections, Latoya Anderson—but although Latoya was their immediate supervisor, since I had been indirectly responsible for the temporary presence of the FBI materials, I wanted to keep tabs on it. Besides, it was fun to see what they turned up, and I always welcomed the opportunity to visit our collections. And since Latoya was away on a long-postponed research vacation, it fell to me to keep an eye on things. Or so I told myself.

Nicholas, a quiet young man in his late twenties with almost Byronic good looks, had been recruited by Latoya to fill the important staff position of registrar. He had previously been working at the University of Pennsylvania, where he had developed a state-of-the-art cataloging system that he had been itching to try on our collections. Since most of our cataloging was mired in the nineteenth century, we'd agreed to give him a chance, and he had made great strides in imposing order on our processing in the short time he'd been here.

The intern was a lovely self-possessed young woman named Alice Price, who had come with strings attached. Her uncle, a well-connected local philanthropist, had promised to fund her salary if we took her on. I had no problem with that, since we'd been planning to recruit her uncle for a board position sometime soon, and doing him the favor of hiring Alice would be . . . helpful. Luckily, Alice had also turned out to be smart and hardworking, and despite her lack of job experience, she had settled in well and was pulling her weight.

The third member of the group was Rich Girard, a part-time postgrad student who'd been hired a couple of years earlier to help catalog the Terwilliger Collection, a massive assortment of documents encompassing everything from the arrival on these shores by the earliest Terwilliger family member in the early eighteenth century to the elaborate business maneuvers of twentieth-century Terwilligers. The gift of the documents had come from several generations of the family, all connected to the Society. The current board member, Marty Terwilliger, was my benefactor, ally, and friend.

Marty was about ten years older than I was and had little patience for fools or fancy dress. She was also smart, determined, and tenacious, which was why she was such a great ally. And she simply couldn't stay away from the Society—not that I blamed her. She was deeply committed to the place, and also related to half of Philadelphia, including James Morrison, to whom she had introduced me. Marty had a finger in every pie in the city and the surrounding counties.

She'd divorced a couple of husbands and had never had kids, so she had plenty of free time to devote to the collections. I was always coming across her in odd corners of the stacks (as a board member, she had a key and free access).

Which was why I wasn't surprised when I found her with the young'uns in the processing room when I walked in. "Good morning, everyone! You all look busy. You keeping an eye on them, Marty?"

"Of course I am. Half of this stuff is the Terwilliger papers."

I settled myself on a stool. I had requested that Latoya and I get basic progress reports on a weekly basis—mainly details like how many items had been processed and what kind—and the trio had been good about doing so. The most recent report was probably sitting in my email in-box at the moment. But reading about something and sitting in the midst of it while talking to its processors were not the same thing, and I liked to check on how they were getting along with each other, and kind of take the temperature of the room. Rich was laid-back, Alice was eager, and Nicholas was . . . an enigma. He was polite and cooperative, but he seldom volunteered a comment or personal fact. Still, he'd walked into a mess—his predecessor had worked for the Society for decades but had only just started transferring our massive quantity of records to a modern digital format before he'd unexpectedly died—and Nicholas had done an amazing job of creating order out of chaos, so I wasn't about to complain if he wasn't warm and cuddly. He was getting the job done.

The group gathered round and showed off their new finds, and Marty and I nodded approval. We were actually ahead of schedule, and we had a handle on what we were working with. Life was good.

Reluctantly I stood up. "I'd better get back to my office. Great job, all of you!"

"I'll come with you," Marty said. "I want to talk to you."

Somehow that was never good news, I reflected as we walked down the hall together, back to my corner office. When we'd both found seats, I said, "What's up?"

Marty gave a snort of laughter. "You look like I'm about to hand you some nasty medicine. I'm not always the bearer of bad tidings, am I?"

"Let's say the jury's still out on that. Was there something specific you needed?"

"Nope. I just wanted to say how well it's been going, our taking on the materials the FBI reclaimed and bringing in those two to work on them. Never hurts to have a favor owed to us by the FBI, you know."

"Especially since we've created so much trouble for them in the past?"

"Yeah, well, there is that. But on average they've come out ahead, so everybody should be happy. You and Jimmy doing okay?" Since they were cousins, Marty could call him "Jimmy" and get away with it, while he twitted her by calling her "Martha," which she hated. Me, I preferred to call him James—more fitting for a dignified FBI agent.

"We're doing fine, thank you very much, and that's all I'm going to say." I smiled at her.

She smiled back. "Okay, I won't pry." She bounced up abruptly. "I'm headed back to the processing room before I lose the thread of what I was doing. See you around."

"Bye, Marty," I said as she disappeared. I heard the phone on Eric's desk ring, and in a moment he came to the doorway. "Agent Morrison for you," he said, pulling the door closed as he retreated. Eric was still fairly new at his job as my assistant, but he'd quickly made himself indispensable, and his polite southern accent soothed a lot of my more demanding callers. He'd long since picked up on my relationship with Special Agent James, although he couldn't always tell whether James's calls were business or personal.

James's ears must be buzzing, I thought as I picked up the phone. "Good morning, Agent Morrison. How can I help you?"

"Good morning to you, Ms. Pratt. Though maybe not as good as yesterday morning," James said. Yesterday morning, we'd awakened together. He cleared his throat. "Actually, this is business, or almost business. Sorry to be so vague, but what can you tell me about Adeline Harrison?"

"Mainly what I read in her obituary this morning. I knew her, but only slightly. We met maybe two or three times, when I first started at the Society, but she was on her way out then. It was a gracious exit—I think she felt she'd outlived her usefulness to us, or maybe she was cutting back on all her activities. She wasn't exactly young."

"Tough old stock, though. I'm guessing you'll have a file on her?" James asked.

"Of course. She used to be a board member here. We keep files on all former, current, and potential future members."

"Can you take a look at hers and give me the high points?"

"You want it now?"

"No rush—how about after work? Meet me at the hotel bar on the corner?"

I mentally reviewed my schedule. Blissfully empty.

"Sounds good. I'll make copies of what I find. But you didn't tell me why you wanted to know." Although based on the knot in the pit of my stomach, I had a feeling I could guess. The FBI wasn't usually idly curious about death from natural causes.

"I think Adeline Harrison was murdered."

CHAPTER 2

James's office was on the other side of Market Street and several blocks toward the Delaware River, but the hotel bar he'd suggested was right around the corner from the Society at Broad Street. I didn't mind being James's peephole into the cultural activities of the greater Philadelphia region, and I was happy to provide him with whatever information I could, but I could see that if his superiors knew of our personal relationship, they might suggest that one or the other activity should stop. I didn't want to put James in a position to have to make that choice—or put myself there, either, for that matter.

I finished up my paperwork and made it to the bar before James and snagged a table. I ordered a glass of wine and watched the door for his arrival. I will admit that I sometimes indulged in a little private pleasure, watching him when he didn't know I was doing it. He was good to look at: not so striking that he drew stares (anonymity was useful in his work), but he filled out his clothes nicely, with a hint of hidden strength. He moved as though he was secure in his skin, which I admired. Me, I was always worrying about those last five pounds, and I mainly settled for looking competent and professional.

I saw James walk in and pause to scan the room, before lighting on the table where I sat. Then he smiled like he meant it. As he made his way over to the table and sat down, a twentysomething server appeared in about fifteen seconds to take his order, then left, swinging her hips just the slightest bit. To his credit, I don't think James noticed, because he'd already turned back to me.

"We must stop meeting like this," I drawled. "I feel like a spy in some bad sixties movie. Am I supposed to slip you the secret microchip or what?"

"Hey, that's before my time, Nell, and yours, too." He laughed. "Most spies these days send their information electronically in encrypted files, or so I've heard. I was only looking for some background, and it's more fun talking to you than Googling the deceased."

His drink arrived and we both took a brief time-out to fortify ourselves. Then I said, "Why don't you tell me what you're looking for?"

James contemplated the depths of his drink for a few seconds before responding. "Nell, I've got a bad feeling about this."

Even though I'd been expecting something like this, his statement chilled me: if he was worried, then I should be, too. "Why?" I prompted.

"Maybe being around you has made me more sensitive to anything to do with the cultural community, but I get nervous when the people involved start dying."

"What was suspicious about Adeline's death?" Then the fuller meaning of his words hit me. "Wait a minute. You said 'people,' as in more than one person?"

"Tell me what you've got on Adeline first, and then I'll fill you in."

"All right. You know that Adeline was a former Society board member, so of course we have a full file on her. She's been a consistent supporter since she left the board, and she came to the occasional event. There's nothing out of the ordinary in her file for someone of her age and social profile. Widowed, left comfortably off. No children. A nice home, inherited, filled with some lovely things, or so say the notes in her file—I was never in the house. We're hoping for a modest bequest from her estate, but we weren't her only interest, so whatever she left may be spread around. Does that tell you anything?"

"It's more or less what I expected."

"Then what are you looking for? When you called me up to ask for background information, I had to assume it wasn't just a burglar breaking into her home or a mugging on the street."

He nodded. "What I've learned corresponds to what you just said. Adeline Harrison lived in an old home out in Delaware County. Lived alone, but she had someone in to clean for her twice a week. No local family checking in with her regularly, although she has some scattered grandnieces and -nephews. The cleaning woman found her when she arrived in the morning, two days ago. I got the preliminary results for the postmortem from the county ME a couple of hours later. No sign of trauma, but of course the toxicology reports will take a while."

"Poor woman. What leads you to think it was murder?"

James sat back in his chair. "I wouldn't have, except that I remembered another case in New Jersey, a few months ago—one Frederick Van Deusen. Ring any bells?" When I shook my head, he went on, "Same scenario: older person but male, socially connected but no near relatives, active in good works and was or had been on a couple of nonprofit boards, no sign of trauma. It certainly could have been a natural death, and no one would have thought twice about it. But since it was an unattended death, a full autopsy was done. Nothing out of place in the man's toxicology screen, just the usual medications a person of his age would be taking, all duly prescribed, although some of the levels seemed a bit high. By the time anyone became suspicious, there was no crime scene to check—the house had already been cleaned up and was on the market."

"Anyone being you, I take it? What made you think there was anything suspicious about this death?"

He smiled to himself. "Since I've met you, I've been more aware of the extended cultural community around here—I've got a computer program set up to search on certain specific terms, and I take a quick look at whatever pops up. Van Deusen fit the profile. That's why I took a second look at the case, and why I noticed the elevated medication. But it wasn't significant enough to pursue."

"But I still don't understand. Why were you involved at all? Even if that was a murder, shouldn't it be a local matter in New Jersey?"

"It was. But I knew enough about that other death that when I learned of Adeline Harrison's death, I noticed the similarities, and I asked the ME to check what prescription drugs she was taking. Turns out it was the same one that registered high in the New Jersey case. It could be nothing, because it's a common enough drug that plenty of older people use, although there are only a few of those that can be dangerous if too many are taken. But to get back to your question, if these deaths were both murders, that makes it an interstate matter, and therefore the FBI can and should be involved."

"So now you're drumming up work for the Bureau?" I asked.

"Not exactly—just being conscientious. If nothing comes of it, no loss. As I said, being around you has made me pay more attention to cultural matters and connections. And when I saw that Adeline had been one of your board members . . ."

"You naturally assumed the worst." I finished his sentence for him. "You do know that some people actually die from natural causes?" I thought for a moment. "Do you have any more information on that New Jersey death?"

"Now you're curious? I don't have the file yet. It's on its way."

"Anything like that death going back further?"

"Nell, I just learned about the Harrison death this morning. I haven't had time to look into the details, or for other incidents. This may be nothing."

"But you called me, just in case? Should I be flattered?"

He smiled. "I knew you'd know something about Adeline. And I knew I could trust you not to talk about this."

"Fair enough. So you don't have anything else, beyond a vague suspicion?"

"Not yet. And I'll admit, if they're both murders, there's no obvious motive for killing either of them. After all, both victims were well into their eighties. Why would anyone want these two nice, harmless old people dead? Why not just wait for old age to do its work? Unless someone out there just likes killing people and picks people who can't put up much of a struggle."

"Odd, and sad, too. But I suppose I'm more used to it, given the demographic of most of our members." I reached into my bag, pulled out a slender envelope containing the materials I'd gathered on Adeline Harrison, and passed it to James. "Nothing in there jumped out at me. She seems to have led a blameless life, managed her finances well, and served quite a number of mainstream good causes, as was typical of her generation and social group. I'm not sure that will help you much."

"I suppose it eliminates some possibilities. I know how thorough the Society's research is."

"Sure, we like to hunt down people with ill-gotten funds or secret babies and blackmail them into giving us lots of contributions and serving on the board," I replied, tongue firmly in cheek. "Or leaving us the entire contents of their family homes, sight unseen. Did Adeline have any nice old furniture? Silver?"

James smiled again; I liked being able to make him smile. "That's not exactly what goes into the preliminary report. 'Victim was found lying in a north-south direction approximately eighteen inches from an exquisite Chippendale chest with original hardware.'"

I chuckled. "Maybe you could suggest that. Who knows what such details might reveal? Did you have plans for dinner?"

"Sorry, I've got to go back to the office. Rain check, definitely."

"No problem." I hesitated a moment before adding, "I'll look at the New Jersey file, if you want to send it to me. If you think it might help. We might have something on him—a lot of our members live in New Jersey."

"I'll send you a copy once I receive it. You ready to go?" James asked. "May I walk you to your train?"

"I would be delighted, sir."

Outside it was still bright—the longest day of the year was fast approaching. We stopped at City Hall Plaza, where I would descend to the train platform that lay under the plaza.

"I should get the New Jersey report tomorrow, or maybe the day after. Maybe you'll see something that I wouldn't."

"It's been known to happen, you know." I grinned. "Don't work too late."

"I'll be fine. Good to see you again, Nell, even if it was over the report on a dead woman."

"Anytime. You know that."

I watched him as he strode off, headed for his office on Arch Street. Definitely worth watching. Then with a sigh, I turned to enter the station and wait for my train home.

CHAPTER 3

The next morning it was overcast, as was my mood. A death in the "family"—that is, the small community of museum administrators and all the personnel who kept such places going—was always a sad event, no matter how long expected. Philadelphia was an old city, one that still retained a certain Quaker reserve; a city that had faced down bankruptcy a decade or two ago, and whose interest groups still fought tooth and nail for whatever funds were available. It felt crass to peruse obituaries to see who might have left us something, but "Bequests" was a line item in our annual budget, and we needed to keep our eyes open. It occurred to me that maybe James had been asking indirectly if any museum administrator would be likely to hasten the death of someone who was expected to leave a tidy sum in her will. I sincerely hoped not, although I certainly knew of some presidents or board chairs who spent more time hand-holding high-dollar donors than they did with their own families. If one had a standing date for tea and crumpets at elderly Mrs. High-Dollar's house, how hard would it be to slip something extra into her cup of Darjeeling? And if an eighty-five-year-old woman dies, apparently in her sleep, is anyone going to do a battery of tests looking for an exotic poison? Not likely. Such grim thoughts occupied me for the balance of my ride into the city.

And gave me an idea.

I arrived at the Society feeling more energized than when I had left home. I greeted Eric, nodding at his offer of coffee.

"Remind me what's on the calendar for today?" I asked.

"You have a meeting scheduled at eleven with Phebe Fleming from the Water Works" Eric replied promptly.

"Oh, right—she wanted to talk about some kind of joint project. Let me know when she arrives."

When Eric left for coffee, I went into my office and settled myself at my desk. I picked up the phone to call Shelby.

"Hey, Nell," she answered quickly. "You need something?"

"I've got something I want to discuss with you. Nothing bad, just an idea for some forward planning, and I think you can help."

"I'll be there in two minutes."

Since her office was only twenty feet away, she could have made the trip quickly, but when she walked in I realized that she had intercepted Eric in the staff room and arrived with coffee for both of us. She deposited one mug on my blotter, then asked, "Door open or shut?"

Here we go again. "Shut, please."

She shut the door, sat down, and said, "What's up?"

"I was thinking—" I began.

"Always a dangerous pastime," she said with a grin.

I ignored her. "What do you know about how boards at places like ours are put together?"

"Is this a trick question?" When I shook my head, she said slowly, "Well, I guess I'd have to say there are a few important criteria: members have to know something about and care about the particular specialty of the museum, whether it's art or history or knitting or teapots; and they have to have money, or at least know a lot of people with money. And they have to be a good fit with the other members of the board—or at least, not actively feuding with any of them."

"That's a pretty good summary. And how do we identify prospective board members?"

"You really have been busy with that thinking, haven't you? Okay, to answer you, that's one reason why we keep good records—we can tell who's been here for which event, and what they said to who. And we can tell who's buddies with someone already on the board, so we know who could approach them. We can get a rough estimate of their net worth—things like property values are public information. And if we learn they have a boat bigger than a dinghy, or race their own horses, we can make some more guesses. Why? Are we looking for some new board members?"

"Not right now, but I wondered if we should be more proactive about it. I think most of us here have a mental short list of who we'd like to see join the board, and there's probably a good deal of overlap, but we may be missing some strong candidates and not even know it."

Shelby cocked her head and eyed me critically. "Nell, what's this all about?"

"I'm thinking we might want to put together a matrix of local nonprofit boards, to see who's already committed or even overcommitted, who's doing what for who, that kind of thing. With different criteria, like gender, race, estimated worth, location, whether they give money or great-grandmother's ormolu clock in lieu of cash. I'm just noodling about this, but I think it would help us all focus, and save us wasted effort. I always wanted to do something like this when I was in your position, but I never found the time, and certainly nobody ever asked me. Right now we've got a good board, but I want to look beyond their circle of friends the next time a vacancy comes up. Which won't be soon, I hope."

"I guess we're lucky that most of them are under seventy at the moment. Unlike Adeline Harrison." Shelby looked at me with a gleam in her eye.

I met her look squarely, and we shared a wordless exchange. She was asking if this sudden idea of mine had anything to do with the death of Adeline. While I trusted Shelby—a trust she had earned—I didn't feel comfortable sharing James's gut feeling that there was something murky going on. I couldn't tell Shelby that. "Yes. Poor Adeline."

"She seemed in good health the last time I saw her, a couple of weeks ago." Shelby laid her next card on the table. "She was sharp as a tack."

"Yes, she always was," I agreed.

"That's why I was surprised that she passed so suddenly." Shelby made one more try to get me to say something more.

"It certainly was unexpected."

Shelby stood up. "I don't have anything pressing on the calendar. I can get right on this today. In case anybody else wants to take a look at it." She raised one eyebrow.

I kept my eyebrows firmly under control. "That's great, Shelby. It would be good to have it soon."

"Of course. I'll let you know what I come up with, Nell." She left and headed down the hall to her office.

Who belonged to which board was not secret—it was usually available on an organization's website, or if they were a nonprofit, through a publicly available IRS Form 990. The issue was taking the time to assemble the information and line it up so we could see the big picture—and so I could share it with James.

I was pleased that James had come to me with his suspicions. At the same time, I was pretty sure we both hoped that the similarity in the two deaths was nothing more than a coincidence. Why would anybody kill off aging board members or elderly members of the local upper crust? In most cases, board members didn't get paid by institutions, and they didn't wield a whole lot of power. Some of them had little active participation in the institution they governed—they might have joined a board because it gave them some social standing. They got their names in the paper now and then, and maybe a picture in the society section in the local papers. As far as I could remember, Adeline Harrison had been a thoroughly nice person who had done no harm to anyone. Maybe she was hiding a deep dark secret or two, but in recent years her life had been blameless, or so it appeared. Who could possibly want her dead?

I assumed I would be hearing from Marty Terwilliger about Adeline's death, and I didn't have long to wait: she popped up in my doorway a few minutes later. She came and went as she chose, and Eric had given up trying to stop her from "dropping in" at will.

Her mission was obvious when she shut the door behind her. "I'll cut to the chase: Jimmy told me about Adeline."

"He called you?" I said, stalling.

"Nope, I heard about it and I called him. I saw her recently, and she was in fine form. I wondered if there was something more going on."

"Why would you think that? After all, she wasn't young."

"Maybe I'm just naturally suspicious. I wondered if Jimmy had heard, and when he said yes, he sounded kind of funny."

"What did he tell you?" I countered cautiously.

"That he's suspicious, too. He tried to duck the question, but Jimmy's never been able to lie to me, not even when we were kids. I don't like it when Jimmy is suspicious, because he's usually right. What are you doing about it?"

I contemplated her for a moment before answering. Marty could be a steamroller, and she had no patience with evasions. She usually got what she wanted, and it saved time (at least for me) if I just went along with whatever that was.

"James wanted to know what we have in our files about Adeline, which I've already given him. He mentioned an earlier death that he thought might—repeat, *might*—be connected, and said he'd send me what information he could on that one as soon as he received it. You have anything more?"

"Apart from being ticked off that he didn't come to me first? He knows I know everybody, and I know about a lot of the details they hope they've buried. I probably know more of the good stuff than your crowd here does. Not that I'd ever use it for anything crooked, but it comes in handy when I'm asking for a substantial contribution."

"So it's not really blackmail, eh?" I said, and when she started to protest, I held up a hand. "Now, I'm not complaining, since the Society is on the receiving end of most of those contributions. Are you saying you have dirt on Adeline?"

Marty dropped into the chair that Shelby had vacated, looking deflated. "Nope. She was exactly what she appeared to be—a good and decent person, the type they don't make many of these days. Not a smudge on her reputation, not a blot on her record—nothing."

"So you think she died of natural causes?"

Marty shrugged. "She was getting up there, goodness knows, but her father was ninety-six when he died, if I remember correctly. Question is, what's got Jimmy's knickers in a twist?"

"Does that expression apply to men?" I asked innocently.

Marty glared. "You know what I mean. Why is Jimmy even looking at this?"

"It could be the FBI's investigation if this other death he's heard about in New Jersey is related."

"What, Freddy Van Deusen? Lifelong smoker, diabetic,

and lazy to the bone. I knew him for forever. Why would his death be suspicious?"

"Why am I not surprised that you knew that guy, too? I have no idea what makes James think his death is suspicious—maybe the pricking of his thumbs. He mentioned the case to me and said he hadn't seen the file yet. You're betting on natural causes? If that's true, then the whole thing would go away. Which would be for the best."

"Of course," she said crisply. "The Society has had enough bad press over the past few months without going looking for trouble, and if Adeline's death is suspicious, we've got a problem. But, heck, if someone is going after the people who run nonprofits around here, I might be next on the list." She looked remarkably cheerful at the idea.

"Like that old book *Someone is Killing the Great Chefs of Europe*? Just substitute regional philanthropists for the chefs?"

Marty gave a short bark of laughter, then looked away. "I liked Adeline," she said, her eyes on the corner of the room. "If her death was natural, I'll go to the funeral and I'll mourn her. But if it wasn't, something should be done about it." She was silent a moment, then swiveled back to me. "So we wait to see what Jimmy turns up?"

We? "Sounds like a plan. Are you headed back to the processing room?"

"Yup. I need to keep an eye on Rich."

I had a sneaking suspicion that Marty's presence there slowed things down rather than speeding them up, but I wasn't about to interfere. "If Nicholas is there, could you send him to me?"

"Sure thing. By the way, how's he working out?"

"Fairly well, I think. So far he's lived up to his own billing—he really does know his software, and he picked up right where the former registrar left off."

"Glad to hear it. If I see him, I'll let him know you want him."

"Thanks, Marty."

CHAPTER 4

I started sorting through the correspondence on my desk and had barely gotten into drafting a reply to one letter when Nicholas rapped on my door. "Marty Terwilliger said you wanted to see me?" He stood, waiting, until I beckoned him in.

"Yes, I did. Please, sit down. How's the work going?"

He sat and regarded me gravely. "I'm still importing some of the existing data into my system, and I'm more or less splitting my time between that and cataloging the new material that came in. Is there a problem?"

"No, not at all. I think you're doing a great job. I'm even beginning to think we'll see the end of it during my lifetime." I waited for a response to my mild joke, but he just stared at me blankly. Nicholas did not have any sense of humor that I could identify. I sighed inwardly. "I wanted to enlist your help on a special project. I know it's kind of a digression from what you've been doing, but

I'd like you to find the time. You're familiar with the Water Works?"

"On the river? Yes, the place is hard to miss. What about it?"

"One of my colleagues at the Interpretive Center there is coming in for a meeting in about five minutes. She requested the meeting—she said they want to do an updated history of the Water Works, with an emphasis on how the river has been cleaned up in recent years, and they want to know what we have in our collections about past efforts. Not just about the site itself, but maybe reports on the state of the river, or waterborne illnesses, that kind of thing."

"Surely they've been through our materials before?"

"No doubt, but you know what staff turnover is like, so assume we're starting from scratch. Do you think that would be a good demonstration of your software?"

"Of course, not that it's a particularly difficult search. When do they want it?"

"Phebe and I didn't get into the details, but probably soon. She did mention that they want to take the project to the city for funding, and of course the deadline is only a few weeks away, at the end of the budget year. Nothing unusual there. Sound good to you?" Since I was his boss, although not his direct supervisor, I asked purely out of courtesy. I thought it would be a good chance for him to show off what he'd accomplished in the few months he'd been working with the Society's collections.

"I'd be happy to do it."

"Great—she'll be here any minute. Sorry to dump it on you without warning, but she didn't give me much, either."

Eric called out, "Ms. Fleming is here. Should I bring her up?"

"Thanks, Eric—go right ahead."

Eric returned quickly, and Phebe walked briskly into my office. "Hi, Nell—thank you for seeing me on such short notice. Somebody up the line got a bee in his bonnet and decided this was a great idea and we should do something with it, like, immediately."

"Hi, Phebe." When I was development director, we ran into each other periodically at various events and conferences around the city, and I'd always enjoyed her company. I was pleased that she'd reached out to the Society for this project—it never hurt to earn some goodwill from a city department. "I know how that goes. I hope we can help. Let me introduce you to one of our newer staff members, Nicholas Naylor."

Nicholas took a step forward and extended a hand. "It's nice to meet you, Ms. Fleming."

"Phebe, please."

"Nicholas is overhauling our electronic cataloging system and database," I said, "which, as you might guess, is a huge task, and we're glad to have him. I thought he could use your request as a kind of test case. So, what are you looking for?"

Phebe leaned forward in her chair. "Confidentially, the Water Department has had an offer from a large local corporation, which shall be nameless, to give us a nice contribution to support this project. They're trying to polish up their public image. What they want is to retroactively present themselves as ecologically sensitive, or if that's not possible, then they want to look proactive now. There may be a good case to be made, but we want to be able to back it up with documentation, so this doesn't come back to bite us. What do you think, Nell?"

"I can see where they want to go with this, but I can't speak for what's in our collections. Don't you already have a scholarly history for the Water Works?"

"We do, but it's kind of dated. And now we want to take a different slant, pushing the health and safety aspects."

"Nicholas, what do you think?" I asked.

"How detailed do you want this to be, and when do you need it?" Nicholas didn't beat around the bush, I noted.

"The good news is, the city is willing to give us a break—it's already past the deadline for submitting requests for funding, but they want to keep this corporation happy so they're bending the rules for us. The bad news is, they want the information and proposal by the end of the next week. Is that doable?"

Nicholas glanced at me briefly before replying. "Let me see what I can pull quickly. I can give Nell a summary of what I've found, say by the end of this week, and then you and she can confer. Would that suit you?"

"Sounds good to me. I've got my people working on the rest of the proposal. Nell, do you approve?"

"Sure. We can talk when Nicholas has had a chance to pull some things together. Actually I'd like to know more about the Water Works, so I'll look forward to seeing what we have in our files."

Phebe bounced up. "That's great! Thank you so much—I know it's a pain to have things dumped on you unexpectedly, but we only just found out ourselves. I'll owe you one."

"I won't forget. Let me walk you out." As I escorted Phebe down the hall to the elevator, I saw Nicholas slip out of my office, heading toward his cubicle down the hall. When I'd waved good-bye to Phebe at the front door, I went back to talk with him.

"Think you can handle this?" I asked

"Of course. I think I know what she has in mind, so I can tailor my search. I'll have something in your hands in a couple of days."

"That would be great, Nicholas."

CHAPTER 5

Anyone who approaches Philadelphia by way of Amtrak or in a car on the Schuylkill Expressway would have to be blind not to notice the Fairmount Water Works, which stretch along the river in all their Neoclassical glory, next to the more garish illuminated Boathouse Row. Philadelphia was the first major American city to consider safe municipal water as the city's responsibility, spurred by the yellow fever epidemics at the end of the eighteenth century (reading the Society's documents about the victims, often letters to and from affected loved ones, can be heart-wrenching). Of course, the city fathers didn't settle for building a humdrum and utilitarian monument. Instead they created a three million gallon reservoir on the hill where the Philadelphia Museum of Art now sits, and a pump house with two steam engines. Then they built a dam along the Schuylkill, which directed the water to a mill house with waterwheels to replace the steam engines, and later turbines to lift the water. The whole thing was embellished by a Classical Revival exterior, and it became a major tourist attraction. Sometimes I wished for simpler days, when an excursion to look at some pretty water pumps was enough to please travelers.

The place was closed in 1909, and languished for decades, housing a variety of organizations such as an aquarium and a swimming pool. Then a major restoration was undertaken, an interpretive education center was added, and behold, it became a tourist destination once again, complete with a highly regarded restaurant.

I was always surprised that Ben Franklin hadn't had a hand in it somewhere, since he seemed to have prompted almost every other "first" in the city and even the country. He missed the "Watering Committee" by only a few years, since he died less than a decade before it was created.

Asking Nicholas to work on this project was not just me creating busywork for him. Phebe and I had posed an interdisciplinary question to test the scope of his data management software, and also to give him a taste of the kind of real-world questions we regularly faced from patrons and scholars. And while it wasn't listed anywhere in the job requirements, I wanted to see him show some passion for the materials he was working with, beyond the mere physical descriptions and categorizations. Not for the first time I wished that he would show some sign that he was enjoying his work, maybe even a smile from him once in a while. But if he was doing his job well, I wasn't going to complain.

I sighed. Being part of upper management, even in a small place, carried a lot of different responsibilities, including supervising employees and making sure they all worked well together. Not an easy task, I had come to realize.

The rest of the day passed in a blur. No major crises, no big decisions to be made. The next board meeting was still a few weeks off, and I looked forward to reporting that we had had a quiet and productive quarter. Then I knocked on the wood of my desk: the quarter wasn't over yet.

At least the day was broken up when Eric informed me that there was a Jacob Miller downstairs and he wanted to see me. "Who?" I said, searching my brain for the name. "Does he have an appointment?"

"No appointment. He says he's with the firm of Morgan, Hamilton and Fox? He promised not to take much of your time."

Whirr, click—that name I recognized. Morgan, Hamilton and Fox was the Society's law firm, when we needed one for institutional business. Not that we'd had any legal problems recently, thank goodness, because they charged by the minute. "You can bring him up, I guess."

Two minutes later, Eric returned with Jacob Miller in tow. "Sorry to barge in on you unannounced," he said, his smile ingratiating, his hand extended.

Since I hadn't met him before, I studied him for a moment before I stood and shook his hand. He was young, eager, nicely dressed, and clean-shaven—just what I'd expect of a baby lawyer at a major law firm. "Please, have a seat. What brings you here?"

"Nothing bad, I promise you! I'm an associate with Morgan, Hamilton and Fox," he began. From the way he said the name, I guessed he was still enjoying the novelty of it. I knew it was a prestigious, long-established firm, and he must be smart if he'd landed a job there. "I've just been assigned to help Courtney Gould with the Society's business, and I wanted to take this chance to introduce myself, since I was in the neighborhood. You're the president of this organization?"

"I am, for the last few months. You've gone over our files?"

"I've just begun."

"What exactly has Courtney asked you to do?" I'd worked with Courtney on and off for several years, and I had found her efficient and pleasant, although I wouldn't call her a friend.

"First, familiarize myself with the scope of your needs. Then she wanted to do a review of the legal status of some of your internal trusts. You know—laws keep changing, and as I understand it, some of your funds and bequests are virtually moribund. If their terms permit, there might be a way to consolidate and streamline your holdings."

I didn't doubt that what he said was true, but I had to wonder if he was here trying to generate billable hours for himself and the law firm—and I didn't want to incur any more bills right now. But that probably wasn't something I should take up with this young, eager lawyer. I made a mental note to check with Courtney before he got too carried away. "That sounds like a good idea," I said noncommittally. "Are you interested in history?"

"Oh, sure. I love old buildings and stuff. Maybe you could give me a tour of this place? Not today," he hastened to add, "but sometime?"

"Of course," I agreed. "I love to show this place off." And it wouldn't hurt to keep our lawyers happy and show them that we had nothing to hide. Just not right now.

He said quickly, "I won't keep you any longer, but I'll hold you to that. Great meeting you!" He all but jumped out of his chair to shake hands yet again.

I came around my desk to take his hand this time, and gently guided him toward Eric's desk. "Eric, will you take Mr. Miller downstairs, please?"

"I'll be happy to."

I watched them go down the hall, and returned slowly to my desk. I couldn't even remember what I'd been doing before Jacob Miller had appeared. Great. I scribbled a note to myself: *call law firm.* I wasn't sure whether Court- ney was trying to send a message by stepping back and letting a junior member take over our business, or if she was just busy and needed some help, but I thought I should find out.

Shelby came by late in the day, looking pleased with herself.

"Don't tell me you've got results already!"

"I sure do." She smiled. "Once I figured out where to look, it went fast. I went back as far as fifteen years, which is about as long as people have been putting that kind of institutional information online. Hard to remember the world before the Internet, isn't it?"

I had to agree. "I don't know whether that's good or bad for places like ours. On the one hand, the documents and materials we have will become more and more precious. On the other hand, people will be so accustomed to calling up quick answers and images online that they're going to be less likely to make a trip to look at the real thing. Not much we can do about it, though, except put as much of our stuff online as we can so we look proactive."

"Amen!" Shelby said. "Anyway, I made you a copy of what I've got so far. Consider it a first draft." She passed me a sheaf of papers. "That includes all Philadelphia institutions and those in the near suburbs, and those that kind of compete with us or complement us, like Valley Forge. That's one column. Then there are the board members for each, over the past ten years and currently, with another column for their years of service. What else would you like to see?"

"Great start, Shelby!" I thought for a moment. "How about their age when they joined each board? And when they died?"

"You mean, did they die with their boots on, still on the board, or did they know enough to pass the torch to someone else?"

"You're mangling your metaphors, but yes, I think you've got the idea."

"Want me to add *how* they died?" Shelby asked with a gleam in her eye.

Shelby could see right through me. "Maybe. How about whether the places they'd served were included in the will?"

"Lady, you don't make this easy, do you? How about shoe size and hair color while I'm at it?"

"No, but you might go back through the last twenty or so years of society columns and see who was seen with whom at whose parties." At Shelby's dismayed look, I burst out laughing. "Just kidding. But is there any way to figure out who knew who, retroactively? I know some of that is in our files, and you can check the reports from our annual galas. You could put in a 'Friends With' column."

"I sure hope all these board members don't know that we archive gossip!" Shelby shot back.

"It's not exactly a secret, even if we don't go around pumping folks for information. They can't really think we come up with our funding requests out of thin air, or with a Ouija board."

My phone rang. I checked my watch and was surprised to see that it was after five. I'd heard Eric leaving while I was talking to Shelby, so I picked up and said, "Nell Pratt."

"It's James. We need to talk."

That sounded ominous, and I thought I could guess why. "Another one?"

"Possibly. Can I meet you there?"

"Of course." I thought for a moment before saying, "James, can I bring Shelby into this conversation?"

I could hear his sigh. Heck, Shelby, sitting across the desk, could probably hear it, too. I waited while he thought it through. "I suppose it will be faster to talk to you both and just say this once."

"I think she can help."

"All right. I'll be there in a half hour."

"I'll wait in the lobby and let you in."

When I hung up, I found Shelby watching me with an amused smile. "I knew there was something going on. You going to fill me in before Mr. Agent Man shows up?"

Now it was my turn to sigh. "James thinks Adeline Harrison's death was suspicious and may be related to at least one other death from a couple of months ago.

Apparently now there's a third that he thinks might also be linked. That's why he asked me to sniff around."

"And why you asked me for this information," Shelby said, nodding to the spreadsheets she had given me.

"Yes. And that's why I'm including you now. You've got access to the information he needs, and I know I can trust you. I can't do this all by myself and still run the place."

I was hardly surprised when Marty showed up in the doorway. "Jimmy just called and said we were getting together here. Somebody else is dead?"

I nodded. "So I gather, but I don't know who yet. Marty, I asked Shelby to put together a matrix of local board members, and I'd like you to look at it and see what you can add. If what James thinks is happening really is happening, it may be useful for us to have that information in one place."

Shelby stood up. "Let me run off a couple more copies for y'all." She headed down the hall toward the copy machine, leaving Marty and me staring at each other silently until Shelby returned. She handed Marty a packet of papers and explained to her what she had done. Marty nodded in agreement and made some good suggestions.

I left them in peace while I worried. Marty was right: James was not an alarmist, and he preferred to keep his business life and his personal life separate. At least, as far as I knew—I'd been part of the latter for only a few months. When we did get together outside of work, we both avoided talking about professional issues—him because he couldn't, and me because . . . I didn't think they would interest him, compared to the things he dealt with daily. And because I wanted to get to know him better, and let him get to know me. So we spent a lot of time talking about what books and movies we enjoyed and what restaurants we went to. We also spent some quality time *not* talking, engaged in nonverbal but mutually satisfying activities.

"Yo, Nell!" Marty's voice interrupted what had been becoming a very nice daydream. "You going to go downstairs and let the man in?"

Where had the time gone? "Oh, right. We can use the old conference room downstairs to talk." The ground floor of the Society was long on grand, soaring spaces but short on places to meet privately, to sit and talk. The exception was the old conference room, tucked under the sweeping mahogany and stone staircase. "Let's head down there now."

Our timing was perfect: by the time we emerged from the sluggish elevator and reached the front door, James was waiting on the front steps. I let him in and wished that I could greet him with proper enthusiasm, but we had an audience (who knew perfectly well what was going on between us, but still) and this was a professional call.

When we were settled around the conference table, I said, "All right, James. You requested this meeting. Tell us what's going on."

"Let's talk about Adeline Harrison first. I have the preliminary results for cause of death: an overdose of a prescribed heart medication. We were lucky, because all her medications were neatly lined up in her bathroom cabinet, and we talked to her primary doctor. Marty, you knew her. Was she getting forgetful? Could she have miscounted pills or taken a dose twice?"

Marty shook her head vehemently. "I saw her a few weeks ago and I didn't notice anything like that. We talked about a bestselling nonfiction book she had read recently, and she made some excellent points about its weaknesses. And before you bring it up, I don't know of any reason why she could have been suicidal. Unless her doctor told you about some terminal illness?"

"No, nothing like that. Then there was the earlier case that I mentioned to Nell. I can't give you the official records, but I can summarize. Frederick Van Deusen, age eighty-three. Impeccable social connections, served on various boards, lived in north Jersey. Not particularly wealthy. Tox screen showed only the drugs you'd expect, including the same heart medication that Adeline was taking, and the level of that one was a bit higher than it should have been. Nothing out of place in his home. Wife's been dead for years, grown children who live out of state and aren't in financial trouble. Again, no motive, and no evidence, except for slightly elevated drug levels in his system."

"I knew Freddy," Marty said. "He was about as interesting as oatmeal, but a nice guy. I never heard anyone say a bad word about him. I went to his funeral."

"So no secret life, no blackmail?" James asked with a small smile.

Marty snorted inelegantly. "Freddy? Not likely."

"Was he ever on the board of the Society?"

I looked at Marty, since her memory went back further than mine. "Nope. Don't even think he was asked. Freddy, rest his soul, was kind of thick, and he had no interest at all in history. That's not to say he didn't have other interests, or get involved in something in New Jersey."

"Marty," I interrupted, "how *did* you know Freddy Van Duesen?"

"His father and mine used to own a boat together—sold it years ago. The Van Duesens had a place on the Jersey shore, and that's where they docked it. Took Freddy and me out a time or two, until we both made it clear that we hated sailing. But I think he was still on the board of some yacht club, thanks to his father—I went to a fund-raising event there, maybe a decade ago."

It figured. Marty continually surprised me with the breadth and depth of her social network—the real one, not the digital one.

James nodded once. "So Freddy had local social connections. That's about what I figured. It's a pretty thin file."

"Then why did you even bring him up?" Marty demanded.

"Because he's part of your crowd, and I'm getting leery of anything that involves the greater Philadelphia cultural community. I wouldn't have given him another thought if it hadn't been for Adeline's death, which is remarkably similar."

"Similar in that there's nothing suspicious about either one?" I asked. "That's an odd reason to look at anything."

James looked at me in turn. "I was prepared to write off these two deaths as a coincidence. As you've pointed out, they were both far from young, and there's no damning evidence, apart from elevated levels of a legally prescribed medicine. Look, I don't mean to be an alarmist. I'm trying to be thorough. Two elderly people die, months apart, from an overdose. Nothing extraordinary there.

Then I find that both had various ties to local cultural institutions, and that Martha here knew both of them. And then Adeline ties into the Society. Can you blame me for wondering, at least off the record? And when I go looking for additional information, I find that since everything looked so simple, nobody bothered to do a thorough investigation of either of them, and now there's no way to retrieve evidence. Dead ends, both, if you'll pardon the expression."

"Do your bosses know about this?" I asked.

"No, and I wasn't planning to say anything to them—I was just satisfying my own curiosity."

"But you said there was a new death?" I prodded gently.

"Yes. Benton Snyder was found dead this morning."

Shelby gasped, and Marty paled. "Benton?" Shelby said. "But he's a neighbor! I saw him just last week, when he was weeding his window boxes. What happened?"

"Found dead in his bed, no signs of forced entry, no struggle. Marty, did you know him?"

"Sure. We used to play bridge together, but I haven't seen him lately. But Jimmy, why do you think his death is suspicious?"

"I asked the coroner to check to see if there were elevated levels of any of the prescription medications we found in his medicine cabinet. The coroner's a good guy, so he did that quickly and then called me. Same prescription." He turned to Marty. "At the risk of repeating myself, was Benton ever a Society board member?"

"No, but I think he was on the board of the Art Museum some years back. He had more money than Freddy—or me, for that matter. Decent guy, though, and a wicked bridge player. He could look you in the eye and finesse your face cards like nobody's business."

"And you think these three deaths are connected?" I asked.

"Either they're an extraordinary coincidence, or there's a fairly subtle serial killer running around."

CHAPTER 6

We all stared at each other, James's last words hanging between us like a physical entity. It seemed absurd: a serial killer preying on the elderly Philadelphia cultural elite? Besides, I didn't want to see anybody else die before their time, elite or not. It wasn't their fault that they'd been born to long-established families and raised in a privileged environment and grown old with their peers. I sneaked a glance at Marty: she fit the description, except for her age. And to give that community its due, the elite had largely used their money generously, supporting good causes and institutions—like the Society—that might otherwise have floundered. What's more, they gave of their time and connections.

I was the first to break the silence. "Shelby, show James what you've been working on."

"Does this mean I'm a consultant for the FBI now?" she asked him directly, dimpling.

"If you like," he said with good humor. "What is it?"

Shelby handed James copies of the board member spreadsheets. "At Nell's suggestion, I've been putting together a list of people who match the general description of your two—now, three—victims. You know, old families, some disposable income, civic-minded. I've been looking at what information we have in our files here and expanding from there. I've come up with a list of local benefactors and their board connections, just to see if there is any overlap between the victims. Or who might be next on the list." She grimaced at adding that last thought.

"Interesting," James replied, leafing through the pages.

Shelby continued, "Our secret weapon is our own in-house 'who's who.' Who knows who, and how, and why. What clubs they belong to, what charities they support. Where their summerhouses are, and who they vacation with. A lot of that stuff doesn't show up on any database." She sat back triumphantly. Marty winked at me.

James had the decency to look impressed. "Thank you, Shelby. This could be very useful to us."

"And this is only what I've found in one day. There are a lot of blanks to fill in, if Nell wants me to go ahead. Or if there's something you'd like to see added."

"Please, continue what you've started. That is, if Nell can spare you?" He looked at me with a smile.

"Of course. Anything to help."

"Hey, I'm in too," Marty protested.

"I never doubted it, Martha," James said drily. "All of you, I appreciate the help. If we can find out what connects these people, apart from their social status, maybe we can start working on who would be killing them.

But"—he glanced at me briefly—"please keep this quiet. As I keep reminding Nell, the Bureau frowns on using, uh, outside personnel in its investigations."

"You mean amateurs like us," Marty said bluntly. "We know. But is it even an official investigation yet?"

James looked pained. "Not unless either the local police invite us in, or I can prove a connection between the three deaths. I haven't got a lot to work with here. That's why I'm using you three—no paperwork, and your price is right."

"Gee, thanks. I love being exploited by government agencies." Then I added, more somberly, "We don't take this lightly. If we can help, we want to. Right, ladies?"

Nods all around. "All right, then," I said. "Marty, why don't you take Shelby's charts home, look them over, and add what you can. Shelby, tomorrow you can go back to fleshing out your information. Your first pass is great, but I'm sure there's more information in the files and from outside sources. James, you let us know if there are any new developments, or if you want us to look at another angle. Is everybody clear on that?"

"Yes, ma'am! Will do, ma'am!" Shelby barked out like an army private, but she was smiling.

"I'll work on the list tonight," Marty said. "It's a great idea that you and Shelby cooked up—and Jimmy didn't even think of it." She looked pointedly at him and he ducked his head.

Marty and Shelby gathered up their things and exited together, leaving James and me alone in the darkening room. "What if we don't come up with anything? What then?" I asked.

"At least we'll have covered all the bases. As I've said,

it may all come to nothing, and these people's time had come. Or maybe this represents a cluster of suicides—they do happen, you know."

"I thought that was usually at colleges, or someplace like the Golden Gate Bridge in San Francisco."

"Not all suicides are as obvious. You have plans for dinner?"

The quick change of subject confused me for a moment. "Nothing out of the usual. You have some ideas?"

"How about takeout at my place?"

"Sounds good to me, as long as I can catch a late train home."

"I think that can be arranged." He smiled.

I took home a substantial doggie bag. Somehow we never quite made it to dinner.

———

On the train to the city the next morning, I reflected on the nebulous problem James had handed us. Three deaths, in two different states; one in the city, one in the suburbs, the third someplace I knew nothing about. Three people close in age, linked by a history of social involvement. None married, or at least not when they died. I made a mental note to ask Shelby to include a column on marital status at time of death, or if there was anyone else living in the deceased's house.

I tried to recall the few times I'd met Adeline. I thought we'd had one conversation at an event outside the Society where we had discussed historic preservation. Maybe something about the Somerhof Museum? Furniture refinishing? Or needlework seat covers for antique furniture? I couldn't bring the memory into focus. Of course, at the time I had had no idea that the passing conversation would figure in a possible criminal investigation into her death. But no one could remember every casual chat they ever took part in. We picked out what interested us, stored it as a memory, and threw out the rest.

Marty had mentioned that Benton had played bridge, an activity that could have brought him into contact with a number of people—although I'd never heard of anyone being killed over leading with the wrong card. Maybe he'd been kicked out of his bridge group and committed suicide because he couldn't stand the shame?

The first victim, the one from New Jersey, I knew nothing about. Luckily, Marty seemed to know everyone everywhere, so she could fill in a lot of the blanks. If she didn't know a person, that person wasn't worth knowing, at least under the umbrella of Philadelphia society. Not that she was a snob about it. It was just that she'd grown up with a lot of interconnected family, attended local schools, and was fully immersed in city history. On the one hand, Marty tended to be direct with her questions and peremptory in her judgments on occasion, but while she was what I would call tact-challenged, she always got the job—whatever it was—done.

I relished my walk from the station to the Society. The mornings were still cool; later in the summer, when all the stone and concrete in the city held the heat, it could be steamy before nine, but we weren't there yet. As I walked, I mulled a few things over. Work at the Society was going well. We were fully staffed for a change; we had the treasure trove of FBI-recovered objects and documents to sort through; and we had no major events looming. June was usually peaceful—later in the summer we would have a higher percentage of visiting scholars or genealogists using their precious vacation weeks to fill in an entire family tree. Of course we welcomed them, but it was also nice when the building was cool and quiet.

On that warm and fuzzy note, I walked into the Society, smiled at Front Desk Bob, and made my way to the elevator, greeting Edwin while I waited.

Upstairs, I had barely settled in my chair when Shelby came bustling in, looking excited.

"You're in early again," I said. "Should we get some coffee?"

"Like I'm not wired enough already? But sure, if you want some."

We strolled down the hall and made the first pot of the day, since I'd arrived before Eric for a change. While we waited for it to brew, I said, "Any luck with . . . that project?"

"I think so. I woke up with some great ideas, and that's why I came in early." She glanced around to make sure there was no one else who could hear. "This is so cool, helping out the . . . you-know-what."

"It is. And we kind of owe them, what with that wealth of stuff they dropped in our laps this year."

"Found anything good? As in, we really hope to keep it?"

"You'd have to ask Nicholas. He's in charge. I try to stay out of the way, but it's hard because I love to see the new stuff. Oh—good morning, Nicholas."

I hadn't heard him approach, but he was light on his feet. His cubicle was just down the hall, close to the staff room, with only the staircase between.

"Good morning, Nell, Shelby." His manner was almost courtly, but he didn't smile. Nicholas seldom smiled.

"Coffee will be ready in a minute. Shelby was just asking about how the processing of the FBI materials is going. I could give her numbers, but maybe you could tell her what your overall assessment is, for the materials you've looked at?"

He appeared to consider the question carefully before replying. "As you might expect, it's a hodgepodge. The FBI provided lists of what they'd found, or thought they'd found, but of course their descriptions are all but useless. They also identified which items they knew or guessed had been stolen, mainly from information provided by the owners—but not surprisingly, the two lists are impossible to compare. So it's a slow process."

"Have you found much that doesn't appear on the lists of missing items that the owners reported?"

"Some. Perhaps. You're thinking that we'll have a shot at keeping the unclaimed items?"

"That's what I hope, even if we have to consider them a long-term loan in the event someone might come forward in the future to claim them. I'm no expert on the legalities. What I guess I need now is a sense of the scope of those items—ten percent? Twenty? And what categories they fall into, if you can give me that. We'll need to start thinking about where to store them, going forward."

"Of course. I think you're right—it's probably between ten and twenty percent. I'd have to check the categories of the articles involved. Excuse me, the coffee's ready." He stepped between Shelby and me and filled a mug, then turned and left without further comment.

"Is it just me," Shelby drawled, "or is that boy a little rough around the edges?"

"What he lacks in social graces he makes up for in technical skills. At least, that's what I keep telling myself." We filled our own mugs and went back to my office.

Once we were settled, I asked, "What have you come up with?"

"A few other categories that might be helpful, like other organizations the people belong to. I've split that between public ones and less formal ones, like the bridge players Marty mentioned. People might have different intentions and different levels of involvement, depending on why they joined. You know, duty versus fun."

"Good point, and I was thinking along the same lines myself. Anything that gets us closer to linking these people, on any level, will be helpful. Although where you find some of the informal organizations is beyond me."

"Well, as you've said, a lot of that is recorded in our files, based on conversations staff members have had with them now and then. Plus, if I go looking online in the *Inquirer* and search on each name, there are often mentions of events they've attended. Like the Flower Show, for example. They may not have any official involvement with the organizing committee, but if they show up there year after year, maybe they actually like flowers, or even belong to some gardening group. Of course, this is all pretty time-consuming."

"I can see that. How many names have you put together so far?"

"Probably around three hundred."

I didn't know whether to be buoyed or depressed by that piece of information. Three hundred people was a lot to sift through for small but potentially significant details. "Why don't you wait until you can sit down with Marty and go over the list with her? I'm sure she'll have plenty to add. That could save you some time."

"You expect to see her today?"

"You couldn't keep me away," Marty announced from the doorway. "And I might have something."

CHAPTER 7

"That was fast!" I said. She'd had the spreadsheets for barely twelve hours. "So, tell us!"

"Maybe we'd be more comfortable at a table. Is the boardroom free?"

"I think so. I'll ask Eric." I stood up and walked around my desk and out into the adjoining room, where Eric was already setting up for his day.

"Mornin', Nell."

"Morning, Eric. Can we use the boardroom for maybe a half hour? There's nothing scheduled in there, is there?"

Eric flipped through his desk calendar. "No, ma'am, it's clear. You need coffee?"

I smiled at him. "Way ahead of you, Eric. But help yourself to what's made."

Marty, Shelby, and I trooped down the hall to the boardroom, a windowless space that lacked charm but did have a door that closed, giving us some privacy.

Once we were seated at one end of the large table, Marty turned to Shelby. "I'm no expert on spreadsheets, but you can sort them by whichever column you want, right?"

"That's right." Shelby nodded, looking puzzled. "You want to sort them by something other than name?"

"I do. I couldn't do it at home, but when I started filling in some of the details that I knew off the top of my head, a couple of groups kept coming up over and over again."

"Such as?" I pressed.

"Well, the Society, of course. We've got the most information on those people. There must have been at least ten names on the list who were once on the board here, who aren't anymore. Then there's the Art Museum, which has a *huge* board, and I'm sure you'd both recognize most of the names on that list. And there's one real outlier: the Edwin Forrest Trust."

I stared at her and said slowly, "Edwin Forrest, as in the statue out by the elevator? I should know about that one, shouldn't I?"

"You should, because we have half of their artifact collection on indefinite loan. Plus a tidy endowment to care for it."

"Ah yes, *that* I remember," I said.

"So that whopping big statue downstairs near the elevator doesn't really belong to us?" Shelby asked.

"Nope," Marty said.

Shelby was looking back and forth at us. "Who's Edwin Forrest?" she said plaintively.

Marty and I exchanged a glance and grinned. Marty said to Shelby, "For shame! Of course, you're not from around here, but that's hardly an excuse to be ignorant of the first great American-born actor. He was the George Clooney of his day, and more. And he was born here in Philadelphia."

"Well, his publicist is doing a lousy job! So what's this trust all about? I assume he's been dead for a while?"

"I don't know the details of the trust," I said, "apart from that nice line item on our budgets. Weren't there strings attached, Marty?"

"There were, and still are. The income from the trust's endowment could be used only to preserve and make available to the public the items from the collection. The Society does have other papers and such that didn't come through the estate, which complement the pieces nicely, but we've done bupkes about presenting them."

I had a small brainstorm—probably the caffeine kicking in. "Shelby, why don't you pull together a brief summary of what we have on Forrest, and the details of the trust. That's not under the table or anything—it should count as regular business, especially if we've been failing to live up to the terms of the agreement so far. It sounds as though we could all learn something about the trust."

"Yes, ma'am," Shelby replied.

I turned back to Marty. "So, what's the connection between the names you've highlighted and our victims?"

"All of them are, or were, current trustees either here or at the museum or on the trust. One or more of the three."

"Any overlaps with the Society, apart from Adeline?"

"Sure. Just look at the museum list—it's loaded with our board members, past and present."

"And you don't think anyone has targeted museum board members?" It would be a daunting task to review that board—the list of current trustees went on for pages and looked like a mini Philadelphia Social Register. And that didn't even take into account former trustees.

Marty shrugged. "I don't know. We only just started looking at this problem. We'd have to go back a few years to see if our three victims have been on the museum board anytime recently."

"I can do that," Shelby said. "But none of this makes any sense. What's the motive? Somebody's got it in for patrons of the arts? High-profile society figures? I thought Philadelphia was pretty laid-back these days about that kind of thing. And I've never heard a bad word about the museum. What's there to complain about? Is there some guerrilla group that thinks it should be free for the public?"

"It *is* pricey, unless you're a member," I admitted. "They do open for free one day a month."

"How nice of them," Shelby said with a trace of bitterness.

"I know what you're saying, Shelby, but they must have massive expenses to cover. It costs about half as much for someone to use our library, and still our members and visitors complain if we try to raise admission by a dollar—and you know how much we need the income."

We were all silent for a moment, contemplating the irony of trying to juggle our admission prices to both cover costs and allow more people to enjoy what we had.

Finally I said, "So, next steps. Marty, give Shelby whatever notes you've made, or set up a time to sit down with her and go over the rest of the list. Then maybe you can take a harder look at the Art Museum list. Shelby, dig up what we've got in the Society files on the Forrest

Trust. As for me, I guess I'll take the Society list. If I don't know all the people on the list, I should, so it will be a good exercise for me. I'd hate to think the Society figures in this problem."

"Not *all* the victims have been associated with the Society," Shelby said.

"*If* we are looking at victims rather than coincidences, or suicides," Marty responded promptly. "Maybe there are other connections. Maybe Benton and Freddy were working behind the scenes to close us down, without our knowing it, and the killer thinks he's doing us a favor by shutting them up, permanently." Marty folded her arms and sat back in her chair, challenging me. Shelby just looked distressed, as though she was a child watching her parents argue.

I chose my words carefully. "Marty, I recognize the validity of your arguments, and I'm appalled at how easy it is for you to come up with a variety of possible explanations. But I think we're getting ahead of ourselves. We've been looking at this for only a day, and we've barely scratched the surface. Let's fill in some more of the blanks before we start weaving together pretty theories. It may turn out to be nothing, after all." I hoped. But somehow I didn't believe myself. Maybe James's bad feeling was contagious.

"Are we done here?" Shelby said. "Because I can see I've got a lot of catching up to do."

I nodded. "We all have our assignments. Let's plan on getting together like this again tomorrow morning."

Marty and Shelby stood up and headed off together toward Shelby's office, leaving me sitting alone at the table.

I hadn't been raised in Philadelphia or even its suburbs, so I hadn't been absorbing this kind of who's who knowledge through osmosis since childhood, the way Marty had. As development director for the Society, I had done enough research to know who the power brokers and players were these days, and a bit about the elite citizens of the past. For a long time in the twentieth century, Philadelphia had looked like a dowdy cousin compared to its nearest competitor, New York. Part of that might have been due to the lingering Quaker influence in Philadelphia, which condemned ostentation. Then the city had suffered from the flight of much of its industry to the growing suburbs, starting in the 1950s, and as a result had faced serious financial struggles.

But the city had fought back. It had created a world-class convention center to draw in visitors, and a new venue for its sports teams. The Constitution Center had filled in a gap across from Independence Hall. New high-rises like Liberty Place I and II had attracted high-end shops in a central location. Things were definitely looking up for Philly.

But despite my research, I still couldn't match Marty's hereditary and encyclopedic knowledge of the people we were looking at. Thank heavens I knew more than Shelby did, or I would really feel like a dope. Having southern-bred Shelby as part of this team forced us to put a lot of social assumptions into words, which could also be helpful. All the information she would acquire would also make her much more useful as a Society employee.

I made my way slowly back to my office. Eric looked up and said, "Something important going on? You keep disappearing into all these little meetings."

I smiled at him, glad he was at least observant. "Nothing you need to worry about, Eric. Just an impromptu research project that I've asked Shelby and Marty to help me with." Then a thought struck me. "Eric, do you know who Edwin Forrest is?"

"No, ma'am. Is he a member here?"

"No, he's been dead for more than a century—although that might be said for some of our current members. He was an actor born in Philadelphia who went on to be quite famous in the nineteenth century. It seems fame doesn't last very long. Anyway, that big statue downstairs next to the elevator—that's Edwin, in all his glory. Anything else on my calendar?"

"Just the usual: board reports and that kind of thing. I left some letters on your desk for your signature."

What a relief: nice, simple, boring, and predictable things that didn't involve anyone dying. "Then I'll be in my office if anyone needs me."

———

I wasn't surprised when at the end of the afternoon, Marty walked in and dropped into a chair.

"You look frustrated. Have you been working with Shelby all day?" I asked.

Marty scrubbed her fingers through her short hair. "With a quick break for lunch. The good news is, she's got the hang of this research, and she's really into it now. The bad news is, she doesn't know the kind of details I know, so it's been kind of slow, going back and forth and filling in the spreadsheet. The worse news is, we still don't have anything conclusive, so we haven't been able to eliminate any group. Heck, I'm scared we're going to find *more* possible connections. Like former members of the Merion Cricket Club or members of the committee for the Devon Horse Show. You know, I thought the Terwilliger family was kind of tangled, but a lot of these people overlap in the most unexpected ways. And how far should we go? If two people sat next to each other at a mayor's banquet in 1993, does that count as a connection?"

"Well, maybe one of them spilled red wine all over the other, and the spillee has been nursing a grudge ever since."

"Very funny." Marty sighed. "You know, the problem is not knowing whether some piece of information is important or if we're wasting our time. And the Society's." She stared pensively at my ceiling. "Did all three take the same medicine when they overdosed?"

"I don't know. I didn't think to ask. Do you think it matters?"

"Maybe. If the police assumed the death in each case was natural, they might not check prescriptions. Of course, there are plenty of over-the-counter medications that can kill you if you take too much, particularly if you're old or have other underlying conditions. Or if you mix them with alcohol. Why the heck does toxicology take so long in the real world? On these television shows, you get results in about three minutes. If these are murders, a whole lot more people could get killed before anybody even sees the first reports. Stupid, isn't it?"

"I can't argue with that. But everything costs money, and a lot of police departments or government agencies don't have as much as they need, and the labs are underfunded and understaffed."

"True enough," Marty said. "I'll take this stuff home

with me and go over it again tonight. You going to talk to Jimmy?"

"I . . . don't know. I'd rather wait until we had some-thing solid to tell him."

"Good luck with that. See you in the morning."

CHAPTER 8

All the way home, I wrestled with whether to call James. And then wondered why I was reluctant. Okay, I'll admit it—I wanted to hear his voice. I wanted to reassure myself that we were actually together in some way, shape, or form, and I wasn't just fantasizing about a relationship with a hot FBI agent.

But maybe part of the problem was precisely that he was an FBI agent. I felt flattered that he considered me a good resource for certain information, and I was happy to help, but almost every time he called me, I had to ask whether it was for business or pleasure. I felt like a frustrated teenager. *Does he like me? Really like me?*

So here we were in the thick of it again. Someone might be killing Philadelphia board members, with the stress on *might*, for reasons nobody could fathom. Being a board member for a cultural institution is boring, most of the time. Nobody had ever thought it was dangerous, except to your checkbook. You sat through meetings, reviewed budgets (well, you were supposed to—I knew our board members usually gave them no more than a cursory glance), planned events, and hit up friends and peers for financial contributions. The last was probably the most important, and some board members were clearly better at it than others. Was it possible that some disgruntled soul had been asked once too often for a gift and had decided to eliminate anyone who asked? That would be an interesting addition to Shelby's chart: who had asked whom for a contribution. I knew we had some sort of records for that in our own files—development usually assigned board members an "ask" list. But finding that for any other place, like the museum? Not likely, and probably overwhelmingly large, even if the institution was willing to share.

It would be a lot easier to look at this Forrest Trust, because the Society had a direct connection. I *should* know more about it, since the Society currently had possession of some of its objects and money, but since there had never been any problems with the arrangement, I suppose we had mainly ignored it. I didn't know how much the trust was worth, but it couldn't be large, and I doubted that the trustees had much to do. Why kill any of them? There was neither power nor money to be gained.

I went home, threw together an uninspired dinner, then settled down in front of the television for some mindless entertainment. Then the phone rang: James.

"Hey there," I said articulately. "I hope you're not calling because someone else is dead."

"No, I'm not."

"Have I violated any laws?"

He chuckled. "Not that I know of. Have you?"

"Nope. I'm a sterling, upright citizen. But I'm glad you called." I pulled my bare feet under me on the couch, and we talked happy piffle for a while. Nice. Maybe I was too old to be doing this, but I didn't care. Neither, apparently, did James. Maybe he'd had a romantically stunted youth, like I had.

It wasn't until we'd begun winding down that he said, "You're still looking into the boards?"

Back to business, then. "Yes. Marty and Shelby are making great progress. I didn't want to bother you with the lists until we found something significant. I hadn't realized how interconnected Philadelphia society was and still is. Although I don't know why I'm telling you—you grew up with it."

"And I hated the snobbery of it all. Sure, I went to the right schools and knew the right people, but I joined the FBI because I wanted to do something with my life, not just have lunch at the Union League. The rest of my family still hasn't forgiven me."

There was a hint of bitterness in his tone. I felt for him: how peculiar to be forced to apologize for doing something good and useful. "Marty respects you."

"Marty thinks I'm still a snoopy, snot-nosed kid."

"Were you ever?"

"Snoopy, yes. Snot-nosed? I hope not. Although we did have one cousin . . ."

More piffle. In the end I had to end it. "We're meeting again tomorrow morning. Maybe we'll have something for you then. You're still not officially involved?"

"Nope. Like you, I'm waiting until I have more than

a vague suspicion before I ask to be invited to the dance.
I'll talk to you tomorrow, Nell."

"I'll call you no matter how our meeting goes. Good
night."

═══════

The next morning found Marty, Shelby, and me huddled
in the boardroom before nine o'clock. Eric had beaten us
in and made coffee. No matter what I said or didn't say,
he seemed to sense that there was something going on,
but he wasn't going to pry, bless him.

I surveyed my colleagues in . . . what was it we were
doing? Crime solving? FBI research? I settled on "board
candidate analysis," which was nice and neutral sounding
and non-incriminating, just in case anybody asked. Thank
goodness we didn't have to account for our hourly pro-
ductivity at the Society, as I'd heard some businesses
required, because we were throwing a whole lot of hours
at this project, which might end up with little result.

"So, what have we got?" I asked.

Marty and Shelby exchanged a glance; Shelby nodded
at Marty to proceed.

"Not a whole lot," Marty said flatly. "Or maybe too
much."

"Which means?" I prompted.

"Based on our combined input, we have thirty-seven
people who are linked to either two or three of the institutions in question, or by other external factors such as club
memberships or location of vacation homes. And a lot of
other variables that I won't bother you with."

"Isn't that good news? It's a shorter list than yesterday's."

"I suppose. But I don't know what to do with it." Marty really looked deflated.

"Maybe you're too close to all these people, Marty," Shelby suggested. "I don't know most of them, so I can be objective. Nell, I think Marty's reluctant to look at any of her friends as killers, potential victims, or suicidal. I know I would be, if I knew any of these people."

I nodded. "Makes sense. No reflection on you, Marty, but maybe Shelby's right. Maybe this is too personal for you."

Marty sat up straighter in her chair. "Well, if we don't find out something soon, any one of my friends or relatives might be the next victim. I can't just sit here and wait to see who the next person is to die. Maybe even me."

That stopped me. I hadn't considered that she might consider herself a target. Was Marty Terwilliger actually afraid? "But you're not affiliated with the Art Museum or the trust."

"Don't be so sure. My father gave a nice Degas to the museum. And you should know by now that the Society and the trust overlap. They've given us money and collections."

"So you're three for three. I see your problem." Though I didn't see what to do about it.

There was a rapping at the door. Eric called out, "Agent Morrison is on the phone for you."

I felt a chill. Was he calling with more bad news?

I turned back to Marty and Shelby. "I have to take this; I'll be back in a few." Before they could answer, I shut the door behind me and went to my office and shut that door, too. I took a deep breath and picked up the phone. "James? Is . . ."

"Is anyone else dead? No. But I wanted to pass on one piece of news. The three people who died? In each case, the cause was an overdose of a medication that had been prescribed for them. But the numbers don't match up."

"What do you mean?"

"You know when you pick up a prescription, you get a certain number of pills, and the pharmacy keeps a record of that?"

"Sure, and that's why I get reminders from them that I'm running out, as if I can't tell by just looking at the bottle. So?"

"In Adeline Harrison's case, she had called in her prescription but hadn't picked it up yet. The bottle she had at home should have had only one or two more pills in it, but her blood level showed far more. Where did those pills come from?"

I turned that over in my mind. "Did the pharmacy say that she was scrupulous about refilling her prescription on schedule?"

"They did, and all her other prescriptions tracked closely. That's why this one stood out. The one that killed her is the only anomaly."

"Could she have been hoarding them, planning on using them to kill herself?"

"Interesting theory, but in this case, unlikely. She'd seen her doctor recently, and he'd given her a clean bill of health, as far as possible for someone of her age. No terminal illnesses, not even arthritis. She took a number of medications for various complaints, but none of them was life-threatening. Adeline Harrison took good care of herself."

"What was she taking medication for?"

"Low blood pressure. Not unusual in older people, and she wasn't taking a very large dose. Doubling it unexpectedly could cause real problems."

"And you think that means . . . ?" I waited almost breathlessly for his answer.

"That somebody else gave her those pills. Someone brought enough to do the job. That person hadn't counted on the refill still sitting at the pharmacy."

I felt both glad and saddened at the same time. It was progress, at least. "So does that mean you're officially on the case now?"

"Not yet, but it's a step closer. I'll still need more. How's your meeting going?"

"Marty and Shelby have whittled things down to a short list of other possible names who fit the victim profiles, but it's still got close to forty people on it. James . . . maybe I shouldn't tell you, but I think Marty's scared. She's on that list."

"Because she's connected to so many things? Maybe she's right to be scared. Tell her not to accept candy from strangers."

"James, this is serious!"

"I know," he said gently. "I care about Marty. I'm doing the best I can. Tell her to be careful, will you? I'd prefer you didn't tell her and Shelby about the pills, but you can tell them it wasn't suicide. That's the best I can do at the moment."

"It may help. Wait—do you know how the pills were administered? Orally, by injection, inhaled?"

"Not yet. I've got friends at the labs where the analyses

were done, so they tipped me off. But I didn't get the full reports, or maybe they haven't finished the analyses."

"Okay. Look, I think we can clean up the spreadsheets and get them to you later today. That is, if you still want them?"

"I do. I promise I won't blow your chances of fundraising."

"You'd better not, or you'll have to write a check to make up for it. Do you have six figures in the bank?"

"Uh, no comment. Can I come by around five and pick them up?"

"Sure. Give me a call when you arrive downstairs so I can let you in."

"Will do."

After we'd hung up, I went back to the conference room. Both women looked up at me with fear in their eyes.

I hurried to fill them in. "No, it's not bad news. James said I could tell you one piece of information that might be important: Adeline's death doesn't look like suicide, and it at least suggests that the other deaths might not be. He thinks it's murder, but he still doesn't have enough to open an official case."

"Well, at least we know that our work here might be good for something," Marty said. She stood up abruptly. "I'm going to go distract myself by bothering Rich in the processing room."

Shelby stood up as well. "Then I'll go pretty up my spreadsheets. Will you be passing them on to Agent James?"

"He said he'd be here later this afternoon to pick them up. Thanks, both of you. Good work."

I went about my usual business for the rest of the day—appalling how much paperwork was involved in running an institution—and James called about four to say that he was running late, and would I mind waiting until six? I told him that was fine.

Shelby stopped by shortly after his call to give me the spreadsheets. She dropped into a chair and said, "Well, I've learned a lot."

I sat back in my chair. "I can imagine. I won't claim I knew half of what you put together. It does seem kind of incestuous in Philadelphia, doesn't it?"

"Sure does, although I'm sure it's just as bad in other cities. It's all about who knows who, and there's a lot of horse trading that goes on. You know, I'll give to your cause if you'll give to mine."

"Isn't that the truth? I guess it's kind of like a local aristocracy. So I have to work that much harder to make people open their checkbooks."

"Marty is part of it, though," Shelby said thoughtfully. "Do you think she *should* be scared?"

"I don't know, Shelby. In the more than five years I've known Marty, I've never seen her scared of anything, but I think you're right—this has her rattled. Give Marty a tangible problem and she's all over it. But this? It's harder when you don't know if, or from where, an attack is coming. But she's a single woman who lives alone. So I'd rather she was on her guard, just in case."

"Amen. And here I thought this would be a nice cushy job." Shelby stood up. "Well, I'm heading home in a little while, unless you need me for something else."

"Go! I'm going to stick around and hand your information to James."

Shelby grinned. "I think you should go back to his place and go over them in detail. Maybe a bottle of wine would help."

I won't say the same thought hadn't crossed my mind. "I'll see you in the morning, Shelby."

CHAPTER 9

Once the third floor had emptied out, I went downstairs to wait for James. I watched as Front Desk Bob gently ushered out a few lingering patrons who had just one more item they had to look at right now. I sympathized: many people couldn't make too many trips here, and it was frustrating to have so many resources and so little time to use them. We were doing the best we could, making documents accessible online, but it would never be enough. Most of the visitors had no idea who I was, as I smiled and nodded when they went out the door, clutching their precious notes. When the rooms were emptied, Bob looked at me. "You need me to stay?"

I shook my head. "No, you go on. I'm waiting for someone. I'll lock up."

"See you tomorrow." Bob disappeared toward the back of the building, to make sure everything was secure in the rear.

Normally I found the silence of the empty building soothing. The thick walls of the Society building effectively muffled noises from the outside world, even though the street outside was a busy one. It seemed so hard to imagine murder and mayhem in this stately space, but I had learned the hard way that even here, some less than pretty things lurked. I'd come face-to-face with a couple of them. Sometimes I marveled that I could handle coming into work each day.

Because I loved the place, of course. I loved being close to so much history and sharing it with the public. It wasn't the past that was dangerous, it was the present.

Still, I jumped when my phone trilled: James, waiting outside. I gathered up my bag, making sure Shelby's envelope of spreadsheets was still there, and hurried to open the heavy front door, a relic from an earlier time. I armed the alarm system, pulled the door shut behind me, and turned to welcome James.

He looked depressed, and I told him so.

"I keep thinking I'm missing something—something that would convince the right people that we have a serial killer on our hands."

I glanced around to see if anyone, friend or stranger, had overheard the term *serial killer*, but the pedestrians kept moving. "Maybe our list will help."

"If it doesn't, I don't know what I can do next."

I had never seen James Morrison so frustrated or helpless. "Do you want to talk about it?"

"If you're willing, it might help if we went over the list together. I'd ask Marty, but she has a tendency to go off half-cocked."

"I know what you mean, but right now I think she's

really worried. And I've already told her she's too close to the people involved to see the big picture, if there is one. How about we pick up some food and go to your place?"

"I'd really appreciate it."

"Great. Let's stop at that Indian place—it's on the way."

I was always amused at how differently James and I had made homes for ourselves. I lived in a tiny former carriage house in the leafy suburbs, and I had filled it with flea-market finds and a few semi-antiques from my family. James lived in a stark, sparely furnished apartment in an older building near the University of Pennsylvania campus. It was neat and efficient—everything my place wasn't. (He had, after several visits, admitted that he had a cleaning service that sent someone over once a week, which made me feel better.)

We spread out our food on his small but immaculately clean table (why was it *my* table was always covered with salt and pepper shakers, unanswered mail, and a host of things I didn't know where to put?), and he pulled an open bottle of wine from the refrigerator and held it up, raising an eyebrow.

I laughed. "Shelby would approve."

"What?" he said, retrieving two glasses.

"She mentioned that maybe some wine would loosen up our thinking." I took a glass from him and sipped.

"At this point, I'll try anything. There has to be something I'm not seeing."

I doubted that, but maybe he was looking for facts and obvious patterns, while what we had put together was more about nuances and subtle connections. "Why don't you look over the spreadsheets while we eat? Then we can talk about it."

I dished up from the takeout containers and kept my mouth shut while he quickly scanned the pages, nodding occasionally. By the time he'd finished reading, we'd cleaned our plates and finished our first glass of wine.

He squared up the pages and laid them on the table, then sat back and rubbed his face, as if trying to erase his fatigue. I remained silent, waiting for his assessment.

It came quickly. He pulled his chair forward, sat up, and looked at me. "First, I have to tell you this is great work. This is exactly the kind of stuff we probably wouldn't have found, certainly not as quickly."

I was warmed by the compliment. "Thank you. So why don't you tell me what conclusions you draw from it?"

"Before you tell me yours? Okay. It seems clear that the greatest overlap is on three primary institutions: the Art Museum, the Society, and this Forrest Trust. What's this trust all about?"

"I'm not familiar with it, but I've asked Shelby to put together a summary of whatever we have in our files."

"You came to the same conclusions?"

I smiled. "We did. But there were three of us, and it took us longer than it took you."

"So the three people who have died all shared connections, past or present, with these three institutions, or with each other through secondary links."

"Have you talked to a profiler?" I had no idea if the local FBI office had a stable of such people, but I knew James had found one who specialized in arsonists and who had previously been extremely useful to us.

"Since this is not an official investigation, I can't go to them." He got up and started pacing, although in his small place he couldn't go far.

"James, what would it take to convince the police to call it a murder?"

"I don't know!" It looked as though he wanted to punch a wall, but then he controlled himself and said less vehemently, "That's the problem. I have nothing concrete that I can take to the police, or to my bosses, who could override the police. Everybody's so damn budget-conscious these days that they won't look at anything that doesn't have a high probability of producing a solution—it has to look good in the Metro section. And even if everyone agreed that these deaths were somehow connected, we still don't have a motive. Why would anyone want these particular people dead?"

"I wish I could help," I said softly.

James stopped pacing and dropped back into his chair. "You already have, Nell. You put together information that we couldn't. You let me blow off steam. You believe me, and you tell me I'm not imagining things."

"And I mean it. James, we—Shelby, Marty, and me—all agree with you that something hinky's going on, we just can't quite put a finger on it. But why now, all of a sudden? Was there some trigger, or a deadline?"

"I don't know! And I'm getting damn tired of saying that. Marty's right—we don't know who's safe and who's at risk."

Poor James—even with his years of FBI experience, he couldn't figure this out. And if he couldn't, who could? Together we had cobbled together a glimmer of . . . something. But people were dying, and we weren't getting any closer to figuring out where to look next. Maybe sleeping on it would prod something to a higher level of our consciousness. Or maybe a distraction would jump-start our brains into working on the problem. A physical distraction, that had nothing to do with crime or society or museums. And I wasn't thinking of a fast game of tennis.

I stood up, walked deliberately around the table, and held out a hand. James looked up at me, confused, and when he took my hand I pulled him to his feet, and close to me. The man wasn't dumb: he figured out pretty fast where I was going with this.

We succeeded in distracting ourselves, or each other, for, oh, an hour or so. But who was counting? When I finally looked at my watch, I realized I had about thirteen minutes to catch my train. The alternative was showing up the next morning wearing the same clothes, which seemed a little tacky. Lucky men—no one cared if they wore the same necktie two days in a row, and it was easy to keep a clean shirt in a desk drawer.

"I've got to go," I whispered in James's ear.

"Maybe you should start keeping some clothes here," he responded.

"Maybe I will, in the future. But for now, we could both use some sleep. You know, to recharge the batteries and all that?"

"I'll drive you home. I don't have to be in early tomorrow. Besides, you're my consultant. I need to do some more consulting."

I didn't argue.

CHAPTER 10

James and I drove back to the city together in the morning. What would it be like to do this more often? I wasn't sure. I valued my "alone" time on the train, where I could read the paper or a book, or just sit and think. Time alone with the leisure to think was a rare commodity in my life.

At least I'd succeeded in cheering him up. The recharging part had been great, but the thinking part I was still working on. Maybe caffeine would help.

"You can go straight to your office. I'll walk from there," I said as we battled morning traffic going into the city.

"What, you don't want to be seen with me at eight o'clock in the morning?" he joked.

"I need the exercise, and I have to get some serious coffee along the way."

I was going to be a determined optimist and assume

that since James's phone hadn't rung last night, there were no new crises—or deaths. Of course, he might have turned it off, the better to pay attention to me and only me. Which was nice . . . but I made a mental note to check the obituaries again today regardless.

"You know, I've never asked what your average caseload is. I assume you don't handle only one case at a time."

"Of course not. We're busy, and there aren't enough agents to go around. Most often we deal with high-profile stuff—terrorism, drugs, organized crime, corporate fraud."

"And don't forget art theft," I said. We'd first met over his investigation of theft at the Society.

He smiled. "Yes, that, too. Any one of us works on ten to fifteen cases at a time. Not all of those are active. Some may be in the legal queue, and with others we've done all we can do and we're waiting for something new to jump-start it again, but they're still technically open cases. They stay open until we arrest someone. So you can guess how reluctant our office is to take on a case with nothing more than one agent's suspicions to go on, and no hard evidence.

I knew what he was saying, but the FBI's reluctance to open an official case into "our" deaths was still frustrating. "James, what does it take to make this an official case?"

He sighed. "There are standards for initiating an official FBI investigation. Trust me when I say that this case does not meet those standards. Yes, I believe there is a killer out there, but I honestly think that no one else in my office would, not yet. Have crimes been committed here? Probably. But the evidence does not reach a level that demands our action. Unfortunately that's not my decision to make."

"And so a killer gets to bump off his victims and thumb his nose at you?" I said bitterly.

He was angry now, and I couldn't really blame him. "You think that doesn't bother me? It does. Remember, some of the names on that list are people I know; some are even my relatives. Which puts me in an even more difficult position—if anything, I should recuse myself, if this ever does become a case, because of just that personal connection. I'm already working on this on my own time—what is it you want me to do, take justice into my own hands?"

Having an argument now wasn't going to accomplish anything—I knew he took this seriously. "I'm sorry," I said quietly. "I know this is difficult for you. But it's not easy for me, either—this is my community, and it hits close to home for me, too."

James's anger faded. "I'm trying, Nell. We're getting closer. And I have discussed it with my Agent in Charge, but he won't budge. We're already stretched thin, and this case, such as it is, just doesn't fit the criteria, not yet. At least he's listening to me. I hope that soon we will have enough to move forward."

We'd arrived at his office and I hadn't even noticed. James pulled deftly into a parking lot off Arch Street near Independence Hall and turned off the engine. He turned to face me. "I'm not stonewalling you, I swear. It would make me extremely happy to figure out what's going on here and stop it, with or without official permission."

"I know. We'll find the killer," I said, and with that I planted a serious kiss on his lips, then got out of the car and set off toward the Society before he could react.

I arrived a little later than usual, and members and visitors were already milling around the catalog room, trying to decide where to start. It was kind of overwhelming, I knew. I smiled at a few of them I recognized, and nodded hello to Felicity, our reference librarian, who was busy helping someone. The elevator arrived promptly for a change, and I took it to my office on the third floor. I was nearly there when Shelby spotted me. "Hey, Nell, got a moment?" she called out.

Since I hadn't "officially" arrived, I figured I might as well talk to her now. "Sure. What's up?"

"You saw James last night, right? And gave him our information?" she asked.

"I did, and yes. He agrees with our conclusions, but it's still not enough. And he's mad about it—at his agency, at himself, at the world in general. I don't blame him. He's good at what he does, but he has so little to work with on this, and his own agency won't let him do much more."

"Hey, he's got us!" Shelby said.

"And he appreciates that. We're going where no agent has gone before—into the darkest depths of Philadelphia society. Or do I mean heights?"

"Aren't we brave?" She smiled. "What now?"

I considered for a moment. Maybe we were getting too bogged down in the details and missing the big picture. "I'm not sure. Let's talk it through." Maybe a night's sleep had produced some piercing insights. Well, half a night's sleep for me.

"Okay," Shelby began slowly. "Based on the three hundred or so names we've collected, representing the past and present board members serving Philadelphia-area nonprofits, three institutions connect the highest number of individuals: the Art Museum, the Society, and the Edwin Forrest Trust. That's just over ten percent of the names."

I nodded. "Good. Keep going."

Shelby looked a bit perplexed. "I'll try." She chewed on her bottom lip for a moment, then began again. "These people live in different areas, anywhere from Center City to out of state. Of course, they may all have lived closer to Philadelphia or in the city originally, but I haven't had time to check past addresses. Both men and women, although the group is skewed toward men."

"As are the boards," I said. "This is excellent. Keep going."

"Um . . ." Shelby said, clearly thinking while she talked. "Mostly WASPs. Age range is fifty to ninety, so I guess they didn't all go to prep school together, unless it was a legacy thing within a family. For those who held jobs, they were mostly professionals—lots of lawyers, for instance, and some stockbrokers and bank managers. The occasional politician. Most belong to multiple other organizations, like exclusive membership clubs, or the DAR for the women. If I had to guess, I'd say that most of them have been in the same room at the same time with most of the others. Okay, that's not real clear, but you know what I mean."

"I do. Excellent summary, Shelby."

"Thank you, ma'am, but does it get us anywhere? I mean, somebody at the FBI could probably come up with that much without cracking open a file."

"Probably." My phone rang, and Eric said, "It's Agent Morrison." I picked up.

"There's another death," he said without preamble.

I felt sick to my stomach. Shelby was watching, and I nodded then swallowed. "Is that person on the short list?"

"She is. Which makes it an order of magnitude more likely that we're on the right track."

I couldn't decide which question I wanted to ask next. How had this woman died? How was she connected? And was her death enough to convince the police that there should be an investigation?

In the end, I asked simply, "Who?"

"Her name was Edith Oakes. In her eighties. She lived in Wayne. And she's a cousin."

"Of yours and Marty's?"

"Yes."

This was not good. "How is she connected to the others?"

"She has been a board member for both the museum and the Society, although she withdrew from both maybe ten years ago—she had emphysema and stopped going out much. But she's still on the Forrest Trust board, because that requires minimal effort."

"How did she die?"

"Much the same way as the others, as far as we know. It's too soon for any official results—she was only found this morning, although she'd been dead since sometime late yesterday. Nothing overtly suspicious—if you don't know what we know. Or think we know."

"So not enough to interest the cops, I assume."

"No."

"This just keeps getting better and better," I said bitterly. "Any signs of disturbance? I assume she had money, if she lived in that neighborhood."

"The place was undisturbed. The police got involved early this morning, when her brother called them."

"Edith didn't live alone?" Wasn't this the first time that had happened?

"No, she shared a house with her unmarried brother. I understand he was the one who found her, but I don't have all the details yet."

"We need to talk to Marty. I haven't seen her this morning. Have you talked to her?"

"Not yet."

"Let me give her a call. Although if she's in the building, she may not have her cell phone on. James, hang on a minute." I put James on Hold while I fished out my own cell and punched Marty's cell number. It rang and rang, but no one answered.

Shelby had been watching me with growing concern. "What's going on, Nell?" she asked.

"There's been another death—someone James and Marty are related to. And James hasn't been able to reach Marty, and she's not answering her cell phone."

"Oh. That's bad. I'll try her at home," Shelby volunteered, and went through the same procedure using her own cell, with the same result. "No answer. You think she's here in the building?"

I went back to James on my office line. "James, she's not answering either of her phones. Let me go check in the building, and I'll get back to you."

"Let me know if you find her—I'll see what else I can learn about the death."

After I had hung up, I stood, fighting a prickle of concern. "I'll check the processing room."

Marty is a big girl, and she can take care of herself.

That's what I kept telling myself as I walked down the hallway to the processing room. When I entered the room, I was pleased to see Rich, Nicholas, and Alice all hard at work, albeit in different corners. Of course, that reflected the distribution of the materials they were working on: Rich, with a year or so of seniority, had claimed the best space for the Terwilliger Collection; Nicholas, with a higher title and a huge stack of materials from the FBI dump, er—no, there was still no better word than *dump*, at least for the moment—had staked out the back half of the room; and Alice, with few items under her direct supervision, had created a cozy nest in a corner. Alice's was the neatest space, but there was nothing out of the ordinary about the controlled chaos of the rest of the room.

"Morning, all. How's it going?"

Each of them mumbled something like "Good, fine, great." Frankly, I didn't feel like pressing them. Any problems they might have would only complicate my life right now.

"Has anybody seen Marty this morning? Rich, were you two planning anything?"

Rich shook his head. "Nope, on both counts. You know, she's been kind of distracted this week. She hasn't been hanging over my shoulder every minute like usual. Has she said something?"

"No. I just wanted to . . . get her opinion on something. I'm sure I'll see her sometime during the day. Thanks, guys. Back to work!"

I trudged back to Shelby's office. That prickle of worry was fast growing into a full-blown itch. Shelby looked up eagerly when I walked in, and I shook my head. "They haven't seen her today."

"Oh, Nell. Should we be worried? Because of . . . you know?"

Was I ready to jump to the conclusion that Marty had been murdered by the shadowy figure we were chasing? No, not yet. But I'd feel a lot better if I knew where she was. "Let's not get ahead of ourselves. I'll make the rounds of the building and see if I can spot her. You keep trying her phones. If we haven't tracked her down by lunch, I can take a run over to her house and see if she's there. She might simply have decided she doesn't want to talk to anyone, if she's heard about Edith." And if she wasn't at home, or at least, didn't answer the door, should I call James? No, it was premature to think about doing that. Marty would pop up, as she so often did. I was sure of it. Almost.

Through the morning I did my best to keep myself busy, but I didn't do a very good job of it. Midway through the morning I went out to Eric's desk and told him, "If Marty Terwilliger should happen to call, or if you see her in the building, can you tell her that I need to talk to her?"

"Of course. Shelby told me the same thing. Is something wrong?"

Poor boy. He was quick to pick up on my concern, but he didn't deserve to have my worries on his head. But I couldn't lie to him, either. "I hope not, Eric."

I went back into my office without giving him any more details. I sat at my desk and stared at nothing, my mind going in circles. Four deaths in the cultural community. All looked natural on first glance, like suicide if anyone looked more closely. All people who had led blameless lives—surely they each weren't harboring a deep, dark secret; or worse, sharing a single secret? No,

I assumed they were what they appeared to be: good citizens with philanthropic interests who gave their money and time to deserving cultural institutions. Who would want to kill people like that?

But it was happening.

By eleven thirty, I couldn't sit still any longer. I strode out of my office and told Eric, "I'm going to take an early lunch. I should be back in an hour."

When I walked toward the elevator, I ran into Shelby in the hallway. "I'm coming with you," she announced.

"Where am I going?"

"Marty's house, I assume."

"If she's there and looking for a little privacy, she'll be mad at us. But thanks, Shelby. I could use the company."

Together we left the building and turned left toward Rittenhouse Square and the Schuylkill River. I'd been to Marty's town house before. It was a nice brick building on a quiet side street, in a good neighborhood. The house was filled with an eclectic mix of antiques, mostly inherited, and modern touches that Marty had added, and somehow they all worked together. Not that Marty made any apologies for the unlikely mix. Her attitude was take it or leave it, and she really didn't care what anyone else thought.

It took about ten minutes to reach her town house, and I think we were both dragging our feet for the last block. If Marty answered the door, we could go ahead and share whatever new information we had garnered over the last twelve hours, including about the new death. If she didn't answer . . . well, we'd take that hurdle when we came to it.

In front of Marty's place, I walked up the few steps leading to the front door and rang the doorbell. I could hear it faintly inside, so I knew it was working, but I didn't hear any footsteps. Maybe Marty wasn't wearing shoes. I rang again, and waited, Shelby hovering on the step below me. Nothing. I grasped the polished brass knocker and rapped firmly a few times. Silence. Marty was either not there, or not answering for some reason.

"Now what, Nell?" Shelby said.

Like I knew. I called James. He answered. At least *someone* was where he was supposed to be. Since this was business, I cut to the chase. "James, have you heard from Marty today?"

"No. Why?"

"She's not at the Society. Rich hasn't seen her. In fact, nobody's seen her. Shelby and I have been calling her all morning on her cell and at home, and she hasn't picked up. We're at her house now, and there's no answer. Do you have any idea where she might be?"

James didn't answer immediately. I assumed he was turning over the possibilities in his mind, and probably coming to the same conclusions that Shelby and I had, and it wasn't that Marty was indulging herself in a three-hour bubble-bath.

"I have her key. I'll meet you there in ten minutes." He hung up abruptly.

I turned to Shelby. "The reinforcements are coming."

CHAPTER 11

Shelby and I felt conspicuous standing on the doorstep, so we sat down on the top step to wait for James to arrive. It was a delightful neighborhood, with plenty of shade trees and little traffic, yet still convenient to both Center City and the highways that led out of town. There were few people on the street. I kept peering in both directions, not so much watching for James as hoping that Marty would miraculously appear, either on foot or by car. She didn't.

When James arrived, I was both glad to see him and also a little afraid, because he would let us into the house and we would find . . . something. Or maybe nothing. Finding nothing would be only slightly more encouraging than finding . . . something worse.

James looked somber as he approached. "Nell, Shelby." He nodded. "Still no sign of Marty?"

Shelby and I stood up. "Nope, and no sounds from inside the house," I said. "Are we going in?"

He climbed the steps to stand beside us. "*I'm* going in. You two wait here."

I was both frustrated and relieved by his order. Shelby and I stayed put, sitting side by side without talking. Marty didn't believe in wall-to-wall carpet, so I could hear James's footsteps moving slowly through the building, up the stairs . . . and down again. It must have been five minutes before he opened the front door. I turned reluctantly, searched his face, and felt a wave of relief: he didn't look grim.

"Nothing," he said. "No one home, and nothing looks disturbed. Have you considered the thought that she might have gone somewhere of her own volition? She does have a life outside the Society, you know."

"Sure, but can you blame us for worrying? Yesterday she was concerned that she could be a target of this killer that nobody will acknowledge officially, and today she's nowhere to be found. Do you think she hopped on a plane to a foreign country? Does she have a summer place or three where she might be hiding?" I was working up a good head of steam, stoked mainly by tension.

"Nell," James said carefully, "I'm not questioning your concern. I'm here, aren't I? I've checked the place out, and everything looks normal. I don't know where Marty could have gone, but her absence may be completely innocent. Okay, maybe she should have let you know that she was going to disappear, but I can't exactly launch an investigation when she's been gone less than a day."

"Yeah, yeah," I muttered. I knew I was being unreasonable, but I had to do something. I looked at Shelby. "So I guess we return to work, and to worrying." Then I turned back to James. "I'll let you know if we hear from her. If we don't, how soon can you actually investigate?"

"Not before tomorrow. Nell, I'll do what I can, I promise. Right now, I'd better get back to the office."

"Go," I said. Needless to say there was no parting kiss. I knew I had no right to be mad at him, but I needed to be mad at somebody. When and if Marty showed up, I could get mad at her.

Shelby and I had covered a few blocks toward the Society before I stopped fuming. "Sorry about that," I said to her. "I was acting like a brat. I know there's not much that he can do. At least we didn't find her . . ."

Shelby finished my statement for me. "Dead? Hey, I think it's sweet that he came when you called. *And* tried to spare you from finding the body, if there was one, which, thank God, there wasn't. Haven't all the other victims been found at home?"

"Good point. Thanks, Shelby. Want to get some lunch on the way back?"

"Sure. We need our strength."

We settled for a fast sandwich at the small shop down the street from the Society. When we'd taken our orders to a table in the corner, I said, "What do we do now?"

Shelby chewed a large bite of her sandwich. After she had swallowed, she said, "*We?* I seem to recall that you keep dumping a whole lot of research in my lap. I'm not going to pretend that we've covered all the bases with the people on our list. Even if I focus on our three prime organizations, there's still a lot of digging to do. In addition to all the regular stuff for my job."

"I know, I know. I think I'll have little 'I Apologize'

cards made up to hand out—it'll save time. And now you're making me feel guilty, since I'm your boss and I'm supposed to be running the Society." For which I depended a whole lot on Marty's help and backup, but I couldn't say that to Shelby. "Thank goodness we're between major events."

"The Board Bash is next, isn't it?" Shelby asked.

"Yes, but not for months. Why?"

"You know, maybe I could kill two birds with one stone. If I have to look up all this stuff about the Forrest Trust, maybe we could use our Forrest collection as the focus for the event? Didn't I see something in the file about using the income from that endowment to promote the guy? We could easily justify spending the money on the party."

I stared at her. "Shelby, you're brilliant! From what I know, Edwin Forrest was quite a figure. We could really have some fun with it."

"Oh yeah? Tell me a little more about this Edwin guy."

"All right, let's see. He was born in Philadelphia, and his career began here, when he was in his teens. And he was still performing right up to his death in the 1870s. He was wildly popular, and from all that I've read, he was considered a pretty good actor, too—at least compared to some of his more over-the-top contemporaries. He took his fame seriously and tried to use it for good purposes. But he had his share of problems. For one thing, he married an English actress, but when they split up they both sued each other for divorce, very publicly—each claimed they'd found the other in the act of being unfaithful. The transcript of their divorce proceedings goes on for over a thousand pages. Edwin more or less lost, but not before dragging her name and his own through a lot of mud. Anyway, he ended up paying alimony forever."

"Nell, why do you know all this?" Shelby asked.

"He's part of Philadelphia history. And it's an interesting story."

"It is that. That divorce must have been pretty shocking for the nineteenth century. Did it hurt his career?"

"Not hardly. I mean, this guy was a megastar by standards back then. People literally died for him." When Shelby looked at me, I explained, "He had this rivalry thing going with an English actor named Macready, and they were performing in New York at the same time. There were riots in the streets between fans from both sides. And a bunch of people died—there are conflicting reports about how many. Again, Edwin picked himself up and kept on going. And, more relevant to our problem here, he made lots of money."

"That's where the trust comes in?" she asked.

"Exactly. He never remarried, and he and his wife had no children. As he got older, his health went downhill—it's kind of hard to piece together, but gout and arthritis are on the list."

"Maybe we'll skip the gout and arthritis part in the party-planning," Shelby joked. "Do we need approval for the theme? Like from the board?"

"Well, since I, the president, and you, the director of development, both endorse it, I think they'll agree. Let's pull together a presentation and see what we've got in the collection."

"I'm on it."

At least lunch had ended on a relatively cheerful and

productive note. We walked back to the Society, where everybody looked energetic and happy, oblivious to the possibility of a lurking killer. Upstairs I stopped at Eric's desk hoping for a phone message, but there were none from either Marty or James.

"Good lunch?" Eric asked.

"Not bad. I should be in my office the rest of the day. If you've got any paperwork I should deal with, now would be a good time to get it done."

"I'll get the folder out."

Mindless paperwork was a great distraction, I had found. I found myself thinking about the idea Shelby had hatched for our next big event, and I still liked it. The Society holds two major social events each year: a gala, usually in the late fall, and another more relaxed event in the spring. The gala is usually intended to draw in our more affluent members and impress them with what we're doing with their money. The other event brings in a broader slice of our membership and we try to make it fun. The latter was still more than nine months away, but we like to have the theme nailed down by the fall. I was amazed that nobody had thought of using Edwin Forrest before, especially since we were sitting on an abundance of materials *and* the money to help pay for the event, in the name of preserving Edwin's memory. Poor Edwin: he definitely had slipped from public memory, even locally, even though he had been a major public figure for a large part of the nineteenth century—not to mention a very colorful individual.

I knew we had a rather generic finding aid—basically a simple list—for the items related to him that had come with the loan of the collection, but it was probably too vague to be of much use. Our staff processors were all very busy dealing with implementing our new database (Nicholas) and cataloging the FBI collection (Rich and Alice). Maybe I'd save the research for myself. We weren't in a rush, and it had been a while since I'd spent any quality time in the collections. Besides, I rather liked what I knew of Edwin, and wouldn't mind finding out more about my marble friend. I'd start by pulling out the original inventory now, to see what it could tell me about the Forrest Trust and its holdings.

Somehow I managed to get through the afternoon without obsessing about Marty's whereabouts too much, though I'll admit that I flinched every time the phone rang, holding my breath until Eric forwarded the call to someone else. Not the most efficient way to get anything done, but luckily the chores I'd assigned myself didn't take much focus.

Shortly before five, however, I looked up—and saw Marty standing in the doorway. I bounded out of my chair, and practically threw myself at her.

"Marty, where the hell have you been? We've been going crazy!"

Marty appeared bewildered by my reaction. "I thought most of the time you were happy to get me out of your hair. Why the big fuss? You heard about Edith's death?"

"Yes, of course. James called me as soon as he found out. We worried that maybe you were next. I even got James to let us into your house to check, just in case."

Marty gave one of her unladylike snorts. "I'm touched. I was with cousin Harbeson." When I continued to stare blankly, she clarified, "Edith's brother. They shared the family house."

"God, Marty, you could have let James know. Or me."

Marty looked contrite. "Sorry. I wanted to get over there as quickly as I could, and then I had to deal with Harbeson."

James had mentioned a brother. "Where was he when Edith died?"

"He'd been playing golf at his club yesterday, and he stayed on at the bar with some friends. He came home late. He thought Edith had fallen asleep on the couch, so he just went upstairs to bed. He wasn't exactly sober. When he came down in the morning he realized she wasn't breathing, and he called me. I told him to call 9-1-1. Then I headed out there, fast. Harby doesn't . . . handle things well. The police came, then the medical examiner; he pronounced Edith gone and carted her away. Harby wants me to help with the funeral."

"I've got to tell James," I said, picking up the phone. When he answered, I said without preamble, "Marty's here."

"I heard. I'm coming over. Stay there."

I hung up, feeling happier than I'd been all day. "Will Harby talk to James?" I asked Marty.

"About Edith? Why not? Harby knows Jimmy—they're cousins, too."

"Marty, I still don't understand how you could just disappear like that, without telling us. You know that Edith was on the list of board members?"

"Of course I do. That's one reason I needed to get out there. I didn't want Harby to screw up any evidence, if there was any."

"Did you find anything?"

"I never had a chance to look. By the time I got there,

the police had arrived and Harby was dithering, so I had to take charge of him, and by then it was too late to look."

"And what did the police think?" I was pretty sure I knew the answer, but I had to ask.

Marty's expression was bleak. "Natural causes."

CHAPTER 12

Luckily there were few people around when I went downstairs once again to let James in, since it was after five. Otherwise someone might wonder why an FBI agent kept dropping by every other day. I had resisted the urge to tie Marty to a chair so she wouldn't disappear again. Instead, I caught Shelby before she left for the day and told her that Marty was in my office and to keep her there until James could talk to her.

James didn't look happy. "Is something else wrong?" I asked as soon as I saw his face.

"No, not really. But each"—he looked quickly around to make sure he couldn't be overheard—"incident makes it look more and more like a serial killer, and there's *still* nothing I can do. At least Marty's all right. Did she tell you where she'd been?"

I gave him the elevator version on our way up to the third floor. Once I finished, I leaned against him, just a bit. He laid a hand on my shoulder. Neither of us said anything more, but this probably qualified as high passion within these stately walls.

Marty and Shelby were bickering when we reached my office. On seeing James, Marty jumped out of her chair. "What are you, Jimmy? My keeper?"

"Marty," James said with admirable self-restraint, "we had reason to think that something might have happened to you. We were worried."

"Jimmy, I've been taking care of myself for years. Since when do I have to account for my whereabouts every hour?"

"Since someone started killing your friends, and now a relative," I said.

"Oh, no," Shelby gasped.

"Oh." Marty's pique evaporated. "Sorry, I hadn't looked at it that way. You know, when you live alone, you get used to not having to answer to anyone."

"I do know," I said. On some dark nights, I wondered how long my rotting corpse would lie in my house before anyone noticed.

"So what are we doing here?" a chastened Marty asked, sitting down again.

"I don't think you need me for this discussion," Shelby said. "I'll just take myself home now, shall I?"

"I'll see you in the morning, Shelby," I replied. She knew I'd fill her in then.

James waited until Shelby had left before beginning. "All right, here's what I know. Edith Oakes was found dead on a couch in the parlor this morning by her brother, Harbeson." Marty nodded, presumably because that fit with what she knew. "The medical examiner collected the body and his preliminary determination was natural causes, but he was persuaded to carry out a more detailed examination. I asked him to look for a couple of specific drugs."

"Persuaded? Wouldn't he have done that anyway?" I asked.

"Given Edith's age, not necessarily. As they did not in the other cases, initially."

"Jimmy, how did you hear about her death?" Marty demanded.

"You know I've been watching for deaths that fit the profile." He didn't add any further detail.

"You knew about Edith's board service, James?" I asked.

He nodded. "I looked at your list. Marty, when did you get involved?"

"This morning, as soon as Harby found her. He had no idea what to do, so he called me. I made sure he'd call the police, and then I told him I'd be over to help him, and that's where I've been ever since. It finally hit him that she's gone, which is why I was there so long. It never occurred to me to turn my cell phone on or to call you—I had my hands full with him. I'm sorry you had to worry."

James was staring over our heads. "So there's no crime scene to speak of."

Marty gave a short laugh. "Sorry, buddy—nothing useful."

"What now?" I asked.

James sighed. "I'd like to talk to Harbeson, face-to-face. Was he going to stay at the house tonight or with friends?"

"Home, as far as I know. His only friends are golf

and drinking buddies. You planning to go right now?"
Marty said.

"The fresher his memories, the more likely they are
to be accurate. Will he be drinking?"

"Probably," Marty said glumly. "I don't know what
you're going to get out of him. You know Harby—he's
vague at the best of times, which this isn't."

"I have to try, Martha," James said.

"Can I come?" I asked, feeling left out. "After all, I've
never seen the house, and I might notice something that
you wouldn't." A lame excuse, but the best I could come
up with.

James looked at me, and I could swear his mouth
twitched. "I'll take you home afterward. Since we'll be
so close anyway."

"That would be fine," I said demurely.

Marty snorted. "I'll let you two figure things out. I've
had enough of Harby for one day. How any grown man
can be so useless . . ." She shook her head. "Tell him I'll
see about the funeral arrangements in the morning."

"I'll do that. Why don't you call and tell him I'll be
stopping by shortly? And please, keep your phone on."

"Yes, Jimmy, I will keep my phone on at all times,
until you catch this bastard. I liked Edith. She had a great
sense of humor, and I know she wasn't ready to go. And
I will lock my doors and watch myself on the street. I
want to be around to see you do the catching."

"Then let's head out," James said. Marty and I gathered up our things and followed him meekly.

We dropped Marty off at her house, since it was more
or less on the way out of the city to Harbeson's house in

Wayne, and waited at the curb until we saw Marty enter through her front door before pulling away.

"How well did you know Edith?" I asked.

"Not very," James said, navigating the traffic easily. "I mainly saw her at family gatherings, when I was growing up. She was what you would call a 'character,' and her brother, Harbeson, was like the moon in her orbit. Neither ever married. They inherited this big barn of a house in Wayne—I think it has eight bedrooms—and have lived there all of their lives. Harbeson never had to work. I don't really know what he does except play golf, or at least talk about it. They're the last of their generation. I'm sure they never expected their story to end in murder."

"How very *déclassé*," I said sarcastically. "The *right* people don't do murder."

"Exactly."

"I'm glad Marty is all right. I wasn't overreacting, was I?"

He sneaked a quick glance at me. "I don't think so. Better safe than sorry. And that applies to both of you."

On a good day, the drive might have taken forty minutes; this was not a good day. We arrived at the Oakes house in Wayne about six thirty. It occurred to me belatedly that we hadn't eaten, and most likely Harbeson hadn't either. Should we ask him out to dinner? Or order in pizza?

Harbeson must have been expecting us, since all the lights on the ground floor were blazing, even though it was still full daylight. He opened the door as soon as we set foot on the steps leading to the front door.

"Come in, come in. James, thank you for coming. And this must be Miss Pratt? Marty mentioned you were to accompany James."

"Nell," I said, and extended my hand. He took it and pumped it several times, stopped, then started again, as if he had forgotten he'd already done it. "Can I get you anything? I don't know what there is in the way of nibbles. Edith always looked after that. I can offer you a cocktail," he said eagerly.

"Harbeson, please don't bother," James said carefully. "Can you tell me about what happened?"

"I need a cocktail first. I won't be a minute." He disappeared toward the back of the house, leaving James and I standing in the broad front hall.

James led the way into the front parlor. The furniture looked as though it could date from the original construction of the house, a century or more earlier, and ran toward plush-covered horsehair. Dreadfully unyielding and uncomfortable stuff, horsehair, but virtually indestructible. A long settee stood in front of the large-screen television.

James nodded before I could ask. "That would be where they found her."

I could hear Harbeson bumbling around somewhere in the background, and the clink of glass on glass. I looked around the rest of the room: every surface was covered with knickknacks and mementos, all miraculously dust-free. Nothing was knocked over or looked out of place.

"This is your crime scene?"

"I assume." James was scanning the room.

"Anything seem wrong to you?"

"No. It's always looked like this, as far back as I can remember. Woe betide you if you moved a china dog on the end table. Edith would notice as soon as she walked into the room."

"James, why do you know this? How much time did you spend here?"

"Not a lot, but those few occasions are seared in my memory," he replied.

Harbeson finally returned, clutching a tall glass with a few ice cubes and a lot of tan liquor. I could smell it from where I stood. "All set. Please, sit down." He looked around the room as if he had never seen it, hovered for a moment over the settee, and then drifted over to another chair and dropped into it. James and I claimed smaller chairs that proved rickety when sat upon.

"Do you mind telling me what you found when you came home last night?" James began.

Harbeson shook his head, staring at the glass in his hand. "Terrible thing, terrible. I arrived home about nine o'clock, I think it was. I'd been over at the club, met some friends, and we got to talking, and I kind of lost track of time. I'd been out all day, and I'd missed lunch, so we ordered something quick for dinner. When I got home, I let myself in the back door and called out for Edith, but she didn't answer. No, she didn't." Harbeson stopped and took a long swig of his drink. Then he gave a start and began speaking again. "I thought maybe she'd gone up already, but it wasn't all that late, and then I thought maybe she'd fallen asleep watching one of her shows. She does that a lot these days. I came in here and saw her on the couch, covered with an afghan, so I didn't disturb her. When I came down this morning, I saw that she hadn't moved all night . . . and she wasn't breathing. And then I called Martha, and she told me to call the police."

"You did fine, Harby," James said gently. "How did Edith look?"

"Just like she always did. As though she had just lain down and gone to sleep. Well, her mouth was open and she was drooling a bit, which wasn't like her. She was very careful about appearances."

"Nothing knocked over or spilled?"

Harbeson shook his head. "Not that I noticed, but then, Edith always tells me that I don't notice much of anything."

It broke my heart that he kept referring to his sister in the present tense. Despite what Marty said, he clearly still hadn't processed that Edith wasn't coming back.

"And the back door was locked when you came in?" When Harbeson nodded, James went on, "What about the front door?"

He nodded vigorously. "It was locked, too. I had to open it for the police."

"Had Edith said anything about not feeling well?"

"Not at all. She'd had a quarterly checkup only a few days ago, and she was lording it over me that she was healthier than I was. She said the doctor had told her she could live to be a hundred. We had an uncle who lived to be 103, you know. Smoked a cigar after dinner every day of his life. Do you like cigars, Jimmy?"

Harbeson's glass was already half empty, and his attention was waning in direct proportion to what he consumed.

"Not particularly, Harby. Did Edith have many visitors?"

"People who came to see her? Not really. She'd out-lived most of her friends, and the ones who are still around can't drive anymore."

"Had anyone come around lately? Pollsters, sales-people?"

"I don't think so. Not while I was here, but I'm at the club most afternoons. I've got a foursome, and we get in nine holes when the weather is good, and play bridge when it's raining. Wait . . . there was something . . ." Harbeson squinted as if the act of thinking was painful. Then he brightened. "I know! There was a cup in the dish drainer."

"Why did you notice that?" James asked.

"You know Edith. It was a cup she hated. It was from a set that belonged to our aunt Prudence, part of her wedding china. Edith said the handles were in the wrong place and it made the cups hard to balance. I don't know what would have possessed Edith to use one of them. And if she had washed it, she would have dried it and put it away. She always did. She was particular about things like that."

I allowed myself a small spurt of hope: maybe the killer had left something of himself behind on the cup? Fingerprints? DNA?

James must have been thinking the same thing. "What did you do with the cup, Harby?" James said patiently, as if he was talking to a child.

"Well, I put it away. That's what Edith would have wanted. And . . . I didn't want to go back to this room, with Edith . . . you know. So after I called the police, I cleaned up the kitchen a bit, just to keep busy, and I had some breakfast. And then they rang the doorbell in front and I let them in."

James and I exchanged a glance. If the cup had meant anything, it was worthless as evidence now. I could just see trying to convince the police that Edith had been murdered because there was a cup in the kitchen, from the set she disliked, and it hadn't been put away.

"Mr. Oakes, have you eaten since breakfast?" I asked. I worried about him pouring liquor into an empty stomach.

Harbeson smiled at me. "Oh, yes, Marty made sure I had plenty of food. And I have some lovely frozen dinners. I just love those little compartments, you know? So neat and tidy, and nothing to clean up after. You're very sweet to worry about me, my dear. Who did you say you were? Do you work with Jimmy at the FBI?"

Marty may have told him I was coming but not why. "No, I'm a friend of Jimmy's and Marty's. Sometimes I help Jimmy out."

"Marty was so helpful today. Was that today? She's going to take care of Edith's funeral, and contact all our relatives and friends. She's very good at that. Are you sure I can't offer you a drink? Or a pot pie?"

James caught my eye, and we stood up. "Harby, if you think of anything else, please let me or Marty know, will you?" James said.

"I will. She said she'd come back tomorrow to help me. I think I'll just have one of my dinners and watch a little TV. You'll come to the funeral, won't you, Jimmy?"

"Of course I will, Harby. I'll see you soon. Don't get up, we'll find our way out."

On the porch James paused a moment, looking out over the rolling expanse of lawn, seeing nothing.

"Will he be all right by himself?" I asked softly.

"What? Oh, I think so. He's fine as long as he does what he's familiar with. Edith was always smarter than him—she took care of things like the bills and getting the lawn mown. He may need some assistance going forward—I'm not sure he even knows where the super-market is."

"Poor man. Did you accomplish what you wanted to there?"

"Yes. I needed to talk to Harby as soon as possible. You've seen him—would you trust his memory for more than a day? And I wanted to check the crime scene, except there isn't one. Damn. Are you hungry?"

I thought about what I had in my larder: not much. "Do you know the hotel in the center of Wayne? We could get dinner there."

"Fine," he said absently. "Just give me directions."

I took his arm. "First you get in the car . . ."

CHAPTER 13

The restaurant in the old but nicely refurbished hotel in the center of Wayne proved a good choice: there were enough people there to make it sound successful, but not enough that it felt crowded or loud. The crowd was moderately upscale. An author years ago had labeled those who lived in Wayne "Bobos"—bourgeois bohemians—and the label fit. The restaurant offered some light dishes, and that was all we were in the mood for. We sat at a small table in a corner and ordered, and started with a glass of wine each.

I settled more comfortably in my chair and looked at James. He looked . . . tired, distracted, frustrated. "Anything I can do?" I asked.

He finally wrenched his attention back to me. "Sorry, I'm not very good company, am I? I'm just trying to work out a way to get involved with this officially. If there is a killer at work here, he's very good."

"Do you think there's a chance it's an 'if'?"

"No, I don't. There are four people dead. Heck, there may be more, if I go through that list of yours."

"I can ask Shelby to cross-reference the names with obituaries. These people are clearly the type to have had detailed obituaries. That is, if you want more bad news?"

"Comes with the job, unfortunately. I hate to ask for it, but I need to know. But as I started to say, if these people were deliberately killed, our killer knew something about the targets. There have been no signs of violence. All the victims were found in their homes, and either the killer is a brilliant lock-picker or the victims all let him or her in."

"Do you think this teacup thing is important?"

"Maybe. Both Edith and Harby were—or are—very set in their ways. Edith always insisted on a cup of tea in the late afternoon. Always black Indian tea, and always with a splash of milk."

"James, how much time did you spend with her?"

He looked at me and smiled. "You mean, how do I know details like this? Within the family Edith was famous for her insistence on social rituals, never mind that she was the only one left who followed them. If you were in her home at four o'clock, by God you were going to have a cup of tea. I was always terrified that I'd break a glass or drop the sugar bowl."

"You're scarred for life." I took another sip of wine. "But if Harby, who may spend most of his time on another planet, noticed the wrong cup, which Edith would never have chosen for herself, then it must mean that the, uh, guest was there around four and grabbed the wrong one."

James nodded. "Yes. A guest who took the time to fix her a cup of tea. It could have been a man or a woman—clearly these hypothetical crimes don't take a lot of physical strength. So she had her tea, said good-bye to her guest, washed the teacup, started feeling woozy and lay down for a nap, and never woke up. Of course, we'll never know what was in the tea, though, because either Edith or her visitor washed the cup."

"Whatever Edith was dosed with, she was already out before Harby came home," I said.

"I'll check back with the ME and see if he can narrow the time of death."

The waiter arrived with our food, and I wondered what he would make of our rather odd conversation. He retreated quickly; good server manners, or had he overheard too much? I tasted my food: very nice. James looked down as if surprised to find a plate in front of him. "Try the veal. It's excellent," I told him.

We devoted a few minutes to eating, which impeded talking. I think we both needed a little time to wrap our minds around what we'd learned from Harby and what we could infer from it. Did this case really hinge on an out-of-place teacup? How many other small details like that had been overlooked in the earlier deaths?

Both James and I accepted the waiter's offer of coffee, and while we waited for it, I said, "You told me that our hypothetical killer used drugs that had been prescribed for each victim. Have I got that right?"

"Yes, that's right. We already checked whether the amounts of the drugs on hand were about right, given when the prescriptions had been filled. The quantities matched up, except in Adeline's case. Which suggests that the killer knew something about the drugs people in that age group were likely to use."

We both fell silent as the waiter appeared with coffees, sugar, cream, and spoons and set each out.

"Where would he get the medications?" I asked when the waiter had finally left.

"It wouldn't be difficult. On the street, or if he had some medical connection. Most of the time he could have used what he found in the house but the snafu with Adeline's prescription suggests that he may have brought the drugs with him. Maybe he was getting cocky since no one had noticed. But then, he never expected anyone to look too closely at the manner of death."

The poor waiter appeared at that moment to offer a dessert menu. James and I turned in unison to bark "No" at him, and he fled. I laughed. "We'll have to leave him a nice tip. What must he think of us?"

"That either we're plotting murder or we're law enforcement officials. Which at least *I* am. Seriously, Nell, you raise some good points. At a minimum we can say that this killer is careful and methodical. There's only been that one slip. These aren't random victims, as you've already figured out. There seems to be a plan. The problem is, we don't know what the plan is."

"I know. Is there anything else I can do?"

"You've done a lot already. Just keep thinking—and watch yourself."

"Maybe I'm safe. Whoever it is hasn't gone after any administrators," I said.

"Yet. Are you ready to go?"

"I suppose."

We drove along Route 30 back to my tiny Bryn Mawr

home. When he'd pulled into the very small space behind my car, I turned to him and said, "Nightcap?"

He hesitated. "I should get home."

"Why? So you can pace around your apartment and worry? You can worry here. We can worry together. Two heads are better than one."

He smiled. "You've convinced me."

I smiled back. "Good. I hate to think alone—always gets me into trouble."

Inside, I opened some windows for air, then turned to James. "Coffee? Liqueur? Some combination of the two?"

"I'll go for the last one—maybe they'll cancel each other out."

"Coming up." I retreated to my definitely one-person kitchen and set a kettle on to boil for coffee.

James came up and leaned in the doorway. "How is it that you keep getting involved in my cases?" he asked.

"Karma? I bet you never knew there was so much crime in the cultural community until you met me."

"No, I didn't. I still don't understand it. It seems like there's so little at stake. I mean, nobody is getting rich, and there's not much power to go around. Most people in the city walk by the museums and libraries around here without even noticing. And if they do go in, they complain because you charge too much, especially for a stuffy old place that's probably filled with mold."

"All too true," I said, measuring ground coffee into my French press. "I know there are courses and even degrees in arts administration, but I'm not sure what they're good for. I understand that if you want to stay solvent, you have to operate your institution as a business, with budgets and all that. But there are so many variables and so many unknowns. How do you place a financial value on three hundred years of history? What do you do when the roof collapses because you've deferred maintenance for a couple of decades?"

The kettle boiled, and I poured water into the coffee press before going on. "At least you know that your job won't go away—there will always be crime, and we'll need someone to track down the villains and see that they're prosecuted. With a museum, if it goes belly-up, a few people will say, oh, what a shame, and go on with their lives."

"But you love it," James said.

"I do. At least, most of it. I feel like a guardian, fending off the enemies wielding budget axes. I believe that what we do at the Society matters." I turned to pull cups from the upper shelf of my cabinet; James came up behind me and kissed the back of my neck. I managed not to drop the cups, but set them carefully on the countertop before pivoting to face him. "So we make a good team, right?"

"We do." We stopped talking for a while, but managed to peel ourselves apart before the coffee was entirely cool. Heck, it was summer: who needed hot coffee? I filled two cups, handed one to James, and led the way to the living room, which was indistinguishable from the dining room—all one big room. I pointed to the antique secretary—an inheritance from a grandmother—and said, "The liqueurs are in there, in the top part."

Once we were comfortably settled, side by side, I asked, "If you have no physical evidence, does that make motive more important?"

"In a way. Sometimes if you know the why, you can figure out the how. Sometimes it works the other way around."

"That's not helpful. We know the how: prescription drugs, coupled with access to the victims, all of whom were elderly and apparently offered no resistance. We don't have a clue about the why."

"What does the 'how' tell us?" James prompted, looking like he was enjoying himself, leaning back, tie askew.

I thought for a moment. "The killer is intelligent and educated. He either knows something about pharmacology or knows enough to learn what he needs. Right?"

James nodded. "Go on."

I swatted his arm. "Hey, don't I pay tax dollars so you can do this? All right, I'll call your bluff. He has access: he can gain entry to a variety of people's homes without force, and without raising suspicion. He must be presentable, nicely dressed. Well-spoken."

"Good. Maybe you have a future as a profiler."

"Maybe I already am. You have to know people in order to ask them for money successfully." I thought again. "I keep saying 'he,' but as you noted earlier, there's nothing so far that a woman couldn't do. In fact, a woman might have a better chance of not raising the victim's suspicions. And they say poison is a woman's weapon."

"You're right. Anything else?"

An idea was beginning to grow inside me—one I didn't like. Unless James and my diligent crew had missed a huge subset of deaths, this killer of ours had targeted a very specific community. Leaving aside the "why" for a moment, how had he—or she—known who to go after? And where to find them? If we knew that, it might get us a step closer to that elusive "why." I turned to James and said flatly, "He's one of us."

"Us?" James replied, startled.

"He's got to be connected to a museum or a cultural institution, or to fundraising somehow. You agree that he's targeting members of various nonprofit boards? If he's an outsider, why would he even know boards exist and how they work and who is likely to be on them? I'm not saying an outsider wouldn't be able to collect the information over time, but he'd have to know where to start and what to look for. I think our killer already has a connection. He's got to be a museum professional of some sort."

James looked at me, and I could almost see his thoughts spinning around like a roulette wheel, slowing, slowing, until the ball dropped in a single slot. "I think you may be right," he said with something like wonder. "Why didn't I see that? Let's walk through it again. All the people who have been killed are members of local cultural institutions. As far as we know, they have no other links other than general social status."

"Right," I said cautiously. "And the four we're talking about overlapped at only a few of those institutions, and of those, the most likely one is the Forrest Trust. For reasons we don't understand."

"So we focus on the Forrest Trust, at least for now. What kind of assets does it have? Who controls it? Who are the other board members? And you're in the perfect position to do just that, because you and the Society benefit from the trust."

"I am," I said with more confidence.

He grabbed me and planted a kiss on me, which more or less put an end to our brainstorming.

CHAPTER 14

Being stuck in a car with someone in early rush-hour traffic on the Schuylkill is a mixed blessing. On the one hand, the other person is a captive audience and can't go anywhere, so you can hash out whatever you want; on the other hand, if murder is on your mind, and you have no idea who the killer was, there's only so much dissecting of the evidence you can do. We didn't have enough evidence to point a finger. Maybe a whole hand, which ended up pointing in five directions.

"Any brilliant insights by light of day?" I asked James once we were on the road.

"I think your conclusion that the killer is connected to some sort of cultural institution holds up," he said, keeping his eyes on the road and his speed a conservative three miles over the posted speed limit, except when our progress could be measured in feet per minute, which was normal for the Schuylkill at rush hour.

"Great. That limits the suspects to a few hundred," I said, frustration creeping into my voice. "I keep coming back to the question, why? What have these nice older people done to anyone that would inspire murder? How the heck do we figure that out?"

"Look at it as a data analysis problem. You've got four data points, potentially. Isn't it the theory that it takes only two to draw a line? Maybe you should be looking harder and deeper into the points you have, rather than trying to find more points to fine-tune your line. Am I making sense?"

"You mean, shift to digging into the individuals, rather than looking for more possible victims?"

"Exactly. Of course, if I could point to additional murders, I'd have a better chance of making a case to be allowed to participate officially, but that might not give us your 'why.'"

I thought for a moment. "How about this: I ask Shelby to go through the obits, to see if she can find anyone else who fits the victim profile, and Marty and I'll do the deeper digging on the ones we have."

"That could work. At least it's a plan."

I turned toward him, as far as my seat belt would allow. "James, I can't stand waiting around to see who's next. I don't want anyone else to die. And I don't want to think that anyone I know could do something like this."

"I know. I don't want that any more than you do, Nell. Just keep digging, and I'll keep the pressure up from my end. That's all we can do for now."

We were still moving at a snail's pace. I decided to look at things from a different point of view. "Tell me more about the FBI's view of serial killers. Why do these people do it?"

"There's no simple answer to that, because there are a lot of factors that may play a role. But the most important is that the serial killer makes the decision to kill and kill again."

"Well, duh. So this person is not acting on behalf of someone else? Like a hit man? Or what about if he's hearing voices that tell him to kill X, Y, and Z?"

"That's a different category."

"So there's no single profile that fits all serial killers—not even gender or age?"

"Nope."

"Shoot, why do we even need the FBI?"

"Don't be so quick to dismiss us," James said, giving me a quick smile. "The behavioral people earn their salaries. There is consensus about the characteristics of a serial killer. For example, they feel a need for control. They can also be glib, and charming, they lie easily, and enjoy manipulating people. They tend to lack remorse or guilt for their crimes. Most fall under the heading of psychopathy, but not all serial killers are psychopaths—they just share some of the traits. And they like to think they're smarter than the rest of us. But a lot of those same traits are shared by successful businesspeople—heck, most executives on Wall Street. And they're not all *American Psycho*s."

"Great, now I can't even eliminate anyone I know. But again, do you guys know *why* these people kill?"

"We admit that motive is the hardest thing to determine. A single killer might have multiple motivations, or they may evolve over the series of murders. For example, a second murder might be committed to cover up the first, and so forth. And you won't like to hear it, but the experts caution us against working to identify motive rather than looking for the killer."

"Yes, but in this case there's no evidence to work with."

"Nell, there's never *no* evidence. We're limited in physical evidence here, but we could pursue how and where the killer obtained drugs, for example, and how he knew what drugs his victims took. That's tangible and something that can be investigated. And you're looking at demonstrable connections between the victims. In many cases of serial killings, that might not exist, but I'll agree that there's a common thread here—if we're right about all or any of what we've deduced."

"Where's Sherlock Holmes when you need him?" I muttered.

"What?"

More loudly I said, "Sherlock Holmes would have heard about Edith's errant teacup and announced that the killer was a left-handed woman who walked with a limp and kept six cats."

I could see that James was smiling even though he didn't turn his head. "Ah, for the good old days."

We arrived in the city as quickly as we could have expected, and again I asked James not to bother dropping me off but to park as he usually did. I wanted to walk, to clear my head and figure out what my next step was. James needed enough evidence, direct or indirect, to persuade his superiors to make this an active case. By God, I was going to find something. I couldn't do nothing and wait for someone else to die.

After arriving at the Society, I stopped at Shelby's office on the way to my own. Luckily she was already there and the rest of her department wasn't. I hated having to hide things from employees, or to spend too much time behind closed doors, because no matter what the facts were, employees always picked up the negative energy and then started nurturing rumors, which only made things worse.

"Hey, Nell," Shelby greeted me when I walked in. "Nice evening?" She looked at me expectantly.

"James and I went out to talk to Harbeson—you know, Marty's and James's cousin in Wayne?"

"Edith Oakes's brother, got it. Did you learn anything useful?"

I leaned against the doorjamb. "Yes and no. Harbeson is a nice man but a bit dim and he drinks. He wouldn't know evidence if it bit him. I'm not even sure he's processed that his sister isn't going to come back. But we gained one whole theoretical clue: the presence of a teacup in the dish drainer. But it's from a set that Harbeson says Edith wouldn't have used. Either way, it suggests that she had tea with someone shortly before she died. Unfortunately, either Edith or her killer washed said teacup, so there's no evidence to be had from it, and then Harbeson, apparently in shock, actually cleaned up the kitchen, possibly for the first time in his life."

"Unbelievable," Shelby said.

"I agree. James and I were brainstorming over dinner and came up with two new thoughts. One: if we look back a year or two and correlate obituaries with your list, we might find some more cases, and by adding cases, we might narrow the suspects, if you follow my drift."

"And you want me to do the correlating? How many more deaths do you think it will take to make the FBI sit up and pay attention?"

I shook my head. "If—still a big if—the FBI accepts the four we've already got, a couple more could help. I wouldn't go back too far. You can access the *Inquirer* obituaries online."

"I'm on it, no problem—I'm happy to help. What's number two?"

"That if, as we suspect, these victims are linked to each other by their service to the cultural community, the deaths almost have to be an inside job. Someone like you or me who has access to the information we've found, or knows how to find it. So now we've potentially narrowed down not only the pool of victims but also the pool of suspects to the greater Philadelphia cultural community. That should make our job easy," I finished on a sarcastic note.

"You sure know how to cheer a girl up first thing in the morning."

"Sorry. But if I can borrow a tired phrase, it's a matter of life and death. I do appreciate your help, and I'm sure the FBI does. Or will. Whatever. Tell me if you find anything? I'm going to try to get some work done."

I headed for my office. Eric took one look at me and hurried down the hall for coffee. When I walked into my office, I glanced quickly around, expecting Marty to pop out from behind a piece of furniture, but for the moment I was blessedly alone. Now, what was it I was supposed to be doing?

Eric returned, proudly bearing a steaming mug of coffee, which he set carefully on my desk. "Anything I can do?" he asked.

It was pointless to deny that something was up. "I wish there was, Eric. You know I'd tell you if I thought you could help. But thanks for asking."

He nodded, then retreated silently. I continued to sit and brood, although the coffee helped. At least for James, investigating a crime—I was going to call it that, no matter what the FBI said—was part of his normal work. Me, I had a museum to run. Fundraising: under control for the moment. Collections: on hold until we sorted out the combined mess of the Terwilliger Collection plus the FBI collection on top of it. I hated to admit it, but I was grateful that I didn't have Latoya hovering at the moment. Special projects: ah, yes, I'd asked Nicholas to look at the Water Works materials and see what he could come up with. Not pressing, but a nice diversion, and if we presented it sooner rather than later, we'd score some points.

When I finished my coffee, I got up and walked down the hall to the processing room. Nicholas wasn't there, so I circled back and found him in his cubicle. "Got a minute, Nicholas?"

"Sure, Nell. Here or your office?"

"Here's fine." Since Nicholas had only half walls, anybody walking by could hear anything we said, but I wasn't intending to say anything private. "How are things going with the Water Works materials?"

He looked startled for a moment. "Oh, right—I promised you a first report today. I've pulled some of the stuff together. Fascinating material, isn't it? I hadn't realized there was so much controversy about the sources of contagion in the city, even as late as 1900. But that wasn't exactly what you were looking for, was it? They wanted something about 'green,' right?" Nicholas gave me a tepid smile. "It's such a classic case of the past and present colliding—you know, unspoiled nature versus the evils of industrialization. There's a lot of impassioned

Victorian rhetoric in the file about it. Interesting reading. When did you want to give this to Ms. Fleming?"

I had to admit I was impressed by his quick grasp of the information. "Let me call her and set up a meeting for next week."

"Of course. I'll have something on your desk by Monday." Nicholas hesitated, as though squeezing out more words was painful for him. "I'm happy to say that the rest of the cataloging is going well, so we're staying abreast of incoming material. Although, that still leaves the problem of the existing collections."

"One step at a time, Nicholas!" I had to laugh— accurate cataloging had been the bane of the Society almost from its founding well over a century earlier, and nobody expected Nicholas to accomplish it quickly.

I made my way back to my office only to find Shelby hovering in the doorway, and she looked troubled. I sighed. "Come on in. Do we need to shut the door?"

"I think so," she said.

I sat down and motioned her to sit. "Tell me."

"I started checking the obituaries, like you asked. Then I thought it might be more efficient to search by starting with the institutions we've talked about. I didn't even have to do it for the Society, since we have all those records. So it was only the Art Museum and the Forrest Trust I had to look at."

"And?" I prompted.

Shelby handed me a few pages of printouts. "Two more possibles, within the last year. And they were both members of the Forrest Trust."

I felt both depressed and elated. The good news was, I had something to give James that might be enough to use to make the higher-ups take notice. The bad news was, two more people had died, possibly at the hands of a serial killer, and once again there would be no crime scene, no evidence.

"Good work, Shelby. I'll call James."

I picked up the phone and hit the speed dial. When he answered, I said bluntly, "We have two more."

His reply was equally terse. "I'll be right over."

CHAPTER 15

James arrived at the front door in ten minutes, and Front Desk Bob called to let me know. I went down to let him in, no longer worried about what anybody thought about the constant presence of the FBI—by now the staff should be used to it. There were more important things at stake, like human lives. Shelby was waiting for us in my office, and I shut the door as soon as we arrived.

James sat heavily, leaned forward in his chair, and said, "Show me."

Shelby handed him a copy of what she'd given me. James took his time looking it over. After a couple of minutes I couldn't stand the waiting.

"Is it enough?"

"Maybe," James said. "These two fit the general pattern—age, social standing, manner of death—but there's no physical evidence so long after the fact. The victims—if that's what they were—are long buried, and there's no point in digging them up. But six victims make a stronger case than four."

"What about the connection through the Forrest Trust?" I asked.

"You mentioned the trust before. What is it?"

I glanced at Shelby before replying. "Shelby's been filling me in about it. We have information in our files because we have collection items here on indefinite loan from the trust, and they gave us funds for their maintenance. This was all put in place before I started working here, so I've had little or no direct interaction with the trustees."

"How many board members are there?"

I looked again at Shelby, and she said promptly, "Ten. Or there should be. Some of them have been replaced, but they're still not at full strength."

James turned back to me. "And six have died, within the last year or two? We definitely need to focus on the trust, since that seems to be the one common factor. I want to know what the trust does, what kind of money they have, how it's controlled, who they give it to."

"I'll pull the 990s," Shelby volunteered. When James looked blank, she explained, "That's the IRS reporting form for nonprofits. It's public record."

"I'm looking into what information we have on Edwin Forrest," I said. "According to our agreement with the trust, the funds that they have given us specify that we must spend a portion on displaying the Forrest materials to the public, so I can poke around here without setting off any alarms. You know about Edwin?"

James's expression brightened. "That giant marble statue in the hallway? That's Forrest?"

I nodded. "In one of his signature roles—a somewhat obscure Shakespeare play called *Coriolanus*." I stopped for a moment to think. "James, we have to put together a lot of information in-house here, and it's coming from a lot of directions: development, collections, outside sources like the IRS. Why don't we collect as much as we can, then sit down and go through it all in one go? And if you think we have enough, we really should find the surviving board members, talk to them, and maybe alert them that there's a problem. Surely they must have noticed that an unusual number of their colleagues have died recently?"

"I agree. I need to talk to them," James said.

I stared at him. "How do you plan to do that? Knock on the door of some frail octogenarian and say, 'I think someone might try to kill you'?"

"I wouldn't do that. I can be tactful, you know," James protested.

"Why not let Marty and me look at the list? Odds are, she knows most of them, and I can break the ice by talking about our custodianship of the collection items." Another thought popped into my mind. "Will they come to Edith's funeral, do you think?"

"If Marty's handling the arrangements, she'd probably ask them. I can't tell you if all or any of them came to the others' funerals—some of them don't travel much anymore. Why, are you thinking of staging a Sherlock event?"

Shelby raised an eyebrow, so I explained, "I mentioned Sherlock Holmes earlier today, and I'd guess that James is thinking of one of those grand finales when the omniscient sleuth gathers everyone in the library and points the finger at the killer. Right?"

Even James had to smile at my lame description.

"Something like that. Unless you're subscribing to the theory that the killer will show up to gloat over his success, unbeknownst to the mourners."

"Unbeknownst?" I said.

"Well, this whole case does have a slightly archaic flavor, don't you think? A mysterious vendetta for reasons unknown?"

"Well, we are, after all, an historic institution. To answer your question, what I was considering was meeting tomorrow and pooling everything we have. We can use the rest of today to pull together our facts. Marty should have a handle on the funeral by then, too. Shelby, do you mind giving up part of your weekend?"

"No, ma'am! This is important, and I didn't have anything planned."

"Good. I'll put together what I've found on the collection so far. If we can make a strong enough case, can you take it to your bosses and open a real investigation?"

"I'll do my damnedest. I don't like having a serial killer in my own backyard."

Shelby shivered involuntarily. "Sounds more serious when you say 'serial killer.'"

"That's what we're looking at, Shelby," James told her. "If what we guess is true."

"Does that mean we're at risk?" she asked.

"I hope not," James said. "The targets seem to be board members. I can't make any promises, but whoever it is seems pretty sure of himself, and isn't likely to believe that anyone is onto him. Certainly not at this place."

I wasn't so sure. The Society seemed to have become Crime Central over the past year, which clashed with our reputation as a sleepy—all right, stuffy—institution. I hoped that Shelby had gotten the message: be careful. She didn't have her own personal FBI agent to watch her back the way I did. "All right, then. James, do you think Marty is out in Wayne now with Harbeson?"

"Probably. I'll call her. I'll let you know if she has any issues with meeting tomorrow and where she wants to do it. And I'll find out when and where the funeral will be."

We all stood up, awkwardly. Shelby glanced between James and me, then said, "I guess I'll go start looking for . . . whatever. Let me know what the plan is for tomorrow, Nell." She opened the door and left, closing it behind her.

Which left James and me alone. "Are we getting closer?" I asked, hating how plaintive I sounded.

"I think so. You and Shelby have been a big help."

"You can give us a commendation when we find the killer. We *will* find him or her, won't we? With or without the agency's help?"

"I certainly intend to," he said grimly. He crossed the distance between us and pulled me close. "Just be careful, please? We know this guy is smart. If he gets even a hint of what you and Shelby and Marty are up to, I don't know what he might do. I'd rather not find out."

"I get it. I think we all do. Let's hope tomorrow yields some results." I leaned into him, thinking how nice it was not to be facing this alone. What would I have done if something like this had come up and I didn't have an FBI agent in my corner? Well, I realized, for a start I wouldn't have gone digging for other murders. I would have looked at the individual deaths of several elderly people I might have known only slightly and said to myself, *what a shame*, then forgotten about them, never connecting them or looking for hidden motives. I wondered if I would ever be so innocent again.

"Uh, Nell?" James's voice came from some distant place. "I should be going now."

I pulled myself away. "I know. Call me when you've talked to Marty, and we'll decide where to meet. I'll see you tomorrow."

I watched him leave, and I watched Eric watch him leave. Damn, I hated to think what Eric must be imagining by now, but I couldn't say anything. Bad enough that I'd dragged Shelby into this. I didn't want to put anyone else in danger.

But I was my own mistress, and I was already in danger, so I decided I might as well spend a little time checking out our Forrest collection. The artifact collections area would be the best place to start. Fourth floor, then. I grabbed my inventory list and headed for the elevator.

The physical collections actually were the smallest part of our overall collections. Most of what the Society held was paper-based, but often we were given items—like that statue downstairs—by donors, or by bequest. Most were not valuable enough to sell. Many came with strings attached: the donor wanted to know we valued it, so we couldn't just get rid of it, in case that person wanted to come visit the family heirloom. But that created yet another problem: storage requirements for a hodgepodge of physical items—wood, fabric, and a few unidentifiable oddities—were complex, so we kept those collections segregated from the books and documents.

An hour later, I was convinced that either the inventory was way out of date or I wasn't reading it right. I wasn't willing to contemplate the third alternative—that collection items were missing—not after the problems we'd had in the recent past. I had found most of the objects without any difficulty, and I knew where to find the statue, of course, and a gorgeous theatrical makeup case that was on permanent display on the first floor. But some of the paper records—letters, handbills, and the like—I was having trouble finding. Collections-related files were kept outside Latoya's office on the third floor, opposite Nicholas's cubicle. The filing cabinets took up a full wall. I went over there to double-check. Yes, there were Forrest folders, and lists inside them that pointed toward documents filed in other parts of the building. I made a quick copy. The paper files weren't where the finding aid said they should be.

A little alarm bell rang in the back of my head, and I quashed it. Before I started really worrying, I decided to check the sign-out slips. Official procedure dictated that if an employee took something from a shelf to look at, he or she was supposed to fill out a routing slip for it and leave in its place. Likewise, if a library patron requested a document or book, the librarian or the shelver should have left a slip on the shelf. But I knew staff sometimes "borrowed" things without following procedure. Heck, I'd been guilty of that myself a few times. But after a number of items had disappeared, I'd treated the staff to more than one lecture about following protocol, and I'd thought they'd gotten the message. Maybe the Forrest items had simply been mis-shelved? It wouldn't be the first time that collection items wandered around the building.

I made a mental note to ask Felicity, our head librarian,

because she always seemed to know where everything was. Certainly she would know if someone had requested the material recently.

I went back to my office, feeling more troubled than I had been before. Yes, things went missing in this building all the time. It was inevitable in collections that numbered in the millions of items. But it was troubling to me that Forrest items were now among the missing. Coincidence? I didn't think so. I hated to think that the Society was the source of the information that the killer might be using, but in a public institution anyone could access the records and there was no way to prevent that. Of course, the request slips might not tell me anything useful: whoever was doing the research could have used a fake name, but if one name, fake or not, cropped up consistently in association with Forrest items, that would be one more piece of the puzzle.

Back at my desk again, I studied the list. I had verified that most of the physical objects were where they should be; the things that were missing were mainly letters and files. Not good. I put the printout with my added notes in my bag to share with my partners in crime-solving the next day.

I checked my watch. It was after five and probably too late to catch Felicity today. I'd have to wait until Monday.

Before heading off to catch my train, I called James at his office. When he answered, I asked, "Did you reach Marty?"

"I did. Edith's funeral will be Monday. Marty's okay with getting together tomorrow morning, but she's meeting with Harby in the afternoon. Makes sense to get together out your way."

"Since I'm nearer to Wayne, you mean? I guess we can meet at my place." I shuddered to think how my herd of dust bunnies would react to multiple guests. "Can you or Marty give Shelby a ride? She could take the train, but if you're both driving that way anyway . . ."

"Marty's closer. I'll ask her to swing by and pick up Shelby."

"Anything new on your end?" James asked.

I debated about telling him about what I had found—or not found—in the Forrest hunt. I decided against it, for now. "Nothing that won't wait until tomorrow. Have you approached the Big Cheeses there?"

"Couldn't if I wanted to. They're in secret meetings somewhere out of the office. Don't tell anyone, but I'm guessing those meetings involve chasing a little white ball around. They should be in on Monday, if we have something more solid that I can take to them."

"Hurry up and wait, as usual. I'll see you tomorrow, then."

"You will."

CHAPTER 16

After a few hurried stops at local shops to stock my bare cupboards and some halfhearted swipes of the duster, I was ready to greet my—what, coconspirators?—at ten the next morning. I had coffee in the pot and pastries on the table. With four heads working together, I thought we had a decent chance to make sense of this nebulous case.

James arrived first. His only concession to weekend casual was to leave his jacket and tie off, although I suspected they might be in his car. His shirtsleeves were rolled up, and his collar was open, and I wished we weren't expecting company any minute.

"Good morning," he said before he closed the distance between us.

"What you said," I mumbled when he let go of me and went to help himself to coffee.

"Nothing new to report since I talked to you last night. At least there haven't been any more . . . incidents."

"You mean deaths. Don't dance around it—it makes it seem trivial," I snapped and was immediately sorry.

"Nell, I don't take this lightly. Nor does Marty, nor, I suspect, Shelby. We're doing the best we can, all of us."

"I know, I know." I helped myself to more coffee. I figured I'd need it if I wanted to think clearly.

Marty and Shelby arrived a few minutes later. I could hear them laughing as they approached my door. I opened it before they had time to knock and ushered them in. Shelby had never seen my home before, so I gave her a couple of minutes to snoop around. A couple of minutes was all it took: it was a very small house.

"Marty, Shelby, there's coffee over there, and goodies. I'm a firm believer in the theory that caffeine and sugar are essential to logic."

"Sounds good to me," Shelby said, helping herself to a Danish.

When we were all settled around my all-purpose table, equipped with food and coffee, James cleared his throat. "Thank you for coming, Marty, Shelby. This meeting is not officially happening, because if these are murders, and I still stress that 'if,' the FBI and the police have taken no formal notice of them."

Marty gave a short bark of laughter. "Too much work for them, eh?"

"They really don't have enough evidence. That's why we're here today—to see if there's a case we can give them that will make them sit up and take notice. Let me summarize what we do know," James said. He held up one finger. "One, as many as six people have died." He held up a second finger. "Two, their deaths, taken individually, look unalarming. The individuals were all older, and they all died from what could be natural causes on first glance, or which may have been suicide, or which may have been nudged along using their own prescriptions." A third finger went up. "Three, apart from their age and social standing, all six of these people are connected through local nonprofit organizations, specifically the Edwin Forrest Trust. Some of them have other connections, but according to what you've found, the trust is the only one that links them all."

"Jimmy, stop pontificating," Marty said. "We all agree that the deaths weren't as natural as they were supposed to look. Let's just say they were all murdered and move on."

James looked pained. "All right. Six people, all members of the same trust, have been killed. What does that tell us? And what do we need to know?"

"Why don't we start with the trust?" I suggested.

"I can do that," Shelby said eagerly. She pulled out a stack of notes and handed each of us a sheaf of papers. "I won't bore you with all the personal details. What's important here is that because he'd outlived all his family and had no children, Edwin Forrest left most of his money to create a home for aged actors. He saw how many of them found themselves old and sick and without money, and he donated his home in Philadelphia plus a lot of cash so they'd have someplace to go at the end of their lives."

"And that's what's in the trust?"

"What's left of it, yes," Shelby said. "That's the only thing the trust supports, except for the collections and honoring Edwin's memory, but that's only a small portion—that's why we have some of his memorabilia at the Society. The problem is, they've run out of aged actors who want to use the place, and the building needs a lot of work if it's going to be used for anything else."

"All that sounds harmless enough," James said. "Was the will ever challenged?"

Shelby nodded. "It was, but only one blood relative was ever identified—or at least, only one ever received anything from the estate. The whole issue has been dormant now for a century."

"Thank you, Shelby," I said warmly. I turned to the other two. "But it doesn't get us any closer to identifying a reason for killing the trustees."

"The trust is pretty closely held. Maybe someone on the board was dipping into the pot, figuring nobody would notice?" Marty said.

"So if someone, or several others, did notice, the embezzler thought the only way to avoid scandal was to kill the ones who knew?" James said. "Seems thin."

"Well, people are dead!" Marty shot back. "Who ever said motives were logical? They only have to be logical to the person who's doing the killing."

"That's a fair point, Marty," James conceded. "But as I've told Nell, we frown on starting with motive and investigating from there. What we need most is evidence."

"But we've been over and over this, James," I protested. "In each and every case, there is none. Nobody except you, and now us, thinks the deaths were suspicious, so the victims were buried, the potential crime scenes were cleaned up, and everybody went on their way. I can't blame the authorities for not noticing—taken in isolation, each death looks innocent enough. Take them as a group and things look different, and nobody saw the whole picture. It may seem odd to us that the remaining board members didn't think something was unusual about all the deaths coming so close together, but to be fair, the police declared them natural, and all the board members are far from young, so maybe they thought it was nothing more than normal attrition."

"Which is why we're all sitting here getting frustrated," Marty said. "We need a plan. We need to do *something*."

I stared at my ceiling, where the bright June light highlighted some substantial spiderwebs. "Let's look at the most recent death. We think Edith had a visitor on the day she died. Can we prove that for any of the others?"

"Unlikely," James said. "We do know that most of these people lived alone, except for Edith."

"Maybe it was some kind of suicide pact?" Shelby said. "Like, if you think you're ready to go, here's a number to call, and some kindly person will show up and take care of you, painlessly? Like a discreet Kevorkian."

"Not the ones I knew," Marty said flatly. "They weren't ready to go. But like you said, Jimmy, most people wouldn't know that. Me, I knew most of them, and as far as I could tell, none of them were depressed. None of them were short of money. They were all still physically active and enthusiastic about what they were involved in. Not the type for suicide, even assisted suicide."

What a glum group. "Come on, we can do better than this!" I said firmly. "What about the ones who aren't dead? We can still talk to them, can't we? See if anyone has approached them lately, for any reason. It might not have been connected to the trust—it could have been to sell them insurance or to discuss a state-of-the-art tombstone. But if more than one had the same person show up, it could lead somewhere."

"We could check to see if they all used the same mortuary," James said grudgingly. "That would be public information. I can't ask if they all took out new life insurance policies in the last few months of their lives."

"Elwyn can," Marty said. "You know, my brother? The insurance agent?"

James looked pained again—this was fast becoming a standard expression. "Marty, you know I can't ask you to ask your brother to find private information. It wouldn't be admissible in court."

"Who cares about court?" Marty shot back. "We're trying to keep the rest of the board alive!"

"Can you please hold off on pumping Elwyn?" James said. Marty grumbled but said nothing.

"What about the living ones?" I repeated. "Can't we talk to them?"

"Of course you can. There's nothing stopping you," James said. "Do you know any of them, Marty?"

"Yup, three of them. One's in a nursing home. She's sharp as a tack, but she broke a hip recently and she's still recovering. But what the heck are we going to say without scaring them to death? And how can we tell them anything if we can't mention that we think their lives are in danger?" Marty looked exasperated. "Jimmy, these people are old, but they're not stupid. And I'm not going to treat them like they're stupid. I show up out of the blue, pretending to be all nicey-nice and then start asking them about the Forrest Trust, what are they going to think? I have to give something to get something."

James was shaking his head without looking at anyone. "I shouldn't have started this. You're going to screw up an investigation that hasn't even started."

"Jimmy, we're trying to save their lives!" Marty all but yelled.

I laid a hand on his arm. "James, do you have any better ideas? We can't just sit here waiting for the next obituary."

He finally glanced at me and smiled, even if it was a poor excuse for a smile. He turned to Marty. "Who do you know?"

"Rodney Lippincott. Louisa Babcock—she's the one in the nursing home, in Devon. Irving Sedgwick, but he moved to California a few years ago. You think he'll be safe there?"

"Maybe," James said. "So far the deaths have been pretty localized. Where does Rodney live?"

"Delaware. DuPont country."

James shook his head again. "Another jurisdiction heard from. Why am I not surprised?"

"What do you want me to do?" Marty demanded.

"When we're done here, maybe you and the girls can go out for lunch. South of here."

"And visit an old friend I haven't seen in a while?" Marty smiled. "Then maybe also pay a visit to that nursing home? How's that sound to you, Nell?"

"I'd love to meet friends of yours, Marty. I'm sure they're very interesting people."

"Oh, they are, believe me. Shelby, you in?"

Shelby looked between us, torn. "Do you really need me? Wouldn't three visitors at once just complicate matters?"

"I'll take you back to the city, Shelby," James said.

"Oh, would you? That would be great. Do you mind, Nell?"

"Of course not." There was no reason to drag Shelby in any deeper.

"Don't forget Edith's funeral is on Monday morning," Marty reminded us.

"Oh, right," I said. "When and where, Marty?"

"St. Mary's, in Wayne. Not far from the house. It's at ten."

"Why don't I attend and then head into the city after? James, does that work? Or were you planning to go to the funeral? You were related, after all."

"I'm not sure yet," he said, with no further explanation.

"Okay, so it's a plan," I said firmly. "Marty and I will go to Delaware and talk to Rodney, and James and Shelby will go back to the city. Then Marty and I will talk to Louisa after we see Rodney. I'll attend Edith's funeral on Monday, and then we'll all meet Monday afternoon at the Society and figure out what we know. Right?"

"And I don't know anything about your plans, and you can't tell me anything when we have dinner tonight," James wrapped it up.

I loved the way he'd sneaked that last part in. "Uh, okay. Where?"

"I'll drop you back here, Nell," Marty said. "I should stop by and see how Harby's doing, and make sure he has a clean shirt for Monday while there's still time to do anything about it."

"Sounds good," James said.

Only I wasn't sure if anything about this was good.

CHAPTER 17

It was nearly noon when James and Shelby left for the city, while Marty and I planned to head in the opposite direction.

"Marty, how do you know this Rodney Lippincott? He's not another relative, is he?" I asked.

Marty was wandering around my house, picking things up and putting them down. I loved the house dearly, mainly because it was all mine, and every creature comfort within its walls I had created—it had started life as a stable. But I'd seen Marty's house, and this was not in her league.

"Nice," she muttered to herself, looking at my woodwork, salvaged from a local junk dealer and carefully stripped and refinished. "What? Oh, Rodney. No, no relation that I know of. Kind of an almost relation, though, since he was courting my mother before she met my father. One look at Dad and Mom was a goner. But

Rodney kind of hung around the edges of our life, when I was younger. I think he thought a small piece of my mother was better than nothing. That's why I'm pretty sure he'll see me now."

"So he never married?"

"Sure he did, and had six kids. I just think he's a hopeless romantic at heart. Anyway, the wife's gone now, and the kids are scattered all over. Listen to me—kids! They're my age, and they've got college-age kids of their own. Let's hit the road, I want to pick up something to take to Rodney—he's got a sweet tooth."

"Fine by me." I was hungry again, and too antsy to sit still, even in my own living room. Besides, I knew Marty had no patience with small talk; she'd rather be doing something. "How do we get there?"

"Route 1, south."

"Then we can stop at the Brandywine Museum and have a quick lunch and buy some of their goodies for Rodney." I loved that museum, loved eating in the glassed-in lunch area overlooking the Brandywine River. I'd been there many times before, though not recently.

We wended our way southward to Route 1, with Marty at the wheel. Her style of driving was rather dissimilar to mine, to put it mildly. She was prone to jackrabbit starts and abrupt stops, with a bit of tailgating thrown in to add spice. I made sure my seat belt was buckled and tried to admire the pretty landscape and ignore the rest. This end of Pennsylvania was delightful—lots of history, mushroom farms, old stone houses. Past Kennett Square, we turned southeast on local roads.

It took us a bit over an hour to arrive at Rodney Lippincott's home. If I'd been expecting another stately mansion, I was immediately dissuaded: Marty pulled up in front of a very ordinary tract home in a housing development that probably dated to the 1950s. As she turned off the engine she said, "I know what you're thinking. Rodney decided the kids should enjoy the family inheritance sooner rather than later, so he downsized when his wife died. Kept some nice stuff—you'll see, inside—but bought this house outright. It suits his needs."

"Okay," I said, reminding myself not to judge a book by its cover. I also had to remind myself that while Marty's extended family and many of their friends might be well established after a couple of centuries in the area, they didn't necessarily have a lot of money. What they did have was a strong sense of civic responsibility, and that extended to preserving their historic heritage, usually through volunteering to serve rather than writing checks. Hence Rodney and the Forrest Trust, most likely.

"Come on," Marty said, climbing out of the car. I followed, clutching a box of yummy cookies we'd bought to soften Rodney up. Marty knocked on the front door, then knocked again. For a long moment I fought the fear that we might find yet another body, but eventually we heard shouting from somewhere inside the house. Footsteps stopped near the door and there was a flash of an eye at the peephole. Finally the door was yanked open and we were confronted by a rather unkempt man of about seventy, wearing glasses set askew on his nose, with a hearing aid in one ear. "Martha Terwilliger, what drags you down to this forlorn outpost of civilization?"

"We want to talk with you, Rodney," Marty said brusquely. "We brought cookies." On cue, I held up the box.

"Bribery will get you in the door, at least." Rodney stepped back and opened the door. "But don't expect coffee. I'm out."

"Rodney, I don't expect much of anything from you," Marty said, brushing past him. I followed meekly.

"Who're you?" he demanded as I passed.

"I'm Nell Pratt, a friend of Marty's." Marty made a right turn for the living room and I tailed along.

"Come on, Rodney," Marty said. "Come talk to us and you can have your cookies."

"Damn, Martha, you treat me like an idiot or a large unruly dog. Nice to see you, give me a cookie, and tell me what you want." That last sentence came out in a rush.

"Ah, Rodney, I've missed you. Kids all right?"

"Fine. I'm a grandfather five times over. How's your love life?" Rodney shot back.

"As dull as ever." Marty glanced at me. "Rodney, this is serious. This is Nell Pratt, from the Pennsylvania Antiquarian Society. Nell and I need to talk with you because we think there's something funny going on with the Edwin Forrest Trust. You still on the board?"

Rodney dropped into a well-worn chair across from us. "Why would I quit? I don't have to do a damn thing except show up for a meeting every now and then. Why, is there something fishy going on?"

"Maybe, but probably not what you'd expect. Several members of the trust have died recently."

"So? We're all old. Trustees die all the time. It's getting harder and harder to replace them, though—nobody wants to be bothered."

"At first glance it looks like they all died from old age,

or miscounted their pills, or maybe committed suicide," I said. "But we think they were intentionally given an overdose of their medications."

"Rodney," Marty followed up with surprising patience, "we think someone is killing the trustees."

"You're kidding." Rodney stared at her for several beats. "No, you're not kidding. Why the hell would anyone want us dead? We don't do anything!"

"That's what we wanted to ask you. We know some things about the trust, but not enough. For instance, how did you get involved?"

"My mother was a member of the board, back in the day. Nobody minded when she suggested me to replace her, so here I am." Rodney straightened his glasses and looked at me directly. "What's your interest?"

"I'm president of the Pennsylvania Antiquarian Society, and Marty's on the board there. A couple of other Forrest trustees who were found dead were also Society board members or former members, which is how I came to be involved."

"Oh, right—you're the ones with that honking big statue of Edwin." He turned away from me. "Martha, who do you think is killing people?"

"That's the question," Marty said. "Rodney, have you had any visitors lately? Or unusual phone calls? Anything at all relating to the trust?"

"Nope. Well, not exactly. I don't open my door to anybody I don't know—usually they want me to buy something or sign some damn petition. And I don't answer phone calls from numbers I don't recognize—same thing. Usually someone shilling for a candidate, or maybe it's for sick animals. I know all my family's numbers. If somebody really wants to talk to me, I let them leave a message, so I get to decide if I really want to talk to them. Most don't. I get ticked off by these people who won't admit who they are. Seems rude." He sighed. "So, who else is gone? I'm kind of behind on my mail."

Marty ticked off the deaths on her fingers, and with each additional name, Rodney's expression grew more serious. When she was finished, he said, "Damnation. I really haven't been paying attention. Six of us? Something's not right. When did all this happen?"

"Over the past year," Marty said. "Although the pace seems to be speeding up. That's why we wanted to talk to you—to make sure you were all right, of course, and to see if you could shed any light on these deaths."

Rodney ate a cookie, slowly. "Like I said, I don't talk to many people—not worth my time. Last trustees meeting was—let me think—six months ago? We're about due for another one, I guess."

"Anything out of the ordinary going on with the trust, Rodney?" I asked.

"Apart from the proposal to dissolve it, you mean?"

My eyes widened: this was the first I'd heard of this idea.

"What? Wait," Marty sputtered. "Who wants to dissolve the trust?"

"I guess we all do, except we've just started looking into how, with a lawyer. We aren't in a hurry—this thing's been ticking along since 1872. But there's really no reason to keep going. Most of the money went to setting up that home for decrepit actors in Forrest's old house, but no decrepit actors want to go there anymore. Can't say as I blame them—the place needs a lot of work, and we don't want to take on fixing it up to modern standards—kind of a waste of money. But we'd have to break the trust in order to sell the place, or even give it away. Old Edwin was pretty clear about what he wanted."

"How hard would it be to break the trust?" Marty asked.

Rodney shrugged. "I don't know. We've asked a lawyer to check it out, but none of us knows yet. Like I said, there's no rush."

This cast a whole new light on our problem, and I tried to figure out the implications. If the trust was dissolved, who would be affected? What would happen to the objects from his collection? That was, after all, my most direct concern, not that I thought anyone would kill over any of it. The Society might have to give back or try to buy the collections items we housed, and we'd definitely have to give back the money we held, but since it was a restricted endowment, nobody had touched it. Was there anything about the dissolution of the trust that could lead to murder?

Marty beat me to it. "Is the trust out of money, Rodney?" Marty asked.

"Nah. It's been safely invested for forever, and we don't mess with it. I'd say in the neighborhood of a million including the property, but the interest income from the endowment isn't enough to cover maintenance of the Home anymore."

That didn't help me much. I didn't see how anyone could get his hands on that million. "Have you changed financial advisors?"

Rodney turned to me. "Don't think so—we let our attorney handle that side of things. No big changes that I can recall, and we'd have to vote on it anyway."

"You haven't said anything publicly, have you?"

"Nope. Besides, who cares? We're small potatoes."

Who cares, indeed. I wondered what would happen if there weren't enough trustees to vote on the dissolution? At the rate things were going, there might be none within the month. What then? Would whoever was holding the money take over? The attorneys? Would a trust that had been set up back in the 1870s hold up today? All questions for which I never thought I would need answers.

And still no motive, and no additional clues from Rodney, apart from the bombshell about dismantling the trust. A sleepy old trust with modest resources was fading away because it had become irrelevant in the modern world; its original purpose had ceased to exist. Why would anyone care enough to kill?

"Rodney, who's the lawyer that's handling this?"

"One of those three-name places in Center City, starts with an M . . . Morgan something?"

"Morgan, Hamilton and Fox?" I said.

"Sounds right," Rodney replied. "The law firm's been around as long as the trust, damn near. They recently assigned some young puppy to handle it. I'm sure he's smart, but dealing with him is like talking to one of my grandkids, and he thinks we're all senile."

I had to wonder if he was talking about Jacob Miller— the description sounded about right. "Has he made any recommendations yet?" I pressed.

"Scheduled for the next meeting. The secretary at the law firm usually sends out a notice telling us when to show up. Like I said, it's probably soon."

Marty and I exchanged a glance, and I wondered if she was thinking what I was: that the pending board meeting had pushed the killer to speeding up his schedule. How would murdering the board members affect trust procedures? What made up a quorum for the trust?

"Rodney, we're going to go see Louisa Babcock next," Marty said. "You seen her lately?"

"Told you, Martha—I only see family these days. And now you. Life's too short to waste on boring people. At least you've livened up my afternoon. If I have any brainstorms I'll let you know. Thanks for the cookies."

Apparently the chat with Rodney was over, but I didn't believe there was much more to be gained anyway. "Thank you for seeing us, Rodney. And take care of yourself," I said.

"I've survived this long, haven't I?" He gave me a searching look, and I wondered what he was thinking. "Take care of old Edwin, will you?"

I laughed. "I usually say hello to him anyway, while I'm waiting for the elevator. I'll give him your best wishes."

"Ha!" Rodney said. He stood up and shepherded Marty and me to the door, which he closed firmly behind us while we were still standing on the stoop.

Back in the car, I said to Marty, "Well, that was interesting. Did we learn anything?"

"The trustees want to wrap up the trust, and they've talked to their lawyer," Marty said, backing rapidly out of the drive without looking. Luckily there were no kids strolling home from school.

"That's news, all right. But I can't imagine there's enough money there to inspire murder. Unless, of course, somebody's been cooking the books. Didn't Rodney say that it was the lawyer who took care of the financial management side? Or maybe the bank holding the assets has been embezzling for years and doesn't want to be found out?"

Marty gave a short laugh. "There are easier ways to cover up embezzlement than killing half the board. I don't think there are any financial wizards among them, so they'd accept whatever piece of paper was put in front of them. Doesn't feel right."

"I know. So, Rodney is a washout, but at least we've warned him. Are we going to see Louisa next?" It was only two thirty—plenty of time for another call.

"Sure. But we have to stop at a liquor store. Rodney likes his sweets, but Louisa likes to keep a little nip on hand, and the rehab place won't let her have any. Not the greatest thing for someone who's trying to relearn how to walk after busting a hip, but who am I to judge?"

"How old is she?"

"Eighty-something. I think Rodney was the baby of the board—you heard him say that his mother kind of passed her slot on to him. But Louisa still has all her marbles, and she remembers everything."

I hoped she remembered something useful. Maybe the closing of the trust wasn't moving forward quickly, but I wondered if someone might be interested in stopping it.

CHAPTER 18

After a detour to a liquor store, we arrived at Louisa Babcock's rehabilitation center. If Rodney's modest tract house had shaken my assumptions about Marty's friends, Louisa's current if temporary residence more than compensated: it looked more like a pricy hotel than a medical facility. Everything about the tasteful, spacious lobby confirmed my original notion of her friends' wealth. There was a surprisingly large and elegant concierge's desk to the right, with a low arrangement of fresh flowers on one corner, and a well-dressed middle-aged woman watching our every move. "May I help you?" she asked.

"We're here to see Louisa Babcock," Marty said.

"Are you on the approved list?" said the woman whose name tag read Esther. It had never occurred to me that we would have trouble getting in.

Marty apparently knew the drill. "Martha Terwilliger. I've been here before."

The woman behind the desk turned to a sleek touch screen and looked at something we couldn't see. "Ah, of course, here you are. I'm sure Louisa will be delighted to see you. If you'll just sign in? And your guest as well?" She slid a leather-bound register across the desk. Marty signed, then passed it to me, and I did the same.

When I had returned the book to Esther, Marty led the way down a long corridor, turned left, and followed another corridor until she stopped in front of a door half-way down. Along the way I caught a faint whiff of what must be dinner, but it actually smelled tempting; happily there was no smell of urine or illness that I had unfortunately noticed in other facilities of this kind. This place was well-managed on all levels, it seemed.

Before rapping on the door, Marty turned to me. "Louisa's sharp, and she doesn't care for mealymouthed people. You have a question, ask it. Don't condescend to her just because she's old."

"Marty, when have I ever . . ." But she had already turned to the door and rapped sharply on it.

"Louisa? It's Marty. You decent?"

"As close as I get," a gravelly but surprisingly strong voice replied. "You'll have to let yourself in—this damned hip!"

Marty pushed open the door and held it while I entered. Louisa was seated in a classic high-backed wing chair near the window, but she made no move to rise.

Louisa all but licked her lips on seeing me. "Ooh, you've brought me fresh company. I'll owe you one. Who are you, dear?" she asked me.

I resisted the urge to curtsey—my mother did teach me to respect my elders, and Louisa wore her eighty-plus years proudly. "I'm Nell Pratt. I run the Pennsylvania Antiquarian Society in Philadelphia."

"You can stop now if you think I'm going to give you any money."

"Nothing like that." I glanced at Marty, who nodded. "We need to talk to you about the Forrest Trust."

Louisa looked at Marty. "Now that's something I didn't expect to hear. Martha, did you bring my, uh, mouthwash?"

"Of course. Shall I refill the bottle?" Marty asked, holding up an unmarked bag.

"If you would. I'd offer you some, but I need every drop my friends can smuggle in."

Marty went into the attached bathroom, and I could see her transferring the contents of a pint bottle of vodka into a brand-name mouthwash bottle by the sink.

When Marty had accomplished her mission (and hidden the empty bottle in her own bag), Louisa asked, "I could ring for tea, if you'd like?" She looked hopeful, and I turned to Marty for guidance.

Marty winked at me. "Sure, go right ahead."

Louisa beamed, then said, "Just push the call button over there and hope someone shows up." Marty did as requested.

"Sit, sit." Louisa gestured imperiously toward the two brocade-covered visitor chairs in the room. "Now, what's this about the Forrest Trust?"

"You still a member of the board?" Marty asked.

"Yes, last time I checked. Why?"

"Because six of your colleagues are dead, and we think it wasn't from natural causes, although the authorities do."

Louisa's eyes lit up. "Ooh, a mystery! Someone is

killing members of a thoroughly useless charity? Who? When? How?"

Marty repeated our list. I couldn't say Louisa looked devastated by news of the untimely deaths of six of her longtime colleagues.

When Marty had finished, Louisa said, "So you really think someone is taking out members of our little board, one by one? Am I on the list, do you think?"

"I'm sorry to say it, but maybe," Marty said. "You upset by that idea?"

"Martha, my dear, I've been ready to go since I turned seventy-five. Anything past that has been a bonus. And to be part of a conspiracy of murder! What a treat! More than I ever could have hoped. So why did you want to see me?"

An attendant arrived in response to the ring. She seemed to have trouble with English, so it took Louisa a couple of minutes to convey that we wanted tea for three. Either she finally got the message or she gave up trying, because she left us alone again. "The help these days! We may get something, but I won't guarantee what. Now, where were we . . . Ah, yes, what can I do to help?"

"Do you have any idea why anyone would want to kill Forrest trustees?" Marty said.

"Not at all. We're a small group, and we're just living up to the terms of the trust. Nothing has changed since it was written, except for the name of the bank and the faces around the table. There isn't that much money, at least by most philanthropic standards."

"Your colleague Rodney said there was talk of shutting down the trust?" I said. "What can you tell us about that?"

"Ah, Rodney. Such a grouchy man! Yes, we've talked

about it, as recently as the last board meeting. But then, we've been talking about it for years, and you can see how much has happened."

"Is something likely to happen now?" I asked.

"Perhaps. We still have money, but it's getting harder and harder to find ways to spend it, under the terms of the trust—isn't that a strange problem to have? The world that Edwin Forrest knew is long gone. It was kind of him to try to do well by his colleagues who were down-and-out, but it's not possible to carry out his wishes now. End of an era, I suppose."

"Does anyone benefit if the trust goes away? Or, on the flip side, does anyone lose if it does?" Marty asked.

While Louisa was framing her response, the attendant reappeared, wheeling in a rattling cart, complete with china teapot, cups, milk, cream, and a plate of store-bought cookies. Still, Louisa clapped her hands with glee. "Oh, thank you, thank you! We'll ring when you can take it away."

After the woman left, Louisa said to us quietly, "Actually it looks pretty dismal, but you've got to encourage the staff or you'll never get anything again. Martha, you pour." Marty grabbed the pot and started filling cups as Louisa went on, "Now, you asked if anyone benefitted or was harmed if the trust went away. I can't think of anyone apart from a few lawyers and bankers. Poor Edwin, at least he had a good run, and his name's on a few Philadelphia buildings. Do you know much about him, Nell?"

"I didn't, but I've been filling in the blanks lately. You may recall that the Society houses the Coriolanus statue."

"Ah, the noble Roman. Did you know that Forrest kept it in his home, when it was new?"

"Really? It's rather large, so it's hard to imagine it in a home."

"True. Have you ever noticed that it's a tad larger than life-size?" Louisa said slyly. "Edwin was a star, and perhaps he saw himself on a grander scale than most mortals." She took a sip from the cup that Marty handed her. "Lukewarm, as usual." She sighed. Then she looked squarely at me. "You know, if I recall, the Society is sitting on a chunk of our money, and some bits and pieces apart from the statue."

"You're right, we are. But we can't use those funds for anything except taking care of the collection, so we don't lose anything if the trust goes away." Assuming what I read on the Society's financial reports was accurate. The lawyers for the trust were also the Society's lawyers, so if there was anything odd going on . . .

"So there's nothing about the trust that you think could push somebody to wipe out the board?" Marty asked.

"I'm sorry, dear, but no. We're a very dull bunch."

Marty looked frustrated. "Okay, putting that aside, let me ask you this: have you had any strangers come visit you lately? Or call?"

Louisa fixed her with a speculative eye. "You mean killers in disguise, coming to slip me poison? I don't think so. But to tell the truth, I wouldn't really know. You may have observed that the dragon at the desk is very good at screening people. I gave her a short list of people I'd be willing to see—and that included you, Martha, as you know. But I also *excluded* a few of my more obnoxious relatives, and I specified 'no vendors.' You'd be appalled at the people who show up trying to sell you something."

When Marty's eyebrows went up, Louisa added, "Nice young priests who want to save your soul."

"And you said no to them, too?"

"I did. No exceptions. This is *my* recuperation, and I'll manage it on my terms."

Marty smiled. "How's the hip doing?"

"All things considered, not too bad. I may go home next week. Or not. I rather enjoy being waited on here, even if the tea is cold. I'm sorry, I haven't been very much help, have I?"

"Even a negative tells us something. I'll ask the Dragon Lady if you've had any unwanted callers. Anything else?"

Marty and Louisa launched into a detailed discussion of people I didn't know. I zoned out, sipping my tea and studying the room. Louisa had clearly brought some of her possessions with her, and they were lovely. No photographs, though. No close family? I wondered if the killer thought that it was less heinous to kill older people, since they were that much closer to death anyway. Or those with no one left to mourn them or to ask awkward questions?

Rodney seemed safe, if he stuck to his rules and didn't let anyone in, physically or electronically. Louisa I didn't think we had to worry about, since she seemed well defended here. I hoped that by the time she was ready to go home we would have eliminated the threat, although we didn't seem to be getting any closer. Both lifestyles, however, felt like a sad commentary on the modern world, if they had to develop strategies to keep unwanted people out.

Marty signaled that she was ready to leave. I took a

quick look at Louisa, who was beginning to fade, and agreed. "Louisa, it was lovely to meet you. I hope you get back on your feet soon."

She nodded graciously. "Come see me when you figure out this puzzle. I love a good mystery, particularly one with a satisfying ending."

"We're doing our best." I hoped that was enough.

I followed Marty back to the front desk, where she stopped in front of Esther the Dragon Lady. "What other visitors has Louisa Babcock had?" Marty demanded.

Dragon Lady drew herself up straighter, if that was possible. "We cannot give out that information."

Marty wasn't about to give up easily. "What I mean is, has Louisa had anyone stop by who asked to see her but who *wasn't* on the list?"

Esther fixed us with a steely glare. "We do not keep records of people who are not welcome."

"But Louisa has so few visitors. Wouldn't you remember someone who asked for her?"

"There has been no such request. Now, if you don't mind . . ."

Mind what? I wondered. We were supposed to feel brushed off, but I refused to give up. "Is there a person who takes your place at night?" I asked.

"Of course. My hours are ten to six. We discourage late visits, however. Many of our guests retire early, after their dinner."

But an outsider might not know that. Marty picked up my cue. "I don't mean to be pushy, but there's a relative who's visiting the area and really wants to see his aunt, Louisa. She probably doesn't know he's coming—you know how bad kids are these days with writing or calling, all this texting nonsense. Anyway, he might have stopped by after you left, some night, and been turned away. Could you leave a note for the night clerk and ask her to call me if she's seen anyone asking for Louisa?"

"Him."

"What? Oh, you mean the person who watches the desk at night is a man. Excellent—would you ask him to get in touch with me? Or better yet, Nell, here? Nell, you got a business card?"

I fished a business card out of my bag and I handed it to Dragon Lady, after scribbling my cell number on the back. I wasn't convinced that the night guy would ever see it, but we had to try. Esther tucked my card under a corner of the leather blotter, and I chose to take that as a yes. "We really appreciate it."

"Come on, Nell," Marty interrupted. "We need to get going. I've still got to visit Harby."

Marty waited until we were back on Route 30 before saying, "Good thinking, asking about people who tried but *didn't* get in to see Louisa."

"I'm just trying to cover all the bases. So we think that both Rodney and Louisa are safe for now. Which leaves us with, what, four other people on the board?"

"I checked. One's in Europe, the other two are on a cruise somewhere with their spouses, and I told you that Irving is living in California now," Marty said promptly, evidently having done her homework. "They're out of harm's way, at least for now, and there's not much point in trying to track them down and talk to them at the moment. So what we've got is . . . what we've got."

"Think it over. Give my best to Harby."

"I will. Poor guy. Or maybe he's lucky, being so oblivious. The drinking helps, too. Never thought I'd say that." Marty pulled up outside my house, and I climbed out of her car. "See you at the funeral Monday."

Marty gave a casual backhand wave as she pulled away.

CHAPTER 19

It was hard to shift gears from trying to track a killer and prevent additional murders, to figuring out what to make for dinner. I definitely wasn't in the mood for cooking, much less trying to impress James with my culinary skills, but we had to eat. We had to keep up our strength if we wanted to stop an elusive killer. What food went well with serial killers?

I was pretty sure wine did, so I helped myself to a glass of Chardonnay while I puttered around, throwing together a corn and cheese casserole that involved few non-frozen or non-canned ingredients. When I slid it into the oven, I glanced at the clock and was surprised to see that it was later again, and James was knocking on the door.

When I opened it I looked quickly at his face: he looked tired but not grim, which I took to mean there wasn't a new report. Our relationship was still new enough I wasn't sure how to greet each other:

when we met at the Society, or at a restaurant or event in Philadelphia, we were usually in business mode—that is, scrupulously undemonstrative. Our time together outside of business was hit-or-miss, usually an evening snatched when slots opened up in both our calendars, which was rare.

But James looked like he needed a hug, so I gave him one. At first he was startled, and then he relaxed into it, and we both stood there in my doorway, kind of leaning against each other. It felt nice.

I was the one to break it off, or at least loosen the grip, so I could look at his face.

"Hello," he said, but at least he was smiling now.

"And the same to you. Come in. I've started dinner. You want something to drink? Unless, of course, this is a business call?" I wasn't sure if I was joking.

"I would love something to drink. And I've turned my phone off. If we talk business, it's off the record."

"Wine?" When he nodded, I headed for the kitchen, and he followed. "Isn't this whole thing off the record? Unless you've got some news."

"Yes. And no. Yes, we're still off the record, and no, there's no progress making this an official inquiry. Heck, if I was looking at this for the first time, I'm not sure I'd give it a green light. Especially if I didn't have the information that you gave me, and the insight into how your world works. At the very least, I probably would never have found the Forrest Trust connection."

"If that's a compliment, I'll take it," I said, handing him a wineglass. He retreated to the bigger room to take off his jacket and tie—and his gun. I wondered where he'd been on a Saturday that would requi knew in my head that FBI agents were supposed to be armed at all times, but it was always a shock to encounter the hard reality of his firearm. I preferred not to think about it.

I checked my timer—still a half hour until the casserole was done. "Why don't we sit down?" I suggested. "I can tell you about what Marty and I did today. I'd rather do it now than while we're eating."

He smiled. "Not good for the digestion?"

"Nothing awful, and mostly dull. Sit."

He sat, falling heavily into an overstuffed chair, and I perched primly on the couch. "You want to go first?" I asked.

He shook his head. "You go."

I launched into a tale of Marty's and my calls on Rodney in Delaware and Louisa in her rehab center, and Marty's report on the other trustees, and by the time I was done, the timer for the casserole was sounding. James hadn't asked any questions, but at least he'd stayed awake through my recitation. "Looks like this is going to spill over to dinner," I said ruefully. "Let me get it on the table."

He got up when I did and followed me, stopping at the door since there wasn't room for two of us in my kitchen. As long as he was there, I made him work for his supper: I ha_____ plates and silverware and pointed him t_____ e. On his second trip, I gave him a fresh _____ a corkscrew, then followed him to the _____. We sat next to each other at one end _____ heritance from a grandmother, and _____ comfortably, eight if they were _____ ished up.

We devoted a few minutes to eating, and then James, looking more relaxed, said, "So, your conclusion is that they're both safe under their current circumstances? And the others are distant enough that they aren't in immediate danger?"

"I think so. Rodney is suspicious of everyone and has kind of walled himself in, and Louisa has guards posted at the gates. I'm sure a thug could force his way in, but our guy hasn't gone that route yet. Maybe he's just biding his time. The problem is, the way these two have shut out everyone makes it harder to know if there have been any attempts to get to them."

"Interesting problem. I think you're right. Our killer has been careful, because he wants these deaths to look natural. But you haven't considered the possibility that the killer is someone they *already* know, and trust?"

I felt chastened. "No, we did not. But if that's the case, that person hasn't made an overture to either of them. I gather that Louisa's list of approved guests is pretty short—we were lucky that Marty was on it. What about the other trustees? The people on the cruise will be coming back sometime. Do you think we'll have figured this out by then?"

"God, I hope so! With or without the immense resources of the FBI."

I looked quickly to be sure he was joking. I thought he was, but it was hard to tell. "Nothing wrong with good, old-fashioned sleuthing," I said brightly, standing up. "Coffee?"

"If you want me to stay awake past nine," he said without moving.

"I do—I have plans for you." I ducked

kitchen and put the kettle on to boil and collected our dishes. I jumped when my phone rang—I didn't get many calls at home. I didn't recognize the number when I picked up the receiver. "Hello?"

"Hello, is this Miss Eleanor Pratt, please?" A male voice, not young, not old, definitely foreign, although I couldn't place the accent.

"Yes, it is. What can I do for you?"

"I am Fernando Rodriguez. I am working at the desk at Bellevue Center?"

The night guy at the rehab center. My senses went on high alert. "Yes?"

"I find note here about people wanting to see Miss Louisa Babcock, I should call you?"

"Oh, yes, I left that note. Thank you for calling." To her credit, Dragon Lady hadn't just blown us off. "Has someone been asking for her?"

"Yes. Man come this evening at time of dinner, ask to see her. I tell him he not on list, cannot come in. He not very happy, tried to give me money to let him in to see her. I tell him no and he leave."

"Did he give you his name?" I asked, hoping against hope.

"He give name. I check Mrs. Babcock visitor list, only two me__ on it, and he not either one."

__ __ __t had been too much to hope for. "What was

__klin Washington."

__bt. "Can you describe him?"

__ars old, six feet. Nice clothes, and he

__hing else to ask about in the way

of identifying features. "Did he wear glasses? What color hair?"

"He wear glasses, baseball cap. I did not see hair."

"Did he bring anything with him, ask you to give Louisa anything?"

"He have flowers, but I don't take them. I cannot leave this desk."

Oh, for a dueling scar or a limp. Still, it was progress: our potential suspect was a young, presentable white male. "Can you let me know if you see him again? And please tell Esther about him, so she can watch for him?"

"Of course, I do that anyway. Always file report. I tell Mrs. Louisa?"

I thought for a second. "No, I wouldn't bother her about it. You've done exactly what she asked—she's particular about who she wants to see. But I really appreciate you letting me know."

"I just do my job. Good night, miss." He hung up.

I turned to find James looking at me quizzically. "What was that about?" he asked.

"That, sir, was the night manager at Louisa's rehab center. He tells me that somebody tried to visit her tonight."

"And you think that's our guy?"

"Louisa doesn't want visitors, certainly not people she doesn't know. I left my card at the desk and asked the gatekeeper to have the night attendant call me if someone else came looking for Louisa."

"What did he say the guy looked like?" I could see James shifting into business mode: he sat up straighter, his muscles tightened, his eyes hardened. Hardly rom_tic, but . . .

"White male, about thirty, glasses, n

marks. Well dressed, well spoken. Came armed with flowers. Gave the name Franklin Washington. Left quietly when he was denied entry, but first tried to bribe the attendant."

"He could fit the profile. I'll run the name, but it's obviously fake. Could the desk guy tell you anything else?"

"That's it, in a nutshell. Hey, don't look so depressed. It's the closest thing to a real suspect we've got. And now we know to look for a male, not too old, not unusual looking."

"Great, that eliminates about two-thirds of the population of Philadelphia. Which leaves us with a mere million or so people to check out."

"Well, he's too young to be a Forrest board member, so that's out. Maybe he's a son or grandson of one of them, and that person has been pinching funds for years and enlisted Junior to cover up the problem."

"It's as good a theory as any. Can you check for descendants?"

"I could if I was at work—that kind of information would be in our files. Please tell me you don't want to head there now."

"Of course not. I thought we had other plans for this evening."

I w   ppy to note that I'd managed to cheer him up, a   uld get to reap the benefits.

=======

ing: bright sunlight flooding through
catch the early summer breezes.
A handsome man across the table.

"Can you get me that information today?" James asked.

Pop went that bubble. "You mean, about sons of trustees? Uh, it's Sunday. The Society is closed today."

"You run the place. Don't you have the keys? And the security codes?" he responded quickly.

"Well, I do, but . . ." Why was I hesitating? For one thing, I'd hoped to have both a little quality time with James, and some time to let my subconscious work on the pile of new information we had already assembled. For another, ever since some unpleasant events this past spring, I was reluctant to be alone in the building. I knew it was irrational, and I knew we had an adequate security system, and I knew that lightning seldom strikes twice, but still . . . "Can't it wait until Monday?" I said plaintively.

"Nell, there's a killer out there. If you have access to information that could help us identify him . . ."

I felt like a wimp, but I resented James putting me in such a position. "Where will you be?"

It finally occurred to him why I was hesitating. "I can work from the Society if you'll give me a desk and a phone. I've got my laptop in the car."

"In that case, no problem," I said, much relieved. "You can drive."

"No problem," he echoed.

"By the way, remember I said I'd go to Edith's funeral tomorrow. Will you be going?"

"Why?"

"Why should you go? How about, to honor Edith? To help your cousin Harby get through this?"

James shook his head. "I'd be more useful at Why are you going?"

"Edith was a former Society board member, and I'm supporting Marty, who's doing the bulk of the work setting this up. If you aren't going to be there, I'll report back on who did show up." I realized I had no idea how many people that might be. Given Edith's age, it could be only a handful, but given the many and varied Terwilliger connections, it could be a hundred, most of whom I probably didn't know. I'd have to enlist Marty to complete the list, once she had Harby settled.

"Are you finished eating?"

My plate was empty, but I had been looking forward to a leisurely second cup of coffee. Not happening, apparently. "Let me put some appropriate clothes on. Give me fifteen."

"Hand me the front section of the paper, will you?" James said.

I showered very quickly, dressed in something a cut above ratty blue jeans, and we set off for the Society. We both fell silent for the rest of the drive into the city.

the office.

CHAPTER 20

The Society and its massive collections are housed in a
building more than a century old, built solidly of stone
and brick, with high ceilings and large windows. It oozes
history and permanence. It's also a heck of a scary place
to be alone in. Like any old building, it creaks and pops
and shifts. There may even be some nonhuman
presences—and I don't mean vermin—although I've
never met anyone or anything unexpected in the stacks.
Well, maybe once.

Which was why I was happy to have James watching
my back and glad he hadn't ridiculed my fears. I wondered if there was anything that scared him, a trained
agent with a badge and a gun. If so, I hadn't seen it yet.
Or maybe I had: he was really suffering now, feeling that
he was powerless to stop these murders from happening,
due mostly to bureaucratic red tape. I could understand

why the Bureau didn't want individual agents haring off on their own; order and process were necessary in law enforcement or we'd be back in the Wild West. But James was a respected agent, one who had demonstrated good instincts and judgment in the past, and I thought his superiors might cut him a little slack if he said he thought he had a serial killer in his sights. As it was, my trusty duo and I were doing all the legwork, trying to put together enough credible information to persuade the FBI to take us seriously.

At the top of the steps, I inserted my keys, pushed open the heavy metal door, and hurried to punch in the code to disarm the alarm system. James followed, making sure the door was shut behind us. Inside, no lights were on, and everything was silent; all was as it should be. I led the way to the elevator. While we waited, I looked up at Edwin, who as usual looked over my head and beyond me. James followed my glance, then smiled. "This is the guy who started all this?"

"Yes, this is Edwin. I'm sure he never envisioned that his good intentions would result in a string of murders."

When the elevator arrived, I inserted the key that would allow us access to the third floor, which was not open to the public. We stepped out into more dim quiet.

"Why don't we set up in the development office?" I suggested, my voice sounding surprisingly loud to my ears. "That's where all the files are."

"Your call," James said.

I led him into the offices at the bend of the hall and flipped on some lights. The room was lined along one wall with tall four-drawer filing cabinets—all full, as I knew.

They held files on individual members and prospective members, board profiles, copies of grant guidelines and past applications, histories of the events we had held here, going back a decade, and more. The paper files went back much further than the electronic versions, but I decided to start with what we had about the Forrest Trust board members in our computer database.

I sat behind our data administrator's desk, booted up the computer, and logged in. Then I pulled out Shelby's list of Forrest Trust board members. Now I recognized all the names, and could guess at their average age— easily past seventy, often past eighty. But as Louisa had suggested, being a Forrest trustee was not particularly demanding or difficult, so there was no reason for members to retire.

It occurred to me, belatedly, that I could actually look at the terms of the original trust. I'd never paid much attention to Edwin Forrest, apart from saying hi to the mighty statue in the hallway, but maybe there was something in his will or the trust documents that might be useful. I ran a search online and came up with a link to a massive biography of the actor written not long after his death that included as appendices both the will and the legal document by which the city had established the Edwin Forrest Home under the terms of the will. Each document was blessedly short, and on first glance, clear and simple. In his will, Edwin had made a few small bequests, and the rest of his estate, which was substantial, went into trust for an institution to be named the Edwin Forrest Home. He had then outlined in detail what the purpose and makeup of the institution should be. There was one key clause, at least for our purposes:

*The said corporation shall be managed by a board
of managers, ten in number, who shall . . . be chosen
by the said trustees, and shall include themselves so
long as any of them shall be living; and also the
Mayor of the city of Philadelphia for the time being;
and as vacancies shall occur, the existing managers
shall from time to time fill them, so that, if practi-
cable, only one vacancy shall ever exist at a time.*

I read on, charmed by Edwin's lofty hopes for his
actors' home: he spoke of preserving the happiness of the
inmates (an odd choice of term, by modern standards);
offering lectures on all manner of subjects; promoting
the love of liberty and country. He outlined plans to celebrate Shakespeare's birthday each year. As far as I knew,
the trust had lived up to his wishes, until the world had
spun too far to make his dreams relevant.

The city's charter, dated a year after Edwin's death,
copied his terms almost verbatim. The only real departure
from the original plan was choosing to place his Home
in his former residence, Springbrook, which he had sold
but which happened to become available at an oppor-
tune time.

So I had confirmed one piece of hard evidence: there
should be ten trustees at any one time, plus the mayor. It
seemed likely that the mayor played a purely symbolic
role and had little involvement with management. According to the agreement, if the number of trustees fell too
low, the mayor could request that the Orphans' Court
appoint replacements. I made a mental note to see if that
process had been initiated, but if the trust was to be dissolved, it seemed kind of moot. And I really didn't think

the mayor had anything to fear from our unknown killer. Should I be warning judges for the Orphans' Court? Ridiculous!

With a sigh, I turned away from Victorian eloquence—or did I mean grandiloquence?—to look at our records for the trustees past and present. The digital files were not detailed enough for my current purposes, as I had suspected, but Shelby had pulled information from a range of sources. The paper files more often included press clippings and records of personal conversations, which yielded more information about offspring. While I was at it, I checked for best estimates of what the trustees had contributed to the trust, and the answer was nothing in terms of dollars, merely a little of their time. No kids or grandkids could complain that the Forrest Trust was draining their inheritance.

In short, I came up with nothing new. I had eliminated some possibilities, but we were no closer to pointing a finger at anyone than we had been when we started.

But maybe I needed to dig deeper or go back further. I understood that there had been challenges to the will, most of them resolved quickly, and without financial settlement. Then, of course, there was his wife, with whom, as Shelby had said, Edwin had held vituperative and prolonged divorce proceedings that probably had left them both reeling, with their individual reputations in tatters. No doubt Edwin had made sure that her claims were long settled when he drew up the will.

Was there someone else who might have had an interest? A century was a long time to hold a grudge, but at the Society we dealt in long periods. Maybe it was worth checking. As Shelby had also noted, only one claimant,

a very distant cousin, had been given any sort of settlement; all other supplicants—and the bulk of those had
been before 1900—had gone away empty-handed.

I went back to the will once again. At the very end,
Edwin had added a pair of codicils. He had given cash
gifts to a few friends, and also to someone identified as
"my beloved friend Miss Elizabeth, sometimes called
Lillie Welsh, the eldest daughter of John R. Welsh, broker,
of Philadelphia." I had to wonder who Lillie Welsh was,
and why she had inherited the bequest. In the second
codicil, Edwin changed the cash legacy he'd originally
left to his friend James Oakes (any relation to Louisa, I
wondered? Would it matter?) to an annuity that would
end with James's death. Then he shifted that cash to Miss
Elizabeth, making her total gift worth ten thousand
dollars—a hefty sum now, and a fortune when the will
was drafted. Now I was even more curious about Lillie.
I wondered what a little genealogical snooping would
turn up. As far as I knew, Edwin had had no children—at
least, no *legitimate* children with his actress wife, Catherine. But from what I'd read about him, I could easily
picture him as a randy devil, and he had traveled far and
wide, no doubt with plenty of opportunities to "sow his
seed." Was Miss Lillie one such result? Was there any
way to find out?

I indulged my curiosity and looked up the 1870 census
for Philadelphia. Yes, there was John Welsh, on Olive
Street, with his wife, Elizabeth; eldest daughter, Elizabeth
(twenty-nine at the time); a few more children; and two
domestics. And there was Edwin at his home, with one
sister and three domestics. Edwin had been worth a hefty
$150,000 that year, or so said the census. I made a quick

Internet detour, just out of curiosity, and found that the $150,000 Edwin declared would amount to well over $2 million in current dollars—not too shabby for an actor then.

I resisted the impulse to dig any further into the mysterious Elizabeth Welsh. It would be a nice diversion, but there were more pressing issues to chase down.

"You know, you're sighing a lot," James called out. He'd settled himself in Shelby's office, where he had a clear view of me at the desk as well as down the hall. "No luck?"

I stood up and stretched. "Not a lot. I've been looking at Edwin's will and how the trust was set up, but it all seems clear enough. The trust is currently in violation of its own terms, now that so many of the trustees are dead, but I'm not sure what the implications of that are. It would probably mean a court battle to sort it out, by which time the remaining trustees would also be dead. I wonder what the internal process for disbursing funds is."

James came out as far as the doorway and leaned on the jamb. "Are you asking if someone has been skimming funds, hoping no one will notice?"

"Or making sure by picking off the trustees, one by one? It's possible. We'd need a forensic accountant to figure that out. What I need to do is talk to the attorney who's been handling the trust, and Rodney told me that he's the one who oversees the accountant, so I can kill two birds with one stone. I'll see if I can set that up tomorrow."

"Is that a good idea?" James said. "If he is involved, you'd tip him off."

"Maybe, but since the firm handles the Society's legal

affairs, too, and we are custodians of parts of the Forrest collection, I have a perfectly legitimate reason to be asking about what's happening with the trust."

"Maybe." He didn't seem satisfied.

I didn't pursue it. "Oh, and it seems the mayor of Philadelphia is an ex officio member of the board."

"And why does that matter?" James asked.

"Because the mayor has the authority to force the trust to shut down, under the terms of the original trust."

"Oh, great. Maybe he's eyeing the money for his next campaign."

"Somehow I doubt it would flow directly to his coffers. But maybe someone in his administration is looking to curry favor and thinks this would impress him? By the way, the trustees were not required to add any money to the trust, merely oversee it. So no motive for grabby grandkids. Skimming funds is a better bet."

Marty appeared in the hall doorway, and I jumped at the sound of her voice. "Any progress?"

"Marty, what are you doing here?" I demanded. "And how . . . oh, never mind." I had long since learned that Marty Terwilliger regarded the Society as her own personal kingdom, and that she had inherited her father's and grandfather's keys to almost any door in the place and knew all the alarm codes.

She eyed me curiously. "A little jumpy, eh? I don't blame you. But that's neither here nor there. I came in a while ago to work on the Terwilliger collection, of course. What about you two?"

"I filled James in on what we learned yesterday, and we were wondering if there were any offspring of the board members who might have a personal interest either in seeing the trust dissolved or in seeing it go on as before without too much poking around in the books. The short answer is no, unless granddad was siphoning off money."

"As far as I know, most of the board members were comfortably off," Marty said, "so they wouldn't have any need for funds. Of course, things can change fast. I suppose you have to consider it."

"I'm not sure I buy into it, either, but I thought it would be a good idea to check." I leaned back in my chair. "Marty, we're running out of places to look. Unless someone shows up at the funeral and lurks furtively around the edges." I turned to James. "The remaining trustees seem to be clean. Their offspring have no vested interest in what happens with the trust. I can't see the mayor hiring hit men to wipe out the trustees just so he could get his hands on a very small pot of money with a bunch of legal strings attached. Maybe the law firm will lose a little income if they're no longer managing those funds, but they're rock solid and they won't miss it. What're the odds that it's a random stranger who thought that this would be a good group to mow down, just for the hell of it?"

"Considering that most of the world doesn't know this trust exists," James said, "that's unlikely. How about from your end? Any museum managers who are itching to get their hands on Edwin's memorabilia?"

"Like you said, I think most of the world doesn't know it exists. And it would cost a pretty penny just to move the statue, which would eat into the trust proceeds."

He smiled. "I have it: you have a mad crush on Edwin, and you want to keep the statue here for yourself."

I smiled back. "Well, I do find him a rather entertaining figure, but I draw the line at cross-generational romances, especially when there's more than a century involved—and one party is made of stone."

"You do know he's dead, don't you?" Marty piped up.

I had another brainstorm. "Maybe he's a zombie and he's risen from his tomb—which, by the way, isn't all that far from here—because he's afraid his name will be forgotten. James, would you recognize the signs of a zombie killing?"

"Not offhand, but I'll take that idea under advisement."

Marty and I burst out laughing, and James joined in as well. After our moment of levity, though, we all fell silent. It was Marty who finally said, "You know, it all sounds ridiculous, until you remember that several people are dead. That's real."

"I know," I said softly. I looked at James. "What now? Our only possible suspect so far is a youngish, educated, personable male who tried to visit Louisa. Not exactly a smoking gun. Whoever this is, is a very subtle serial killer, and has some unspecified connection to someone or something involved in the Forrest Trust. And wants them dead, for a motive we can't see. Not a lot to go on."

"Wait—what young man?" Marty demanded.

"Somebody tried to see Louisa after hours last night, and the night desk person turned him away, and then called me, bless him. His description was pretty vague, but it's better than nothing."

"Young pleasant man," Marty said, shaking her head. "Yeah, that helps a lot."

"Keep digging," James replied, holding my gaze. "If

it's not random, which seems statistically improbable, then there must be some evidence somewhere."

"One thing we haven't tried," I said, talking more to myself than to the others, "is checking who has requested Forrest material from the collections over, say, the past year. I was going to ask Felicity to check for me. It would take a little time—it would be a manual search, because we use physical call slips, so the information is not digitized, although we're working on that. But we do keep them. Maybe someone has been looking for something specific about Forrest. I'll admit I've had trouble finding some documents that were his. It could be poor filing, or it could be that someone has been making off with them. That's still too easy to do, as long as we don't perform full-body searches of our patrons."

"If you track down those slips, they'll tell you who requested the materials?"

"Yes, and the person would have to have shown ID when he—or she—came in originally and signed in. Although that's not to say that that person couldn't have filled in a fake name once he was inside the library."

"You mean, like Franklin Washington?" James asked wryly.

"Exactly," I replied. Marty looked confused, and I added, "The mystery guest at Louisa's rehab center said his name was Franklin Washington."

"Look, I can help with the call slips, see if I recognize any names, if you get them from Felicity," Marty volunteered. "After the funeral, of course."

"Right," I said. "Ten o'clock?" Marty nodded in reply.

"If you're done here, can I give you ladies a lift home?" James asked.

"I'll take Nell home," Marty said. "I've got to visit Harby again anyway, so I'm headed that way."

"Call me tomorrow, after the funeral," James said.

Marty and I exchanged a glance. "We will."

The three of us left the building together, careful to turn off the lights, arm the alarm, and lock the door behind us.

CHAPTER 21

I dressed with care for the funeral. I'd attended several in the past few years, mainly in a professional rather than a personal capacity. The Society's board and many of our best supporters were advanced in age, so I ended up paying my respects fairly often. I refused to regard funerals as an opportunity to network with people of high net worth, nor did I pump grieving relatives to find out what they planned to do with the contents of the library or the collections of the departed—I wasn't that crass. At best I hoped that people would remember my presence at some later, happier time.

I found parking across from the church in Wayne and entered the building to find a midsize crowd. I spied Marty and Harbeson in the front row, but I had no claim on that space, so I slid into a pew toward the back and studied the architecture. Nice building, maybe early twentieth century, reverent but not in your face about it. A closed casket,

I was happy to see. An older minister whose eulogy proved he had known Edith. A respectful assembly, their grief restrained. I recognized a few people from events at the Society or from the society pages in the *Inquirer*, although few acknowledged me. The peril of being a fundraiser: you were mostly invisible, and if you were visible, people tended to shun you for fear you would ask them for a contribution. Too often that was true, but not in my case.

The service was over in less than an hour. It was announced that there would be a cemetery interment for family only, and that was that. I wasn't surprised: even with Marty's help, I couldn't visualize Harby managing a gathering at his house. I waited in my pew as Marty and Harby exited; as they passed me, Marty leaned toward me and mouthed, "We have to talk," before leaving the building. Something new?

I drove to work. The good news was, most of the traffic should have cleared by midday. The bad news was, parking in the city would be sticky. But I had to be there. I needed to ask Felicity, our head librarian and keeper of all knowledge, to review the call slips for any Forrest materials that had been requested, hoping that there would be a clue somewhere in there. I should bring Shelby up to date on the trustee research I'd done on Sunday and ask her to see if there was anything I had missed. I should go stare searchingly at the Coriolanus statue and ask Edwin to give me an answer. I knew he'd had a troubled life and career—and they were inextricably intertwined—so in a weird way it was fitting that tragedy should dog him still. Poor Edwin—he'd wanted to do some good, and now people were dead because of it. It wasn't fair.

I didn't talk to him, of course. When I arrived at the Society, I gave Edwin a nod as I waited for the elevator, but that was all. In my office, I dumped my bag and called Shelby. "A word with you, please?"

"Be right there," she replied, and she was. "What's up?"

"I was here yesterday reviewing the information you put together again. Oh, so was James, if you find anything out of place on your desk. We thought it was worth looking to see if there were any offspring who might worry that the trust was sucking up their potential inheritance."

"The next generation?" Shelby asked. "Or should I say, generations, plural?"

"Exactly. The other thing I'd like to check is whether somebody had been helping themselves to the trust's funds, but I'd have to see a historical accounting for that. I'm going to try to talk to someone at the law firm that manages the trust. Marty was also here yesterday. I saw her at the funeral but she was busy holding up Edith's brother. It occurs to me that I should ask her to see if Edith Oakes had any of the documents at her home that would have been distributed for the trust board meetings."

"Lady, you sure have been busy! So what is it you want me to do?" Shelby asked. "Oh, by the way, James was the picture of discretion when I tried to pump him about your relationship when he drove me back to the city on Saturday."

"All part of the FBI training, I assume." I wasn't about to ask her what he had said. "I guess there's no way for us to check if somebody's been using the trust as a private bank account, but the lawyer should know, or could find out. Just to be on the safe side, could you check the children of the trustees again? But limit your search to any male children between, say, twenty-five and thirty? Maybe if we ever make this official, the FBI can check their records for any suspicious deposits."

"Why male?"

"We have a lead that whoever's been approaching the trustees could be a thirtyish male." I filled Shelby in on the call I'd received Saturday evening from Louisa's rehab center.

"Okay, that helps. So your theory is that either a trustee might have been skimming and is trying to cover his tracks, or one of their male children or even grandchildren is doing the covering-up out of a misguided sense of filial loyalty?"

"Something like that. I know, it's pretty thin, but it's the best I've got."

"I'm on it. James is still stymied?"

I nodded. "He is. It's like chasing ghosts—you catch a glimpse of something out of the corner of your eye but you can't quite see it." I stood up. "I'm going down to talk to Felicity for a moment."

I decided to take the stairs down and walked through the catalog room into the reading room, which looked moderately busy. Felicity was enthroned on the elevated dais (the better to observe the library patrons, who had been known to conceal documents in some rather intimate places), so I approached and said quietly, "Can I have a word with you?"

"Of course," she said promptly. "In private?"

"A quiet corner would do," I told her.

"Ah," she said, "only semisecret."

"Disappointed?" I asked, smiling.

Felicity returned my smile with a more restrained one. "Well, you do come up with such interesting questions."

We found an unoccupied corner. "What I'd like you to do is pull the call slips over the past year or so for any items related to Edwin Forrest. I've been having trouble locating some of the items."

Felicity looked alarmed. "Is there a problem?" She had been extremely helpful when we'd uncovered earlier "disappearances" at the Society, so I rushed to reassure her. "Not that I know of, but let me know if you find anything unusual, will you?"

"I understand—I think." She gave me a long look. "Was that all?"

"For the moment," I said cheerfully. "Thanks, Felicity."

We parted ways at the entrance to the reading room, where Felicity went toward her desk and I went to the elevator. I looked up at Edwin, towering over me, but he avoided my eyes—not that he had much of a choice, since he was looking to his right forever.

I wasn't surprised to find Marty waiting for me upstairs. "You made good time," I said, settling behind my desk.

Marty had already made herself comfortable on my visitor's couch and was forking up a takeout salad. "A couple of cousins are looking after Harby, so I escaped."

"How's he doing?"

"Better than I expected. I gather that Edith ran the household with an iron hand, and Harby has only just discovered that he can do what he wants—eat when he's hungry, watch television six hours a day. He's finding it quite liberating."

"By the way, it was a nice funeral, as such things go."

"Edith was a grand old woman. We won't see her like again. Thank goodness—she used to scare the crap out of me when I was a kid," Marty said.

"That's what James said, too. Was there something else you wanted to tell me?" I asked.

Marty dumped her empty plastic container into my trash can, then sat down again. "Yes. Harby finally remembered that there had been a couple of phone calls for Edith. You can probably guess that he's not into caller ID and all that stuff, so he answers the phone whenever it rings, which I gather isn't all that often. Anyway, there were a couple of times he picked up and it was a call for Edith, usually in the middle of the afternoon." She paused to challenge me with a look.

It took me a moment to work out what she wanted me to see. "You mean, when Harby should have been at the club?"

Marty nodded triumphantly. "Exactly. On at least one of those days, Edith was out with the car, so Harby didn't leave until late. But if the caller had assumed Harby was following his usual schedule, Edith would have been home to answer the phone."

"It could have been a solicitor of some sort. Most calls are, these days."

"It's possible, but Harby thought it wasn't. He said the caller was a nice young man. Polite. Now, 'young' to Harby could be anywhere south of fifty, but if there's a phone record, Jimmy can find it!" Marty finished triumphantly.

At least the vague description of the caller—young and male—matched the visitor at the rehab center. "Isn't that illegal?"

"If it's for some random person. But Harby is Edith's executor, and you know he'd give James permission in a second to check the records."

"Did he remember when the calls came?" I asked.

"He might, if he checks his bar tabs at the club and figures out when he *wasn't* there. Anyway, there were only two that he can recall, so it shouldn't be hard to narrow it down."

With our luck, it would probably turn out to be an insurance salesman, but it couldn't hurt to check.

"You got anything new?" Marty asked.

"Not really. I hate this, not knowing. If the deaths stop, does that mean it really was just a series of coincidences, or that the killer got smart and is holding off? Speaking of which, another thing I think I found out yesterday was that the trust is in violation of its rules because the board is short multiple members, which means that the mayor, on behalf of the city, has the right to step in and ask that replacements be appointed by the court. I'm not sure how to look at that in relation to the proposed dissolution of the trust. Can you shed any light on it?"

"Maybe. I'd be willing to bet that the city has a lot of other things on its platter, and it's not going to bother with a dinky little trust, or at least, not right away, and especially if they know it's going to be dissolved soon."

"What is 'soon'?" I asked. I had only just realized there

might be a ticking clock. "Has anything been filed officially?" Rodney hadn't seemed to think so, but maybe he hadn't kept up with the trust doings.

"I can ask Louisa. Oh, and I looked for Edith's files on the trust."

"I was planning to ask you to look at those. And?"

Marty shook her head. "There weren't any."

I fought a stab of disappointment. I had hoped that those files would shed some light on how the trust actually functioned. "What do you mean? The files were empty? Or there were no folders at all? Nothing?"

"It's like they never existed. Everything else in Edith's desk and filing cabinet was in apple-pie order, neatly labeled, as you would expect. But no files labeled 'Forrest Trust,' or 'Trust-Forrest,' or 'Edwin Stuff,' or anything else. Believe me, I looked. If they were there, they're gone. And given how meticulous Edith was, I'd bet there *were* files."

If it was possible to feel simultaneously elated and depressed, that was my reaction. Depressed because there could have been valuable information in those files; elated because if someone had taken the trouble to locate them and take them away, and even tidied up the remaining files, then we were on the right track and Edith's death did tie to the Forrest Trust. "So whoever had tea with her, took them away."

Marty was watching me, enjoying my thinking process. "Exactly what I figured," she said. "The files that *aren't* there are proof that there is something going on with the trust. Right?"

"That's what I was thinking. I'll let James know."

"You do that," Marty said, standing up. "I'm going to

go bother Rich some more. Let me know what Jimmy has to say, or if he wants me to talk to Harby about the phone thing."

"Will do." When Marty had left, I looked at my desk. While it was nowhere near chaotic, thanks mainly to Eric's admirable organizational abilities, there were still several things that required my attention. My first job was running the Society, which seemed to roll on with or without murders on the side.

The next time I came up for air, it was after four. I leaned back in my chair and stretched.

Marty's talk about Edith's files reminded me that I should take another look for the Forrest files in the stacks. Maybe I'd missed something the first time around. Or maybe I just wanted an excuse to hide out with all the old documents and avoid people. I picked up my annotated finding aid, stood up, and marched out of my office.

"Eric, I'm going to go look for something in the stacks. If I'm not back by five, you go on home, okay?" I said as I breezed past him.

An hour later, I had to admit defeat: I couldn't find a single file, either autograph materials or ephemera or secondary sources from Edwin's day. I reminded myself to talk to Felicity in the morning. Maybe she had found some sort of paper trail.

I knew that some of our board members, and even some longtime researchers, kind of bent the rules, and that's how things get lost or misplaced. But *all* the Forrestiana, if that was a word? Unlikely. This felt like a systematic effort to me.

I went back to my office. Most people had already left for the day. Eric's desk was ridiculously tidy, all ready for the morning. There were no message slips waiting for me on my desk. I picked up the phone and hit the speed dial for James's private number at the FBI.

"You have something, Nell?" he said without preamble.

"Maybe. Can we meet? It won't take long."

"Sixish? I'll buy you dinner."

"Deal."

CHAPTER 22

Over a quick and decidedly non-romantic dinner, I briefed James on what I had found, or rather, *not* found, at the Society, in the way of Edwin Forrest documents, and Marty's equal lack of success among Edith Oakes's records. That some documents at the Society were misplaced would not surprise anyone who has worked with large paper-based collections, but *all* of one set, scattered throughout the building? Not likely, which meant that somebody was probably "disappearing" them. Worse, it had to be somebody with access to our stacks, and with the knowledge to bypass the usual library protocols; it almost had to be an insider. I did not want to contemplate that possibility.

"It makes no sense to me," I complained. "What should I do? Call a staff meeting and ask everybody if they've seen any Edwin Forrest papers wandering around the building?"

"If this person was as thorough as you say, he—or she—has probably already got everything, so all you would accomplish would be to alert the perp."

"So your advice is to do nothing?"

"More or less. Does anyone else know what you've been looking for?"

"I don't think so. The only person I've said anything to is Felicity, because she's the keeper of the tracking records. We know she's discreet."

"What about Shelby?"

"She's only looked for the Society records pertaining to the trust, not for original Forrest documents. So she's clear."

James said carefully, "Is there anyone you suspect?"

"No! I mean, I don't even know why anybody who works at the Society would be that interested in Edwin Forrest or the trust. But once you slip outside of rationality, anything's possible. Right?"

He was watching me, his expression troubled. "Nell, be careful, will you? You're right—the logic behind these killings may make sense only to the perp. Which means anyone and everyone could be at risk." He hesitated a moment before adding, "I don't want anything to happen to you."

For a by-the-book FBI agent in a public place, that was positively romantic, and it warmed me just a bit. "By the way, Marty said that Harby told her that Edith had received a couple of phone calls from a young man, at times when Harby wouldn't usually be there. Could those be related? Can you look into them?"

"I'll talk to Harby again. You're thinking that Harby

will let me get access to those phone records?" When I nodded, he went on, "It may turn out to be nothing."

"James, what would be enough? I'm sorry if I sound selfish, but so far we think we have six victims, and some of those are people I knew, or Marty did, or even you. If we're right, we can guess who the next victims might be, and I've just met two of them. I know you can't personally babysit all of them, but surely there must be something you can do."

James sighed. "Nell, I've told you, I'm doing the best I can. I've asked you and Marty for help, which will not make the FBI happy, but it's probably the most effective way of getting to the bottom of this, believe it or not. Look how much you've uncovered, after only a few days."

"Thank you, I guess. But we still don't have a suspect."

"We have a profile that is getting more clear by the day. Young male, educated, knowledgeable about collections. And apparently lacking in any sort of conscience. Do you know anyone who fits?"

I thought about our staff roster. Eliminating the women and the older men, of which there were few anyway, who was left? Eric, Rich, and Nicholas—all no older than thirty, all educated. Eric's mild southern accent didn't necessarily exclude him. But I was reluctant to label any one of them a murderer. Whatever James's FBI serial killer handbook said, I kept coming back to motive, and none of these three had one, that I could see.

I sensed that James was watching, waiting for an answer. "I'm not ready to point a finger at anyone. Yes, we have some young men on the staff who fit the general description, but it's pretty vague. I want to think this over before I say anything. Believe me, if I had anything solid I'd tell you."

"Fair enough," James said. "Just watch yourself."

"I will. And we don't know for sure that it's someone on my staff. It could just as easily be a board member"—although none of them was young—"or a researcher or a trusted member. There are other people who have that kind of access."

After some small talk, James walked me back to where I'd parked earlier in the day. I was glad for his company: the outdoor lot was poorly lit, and I wasn't sure the parking attendant would be any use if there was trouble. Having an FBI agent at my side was reassuring. We'd grabbed a good-night kiss, then James stayed long enough to watch me pull away before heading off for his own car. I drove home in the June dusk, thinking hard about the young males on our staff. I had known Rich the longest, since he'd been working in his grant-funded position for almost two years. In that time I had found him pleasant, responsible, and competent. Eric I had hired quickly out of a desperate need for an assistant, but he had worked out well. He was a sweet southern boy, with a few minor blots on his record, but he'd been an exemplary employee since he had started working for me. For the life of me, I could see no reason why he would want to murder anybody. Nicholas had been with the Society for only a few months, but he had come highly recommended by his former employer, and he had done a great job so far in creating order out of the chaos of not only our collections but also in the massive load of FBI materials, and I was grateful for that. On a personal level, I knew very little about any of them: Nicholas was civil and courteous, but did not go out of his way to cultivate friendships among the staff; Eric seemed to know everyone, and something about his innocent face led a surprising number of them to confide in him, but he had no roots here in Philadelphia. All I really knew about Rich's personal life was that he was dating another staff member. They all seemed like nice, ordinary young men. How could I suspect any one of them of being a murderer?

I gave myself a mental slap: I had forgotten to call Courtney Gould at Morgan, Hamilton and Fox yesterday, to ask about the Forrest trust. If I requested a meeting, the Society would probably have to pay for it, but we had a legitimate stake in the disposition of the Forrest materials, not to mention the endowment that had come with it, so I had a perfect excuse to talk to her. I put that call on my mental to-do list for the next day.

———

When I arrived at my office in the morning, Eric was already there. I looked at his open, cheerful face and couldn't begin to see a serial killer lurking behind it. "Eric, when you think the offices are open, can you call Courtney Gould at Morgan, Hamilton and Fox and set up an appointment for me, as soon as possible?"

"Trouble?" Eric asked anxiously. I could sympathize with his apprehension. I liked some lawyers as individuals, but somehow involving them always seemed to create more problems than it solved, and we ended up paying for it.

"No, this is Society business. She's the Society's attorney, and I have a couple of questions for her, that's all. Tell her it should be a short appointment—I think that firm bills by the minute."

"Will do," he said. No more than a half hour later, he called out, "Ms. Gould can see you at eleven—does that work for you?"

"Tell her that's fine," I called back. Lucky break— sometimes it took weeks to find a time to get together. I immersed myself in paperwork until it was time to walk over.

Morgan, Hamilton occupied one of those big glass buildings on Market Street, an easy walk from the Society. I arrived on time, conscious of the ticking clock, and was promptly ushered into Courtney Gould's office. Courtney, a slender woman only a few years older than I am, rose from behind her desk and came around to greet me warmly.

"Nell, it's been a while. I hope there's no trouble?"

"You mean like the last few times I've talked to you? No, no thefts or fires this time around. Sorry to disappoint you."

"I'm happy to hear it. Please, sit down." Courtney gestured graciously at the two chairs in front of her desk. "Coffee?"

I sat. "No, I'm fine, and I know you must be busy." And I didn't want to spend three figures of the Society's money drinking a cup of coffee. "I'll come to the point. I have heard rumors that the Forrest Trust, which I understand your firm also represents, is thinking of liquidating. I don't know if you remember, but we hold a number of items that they've loaned to us, as well as segregated funds to maintain them, and I wondered what our legal standing was if they do go ahead and dissolve."

"Hmm. I'm not aware of any discussions about that, but then, that's not my area of expertise. Let me see who's handling the trust." She stood up again and went out into the corridor to talk to her legal assistant, returning two minutes later. "That would be Jacob Miller, an associate. He's coming right over."

I was pleasantly surprised. "Thanks. Jacob stopped by the Society a few days ago to introduce himself. How long has he been handling the Forrest Trust's interests? And the Society's? I didn't know he was involved with both, but it certainly makes it easier for us."

"It does, doesn't it?" Courtney didn't seem the least surprised by my question. "We hired him last year, right out of law school. I think the Forrest Trust was one of his first responsibilities—it was small and not particularly complex. I asked him to help me out with some of my other clients a couple of months ago. Everything else going well?"

"All things considered, yes." We chatted a bit about the Society's next planned exhibition, a small display of early Philadelphia maps, until Jacob Miller arrived.

Seen in this august setting, Jacob looked even younger to me than he had at the Society, barely old enough to have graduated from college, much less have earned a law degree. But this was a fairly prestigious firm, so he must have some solid credentials. On the other hand, I knew that major firms hired scads of eager young associates—then spit out the majority of them after a year or two. It was a cutthroat arena for young lawyers. I wonder how he thought he was going to distinguish himself.

"Hello, Ms. Pratt," he said. "What can I do for you, Courtney?"

"Come on in. Or since there are three of us, maybe we should move to the small conference room?"

Jacob promptly went out to the hall and retrieved a third chair. "This'll do for me." He sat and looked back and forth at us like an eager puppy.

"You already know Nell, I understand. She came to us with a question about the Forrest Trust."

"Of course. What do you need to know?"

"As you are probably aware," I began, "the Society has some items that belong to the trust on long-term loan. I've heard that the board is thinking of dissolving and divesting itself of its physical collections, and I wondered if we had any standing if that occurs."

"Where'd you hear that?"

I evaded the question by saying, "There is some overlap between our boards. One of those members, Adeline Harrison, died recently, and that prompted me to look into the matter. I'd rather know where we stood now than have to deal with the situation when and if it comes up later."

"Good thinking. But I have to tell you, the matter has barely gone beyond the preliminary discussion stage."

"Who have you talked to?"

Jacob looked startled, then wary, at my direct question. "I'm not at liberty to say. More than one member of the trust."

Courtney interrupted, "Jacob, I think you can tell Nell. I'm sure she'll be discreet."

Did I see a flash of something in Jacob's eyes? Anger? Did he think I was challenging him? "I think Rodney Lippincott and Louisa Babcock brought it up, one or the other—they're fairly senior members of the board." He paused for a moment. "That's rather obscure information for you to have."

"Not really. I've been reading up on Forrest, and his

will is published on the web. Besides, since the Society benefits from the terms of his will, however indirectly, I was interested."

Courtney seemed bewildered by my exchange with Jacob. "You've looked at Forrest's will?"

"I have. It's short and to the point—and it's still valid, isn't it, Jacob?"

"Nobody's challenged it in the past century," he agreed. "Look, it's a restricted trust with maybe a million in total assets. Without looking at the original documents, I'd guess that the holding of the trust—property, artifacts such as yours, and, of course, funds—would be liquidated and pooled, and the trustees would determine how to disburse the proceeds. I could approach them on your behalf if you like. Or if you want me to do some more research, I'll be happy to get back to you later. How's that sound?"

"That would be fine, and what you said is what I more or less suspected. Oh, one more question. Who's the auditor for the trust? I want to make sure our numbers add up, if this dissolution goes forward."

"A guy named Alvin Washburn. Works out of his home in Bala Cynwyd. Everything's electronic these days, so he prefers not to have to come into the city. He's not real mobile since the accident."

I caught Courtney's look of annoyance; she was signaling to Jacob that he was saying too much. I was glad, though, since if the auditor was disabled in any way, it was unlikely that he was traveling around poisoning elderly board members. Unless he was faking it. People would generally open the door to someone in a wheelchair, wouldn't they?

"Nell?" Courtney's voice broke into my speculations. "Was there anything else you needed?"

I stood up briskly. "Not right now. Thank you for seeing me on such short notice, Courtney. Jacob, I'd appreciate it if you'd get back to me with more details about the trust, and the status of our agreement with it."

Jacob had risen politely when I had. "No problem. I'm happy to help. Maybe when I deliver them, you can take me on that tour you promised?"

"I hope so, Jacob. I'll find my way out, Courtney. I'd say I hope I'll see you again soon, but since that usually means we're in trouble, I won't."

Courtney laughed. "I understand completely! Bye, Nell."

CHAPTER 23

Back on Market Street, trying to decide if it was still too
early for lunch, I reviewed what I had learned. Jacob had
confirmed that the idea of dissolving the Forrest Trust
had been floated, but not much had been done to pursue
it—or so he said. He was a young man, looking to make
his mark at the law firm. How could he handle the trust
to place himself in the best possible light? Or if he was
on the dark side, had he been dipping into it himself?
Perhaps to pay off what must be hefty law school debt?
*Nell, you're being ridiculous! You meet a perfectly nice
young lawyer, and immediately you start looking at him
as a potential criminal?*

But still . . . He was the right age and fit the vague
definition of the killer. He was certainly in a position to
know all there was to know about the Forrest Trust,
including the identities and whereabouts of the trustees.
I couldn't say whether he had any direct access to the

funds, but I couldn't rule it out. Maybe he and the crippled accountant were colluding in siphoning money out of the trust. But how would killing any of the trustees help? Jacob had admitted in front of Courtney that at least two trust members had put forward the idea of dissolving the trust. Had she known before today's meeting? It was out in the open now, in any case, and she would likely be watching when any audit was done, if Jacob worked for her. If he was the killer, what would Jacob do next?

Nell, you're losing your grip! We had to sort out these murders before I became completely paranoid.

I decided to find a quick sandwich and eat it in my office. I went back to the Society, helped myself to another cup of coffee, then sat down at my desk with my sandwich. Now what? I was frustrated; I hated this waiting, jumping every time the phone rang, expecting to hear that some other person had died because we couldn't seem to figure out who wanted them dead. At the moment, it looked as though the surviving trustees were safe, either far removed or protected. But there were ways to get at people, even those who thought they'd taken precautions. Still, would killing more of them serve a purpose? Right now the trust was vulnerable because the surviving trustees had to fill the vacancies or risk seizure by the city, at the request of the mayor. But if they were planning to dissolve anyway, did that matter? If the city took over by inserting its own representatives, it wouldn't change the terms of the trust, would it?

It was the "why" of it all that troubled me. I couldn't figure out who benefited. If the trust liquidated its assets and had money to give away, where would it go? I'd guess the dispersal would have to be approved by the courts, and I doubted that the trustees would do something frivolous with the cash. Maybe someone at the city thought they could divert those funds to something dear to their hearts—and there was no shortage of worthy projects in the city of Philadelphia—but the trust money was so comparatively small, and the city's needs were so large . . . It didn't make sense.

All I was accomplishing sitting here was driving myself crazy. Six possible murders for no apparent reason, and Marty, Shelby, James, and I seemed to be the only people who'd noticed or cared. I had better find something useful to do, and fast. I took a look at my calendar: my next appointment was a meeting at the Water Works later in the week, and I needed to find out what more Nicholas had collected since our last meeting. Voilà, a distraction.

Since I couldn't sit still any longer, I headed down the hall to find Nicholas. He was at his desk in his cubicle, peering intently at his computer screen. He looked up when I came around the partition to his desk.

"Nicholas, do you have a minute? I want to talk about our presentation at the Water Works this week. You owe me a preliminary report, and we've got a meeting scheduled there tomorrow afternoon."

"I apologize," he said, contrite. "The research took longer than I expected, but that's no excuse. I should have let you know."

Yes, he should have. "Let's use my office—there's more room there."

"Fine." Nicholas gathered up a couple of folders and followed me down the hall. Once we were seated, I said, "What have you got?"

"As I understood it, Phebe Fleming at the Water Works

wanted us to put together historic material that could be reinterpreted in light of current 'green' concerns, for benefit of certain corporate interests. What I've been looking at is things like the Water Works' early recognition of potential sources of infection and how they addressed them with the technology available to them at the time."

"Have you found any examples?"

Luckily I had pressed the right button, and Nicholas was happy to show off the information he had assembled. All I had to do was throw in a reasonably intelligent comment now and then. He had accomplished quite a bit since he'd been handed the assignment, and I could see the potential for an interesting display. As for Nicholas, he was positively animated. Maybe he'd found something historic that actually interested him.

When he finally wrapped up, he looked at me squarely and said, "Again, I apologize. I'll have something on your desk by the end of the day, or tomorrow morning at the latest. I guess I got so caught up in the material that I misjudged my time."

Strangely enough, that was a good excuse. "I understand, and I'm glad that you found it absorbing. That's what we hope for around here, but not everyone feels that way about old documents."

Since he seemed to be in an expansive mood, I decided to press a little further. In fact, he was due for a three-month review, and I did want to hear his opinion about how the work in the processing room was going—without his colleagues overhearing. "So, Nicholas, how's the job going?"

He looked at me quickly. "Have there been any complaints?"

"No, nothing like that. I'd like to hear your general

assessment. Have you mastered what your predecessor developed in the way of cataloging?" Poor Alfred—his heart had been in the right place, but he'd been slow to adapt to the new electronic world.

Nicholas seemed relieved to be on familiar ground now. "Of course. I've already transferred all of his material into the new database. I'm afraid he had barely scratched the surface."

"You didn't need to start over with the items he had input?"

"No, he handled those adequately. But he was old-school, and there are better ways of doing things now. I've now completed his material, and I'd say I've finished maybe twenty-five percent of the new material. You wanted me to begin with the FBI trove, correct?"

"Yes, there are strategic reasons for getting a handle on the contents. One, we need to give the FBI a list that's detailed enough to enable them to compare our listings to reports of missing items. Two, we want to keep them in our debt, so that if anything remains unclaimed we have first crack at keeping it. So getting the information to them sooner rather than later would benefit everyone." Maybe I was telling him too much, so I was relieved when he nodded in agreement.

"I see your point, and I'm happy to expedite the process."

I shifted back to practical matters. "How long do you think it will take you to complete the assessment and data entry?"

"Realistically? Another six months. The balance will go faster because I've familiarized myself with the parameters and adapted my program to the Society's use."

That was about what I had expected, so I wasn't disappointed. "I think you've made great progress, all things considered. After all, you weren't expecting your task to triple overnight." Nicholas had been working for me for months, but I realized once again how little I knew about him, apart from what I saw when he was at work. "Did you grow up in this area?"

He didn't appear startled by my shift of subject. "In the suburbs, mainly."

"Oh? Where? I live in Bryn Mawr."

"Mostly north of Philadelphia—Jenkintown, Abington, that area."

"Ah. I don't know that area well. You live in the city now?"

"Yes, a few blocks from here. I walk to work—it seemed inefficient to waste time commuting."

"What do you like to do, when you're not working?"

"Read, mostly. Books, not digital."

I thought about asking more questions, but this one-sided conversation was too much work. I'd have to give Nicholas points for doing his job well, but he was never going to win prizes for Mr. Congeniality. Still, that had never been part of the job description. His position was glorified technical support for collections management. "Well, Nicholas, thank you for the Water Works update. I'll let you lead the discussion when we're there. And I'll look forward to reading your report," I reminded him.

"Thank you, Nell," Nicholas said.

I stood up as he left, wondering what it would take to get him to loosen up.

Once Nicholas was gone, I wanted to lay my head down on my desk and not think. But that wasn't a good idea—I might drool on the priceless eighteenth-century mahogany with the original finish. No polyurethane here. Then I remembered that I had told James I'd look into any other people associated with the Society who had access to our collections. I thought about asking Shelby to come to my office but decided I needed to get the blood flowing to my head again, hoping that would help. I stopped at Eric's desk and said, "I'm going to have a word with Shelby. You can call me there if anything critical comes up. Or if Marty stops by before I come back, you can send her down."

"Will do, Nell."

I walked down the hall and rapped on Shelby's half-open door. She looked up from a pile of documents. "Hey, Nell. You slumming down here?"

"No, I'm doing a nostalgia tour for the good old days. Got a minute?"

"Sure do. Is this about the . . . you know what?"

"It is. After all, we don't have anything else important to do." I dropped into one of the chairs in front of her desk, after closing the door.

"You sound discouraged," Shelby said, studying me.

"Don't encourage me to feel discouraged. You remember we thought it might be a nice idea to use Edwin Forrest as the theme for the Board Bash? Whenever I've had a free moment, I've been trying to pull together what we had on him so we could take a look at it. And I can't find the documents. I even asked for Felicity's help, without exactly telling her why. All the documents have vanished, although most of the artifacts are where they should be. What do you make of that?"

"That's a stumper," Shelby said. "But how many

people can there be who could get at all that stuff? You've got our board, all of whom have free access to the stacks. You've got a bunch of researchers, mostly local college professors or historians working on a book, plus a few genealogists for hire who come in and out. They're all on record. Maybe someone has been secretly copying the keys of one of those people and using them behind their backs, in which case we'll never find them. And don't forget people who have left over the last few years. Have you collected all their keys? Or had the locks changed?"

"Of course not. We trust people here, which is why we keep losing things," I said bitterly.

"That's what I thought. And then we'd have to look at spouses, roommates, siblings, and so on, both past and present. And don't forget our staff. Even you, Nell. I've seen you eyeing that statue downstairs. Maybe you have an unhealthy passion for Edwin, even though he's dead. You sleep with his correspondence under your pillow."

"I'm *so* glad I've made you discouraged, too. My work here is done," I said. It seemed that my frustration was making me snarky.

"Ha! Well, for your information, lady, I'm way ahead of you—I already have the list of people we know have access." She flipped through a pile of papers on her desk and pulled out two pages stapled together. "Here. You'll probably recognize more names than I would."

"Probably," I said absently. "And I should have told you to eliminate the older ones—I'm pretty sure some on this list are too old to fit the bill."

"Huh?" Shelby said, looking bewildered.

"Oh, shoot—did I forget to fill you in on that?" I quickly told her about the phone calls that Harby had finally remembered, and the mysterious visitor at Louisa Babcock's rehab center. "So we're looking for a thirty-something guy, although I'm sure we have researchers that fit the bill."

I scanned the list. As Shelby had suggested, there were few names I didn't recognize, although I might be hard-pressed to put faces to all of them. As far as I could recall, most were sedate middle-aged people who wanted nothing more than to spend a quiet afternoon sitting in the library reading James Monroe's correspondence.

I handed it back to her. "Okay, I'm out of ideas. Maybe Marty's been killing people because she doesn't have enough excitement in her life. You could mistake her voice on the phone for a young man's. And all we know about any phone calls is what Marty said Harby told her, and if Marty's the killer, she could have made up anything she wanted. Although there was that night attendant at the nursing home . . . I know, Marty dressed up in drag just to confuse people."

"You're right—you're out of good ideas, and you've gone straight to the lousy ones. Speak of the devil . . . hi, Marty," Shelby said.

Marty dropped heavily into the other chair. "You were talking about me?"

"Yes," I replied. "I just accused you of murder. Heck, at this point framing you would be easier than finding the real killer. Please tell me you have something new," I said.

Marty slumped even lower. "Not a thing. Nor have I heard from Jimmy today."

"Neither have I. He's probably busy working on things that *can* be solved. That would be the sensible and useful thing to do."

"So what now?" Marty shot back.

"Marty, I really don't know. Look at us—we're historians, collectors, administrators. It's ridiculous to expect that we can solve crimes." I hated that I sounded whiny, even if what I said was true.

"Nonsense," Marty replied firmly. "We're smart. We're trained in research. Nell, you've been in development, so you must have some skills in reading people."

"I guess, but how far has all that gotten us? The thing I keep coming back to is, what's the motive? Why this group of people, why now?"

"Good point," Marty said. "Because the trust is about to be dissolved? Did that set this off?"

"How many people would know about that?" Shelby asked.

"Not many," I replied. "The trustees themselves, and the lawyer—who I met with this morning. He's an associate and looks about twelve. He's had the file on the trust for maybe a year. And I asked about the appointed accountant working on the trust—he's apparently disabled, which probably eliminates him as an active murderer. And even if people knew about the trust and its potential for going away, why would they care? *Cui bono?*"

"Who stands to lose anything if the trust shuts down?" Marty asked. "We know the Edwin Forrest Home is moribund, and there are plenty of organizations in Philadelphia that could make better use of the space, whether or not it comes with any funding or endowment. Or they could tear it down and build something new on the property, especially if the price was right or it was given outright. Or the trust could really liquidate—sell the property and put the money to some better use. Of course, they'd need court approval, but I'm sure that could be managed."

"Even if some group had its eye on the property, how does killing the trustees help them?" I asked, rubbing the bridge of my nose. I was getting very tired of thinking about this.

"Maybe it accelerates the schedule. Now that the trustees are in breach of the trust terms, the surviving members may be forced to do something. Or at least, the people involved would *believe* they have to do something. They're honorable types. And the simplest solution now is to wrap it up and be done with it."

"But that will take time, right? The trustees would have to vote to pursue dissolution, and then documents would have to be drawn up, and then they'd have to be presented to whichever court covers this, and you know how fast they move. Rodney and Louisa both said that the trustees hadn't gone beyond talking about disbanding, and they'd asked the lawyer to look into the options, and he confirmed it. And from my conversation with him today, he hasn't done much."

"But that's the way *we* see it," Marty said. "Maybe someone else doesn't know all that."

"So you're saying that we haven't looked hard at the possible dissolution as a motive because we know it's not happening anytime soon, but maybe someone else thinks it's urgent?"

"Exactly," Marty said triumphantly. "So we need to know who really has a stake in this. Like you said, *cui bono*? We go back to the beginning and look using that as a filter."

"Can we do that in the morning?" Shelby said plaintively. "Because I really would like to get home in time for dinner."

I checked my watch: well past five. "I think we're burned out today. Let's reconvene in the morning and look at the whole problem with fresh eyes."

"What a brilliant idea, Madame President," Shelby said, grinning. "Let's do that!"

We went our own ways with one assignment: to think. As if I hadn't been doing that. But tomorrow was another day, and maybe things would look brighter in the morning. I hoped.

CHAPTER 24

I find trains soothing, with their rhythmic *clackety-clack* and their stately deceleration and acceleration at stations, and I loved not having to do anything or talk to anyone—I could just sit until I got where I was going, leaving my mind free to roam.

On my ride home, my first thought was: the results of the brief discussion between Shelby, Marty, and me had again made it clear that we had always assumed that a killer did what he did for a rational reason and with a plan. What we had seen from our killer so far suggested intelligence and some skill. After all, he'd successfully evaded detection so far. But if I divorced the method from the rationale for the acts, that opened up a lot of possibilities. The problem was, I wasn't sure how we were supposed to look for irrational ideas.

If this killer wanted only to indulge himself in a few murders, he surely could have chosen almost anyone other than a small group with obscure connections. We all agreed that somehow everything came back to the Forrest Trust. Someone was killing its trustees—but why?

I tried a different angle. Say somebody had buried something precious in the walls or floor of the former Edwin Forrest Home and was worried that a change in ownership might threaten either his chance of retrieving it, or its ongoing concealment? Remotely possible, depending on the timeline. I could probably find out whether the house had undergone any significant renovations in the last century or so, which might have uncovered the mystery item or destroyed it. But what could be hidden that would be so damning? Gold? Diamonds? Another, newer Forrest will? A dead body? It would be rather ironic if someone was willing to kill in order to prevent a dead body from being discovered, but not impossible.

Or how about: someone was offended that callous modern people wanted to break the trust so carefully created by Edwin Forrest? Edwin had wanted his name to live on after his death; he wanted to be remembered. But he did not foresee that there would be no more tenants for the home. Any money left, or received from the sale or transfer of his memorabilia, would be more useful in fulfilling the spirit of the trust and honoring his memory than would a crumbling, empty mansion.

Well, Nell, if you're casting off the shackles of logic, why not go whole hog? What if the ghost of Edwin Forrest was doing it? No, it had to be someone corporeal to carry out the murders. I'd already dismissed the zombie theory. Well, what if someone had gone off the deep end and *thought* that the ghost was running the show? Such a person could be crazy enough to do anything and use the excuse: Edwin Forrest made me do it.

I knew I wasn't equipped to put myself into the mind of a killer; I had trouble killing a spider. Still, there had to be *some* rationale. Money? I could understand that some people might kill for money, especially if it was a substantial amount. But how would it be possible to extract any money from the Forrest Trust, whether intact or dissolved? It had withstood any number of lawsuits when it was new, or so I had read. Was there a statute of limitations? Perhaps the law had changed enough or been reinterpreted enough that the trust might not be so invulnerable now. But I was not a lawyer, and Jacob Miller hadn't expressed any concern when I'd talked to him, although there was no reason for him to share that kind of information with me. I put the whole idea aside to meditate on it. I wasn't planning on doing anything about it tonight in any case. Dinner, a movie on cable, and bed—alone. That I could handle.

———————

Even a good night's sleep brought no new perceptions. I was almost afraid to open my paper on the train the next morning for fear that I'd find that yet another name had succumbed to a death that might look natural but which I knew most likely was not. I was beginning to feel ghoulish.

I like to solve problems and bring them to satisfying resolution. In the Forrest Trust problem, I had a heck of a puzzle but no logical answers. Most of my knowledge of serial killers came from popular media, which aimed for maximum shock value. How many pleasant, ordinary people harbored an urge to kill someone? I'd bet I would never know if I passed one on the street. We were all lucky that only a very small percentage acted on that impulse.

If this ever became an active investigation, James could check phone records, which might show that someone had called each victim before showing up and doing the deed. But if that person was smart, he or she would have used disposable phones that couldn't be traced. Still, if each of the victims' phone records showed a call from the same unidentifiable phone, that would at least reinforce our theory that there was one person behind all the deaths. Marty had said that Harby would be happy to share the records of the landline phone that he and his sister had used, but one phone number wouldn't get us very far. Could James get hold of all the victims' phone records without jumping through official hoops? I tried calling him again from my cell phone, both on his office phone and on his cell. No answer. In the end, I settled for leaving a message, telling him that I would be at the Water Works later in the day. It occurred to me that James knew far more about my job than I knew about his. I wasn't sure if there were restrictions on what he could talk about with civilians, or whether FBI agents in general cultivated an aura of mystery, which made them appear far more powerful than in fact they were. I knew that James never talked about any cases that didn't involve me, and I'd been surprised when he told me how many he and his colleagues handled at any one time. But I could dig up information that the FBI couldn't. Local history, for one thing—most of that would never show up in a

Google search because it existed in only one typescript copy in our stacks. Edwin Forrest had been a local boy who had made it big, yet he had chosen to make Philadelphia his home for most of his life, and he was buried here. Someone had collected all the written documentation we had about him at the Society—looking for something in particular? To keep it out of someone else's hands? But what would be important enough in those records and artifacts to lead to murder?

I was starting to get seriously annoyed. How dare Edwin cause so much trouble this long after his death? I pulled from my bag the meager file of information that I had collected on my own and leafed through it. Forrest's contentious ex-wife, Catherine Sinclair, seemed to have lived out her life in relative obscurity after their very messy divorce. I had come across a newspaper obituary for her that managed to avoid using her birth name altogether, identifying her only as "Mrs. Forrest," even though they had been divorced for years and Edwin had already passed away by the time she died.

I was still curious about the Elizabeth Welsh mentioned in Edwin's will: she was the only anomaly among his bequests. Who was she? Why had he left her money? The logical—or modern—conclusions were that either she was his child by an unknown liaison, or he'd been carrying on with her in his later years, when she was in her twenties. Shoot, maybe he was getting senile and had been taken by a pretty face. Stranger things had happened.

I knew that John Welsh, Elizabeth's father of record, had died in 1874. When I looked at the 1880 census, there was Elizabeth—and a nine-year-old daughter also named

Elizabeth, although no husband was listed for the elder Elizabeth. Edwin's child? Or grandchild? Even if either was true, it was unlikely that I could ever prove it.

I tried to envision explaining to the police or the FBI that there was a serial killer on the loose who was obsessed with the long-dead actor Edwin Forrest. I could only imagine (and cringe at) what they would think.

When I arrived at the Society, Eric was already at his desk, as usual. He looked at me and said promptly, "I'll get your coffee."

"Thanks, Eric." He was right—I needed caffeine. Too bad he couldn't bring some inspiration along with it.

He was back in three minutes. "I made a fresh pot. Don't forget you have that meeting at the Water Works this afternoon."

"Thanks, Eric. I know. Four o'clock, right?"

"Yes, ma'am," he said, and retreated to his desk.

I shuffled through the papers Eric had left neatly stacked on my blotter, and found enough work to keep me busy. Actually it was rather nice to do simple, routine things. Nobody called or dropped by—not James, not Marty, not Shelby. I assumed that meant that nobody had anything new—and that nobody else had died.

It was well past lunchtime when I realized that I hadn't seen the report that Nicholas had promised me. I really should read that before we talked to Phebe Fleming. I went out into the hall. "Back in a sec," I told Eric, and continued down the hall to Nicholas's cubicle. He wasn't there. I scanned his desk for anything that looked like a report. He was scrupulously neat, with everything stacked up in tidy piles, mostly on the credenza behind his desk, leaving his desk clear. One pile looked promising: I knew some of the Water Works files should be a century old, and I recognized the outdated folders and the file coding on them as our in-house system. I walked around the desk and picked up the top folder of that pile and opened it.

And nearly dropped it: it contained handwritten letters—signed by Edwin Forrest. I froze, my mind racing, even as I admired the clear, bold handwriting, and the purple ink. Why would Nicholas have Edwin's letters?

I could feel a seed of suspicion germinating. I laid the folder down where I had found it, neatly squaring the corners. I found a scrap of paper and made a note of the call number, and then I walked calmly down the hall, past my office, and toward the elevator. I had to talk to Felicity—now.

Luckily, Felicity was already at her high desk in the reading room. "Hi, Nell," she greeted me. "Is everything okay?"

So much for my poker face. "I hope so. Listen, did you have time to check the Forrest call slips?"

She cocked her head at me. "I did. The original materials haven't been signed out for quite some time. Everything appears to be in order. Did I forget to give you the list? I know it's here somewhere." She rummaged through the neat piles on her desk. "Oh, here it is. Is there a problem?"

I took the papers she handed me, although I wasn't surprised by what she had told me. "No. I was just following up. Thank you." Before she could ask any more questions, I turned away and went back to the elevator. Edwin ignored me as I waited for it to arrive.

Back at my office, I wondered what I was supposed to do next. Now I knew that Nicholas had been looking at

Forrest documents, and he hadn't signed them out officially—although he hadn't taken them very far. They weren't hidden, and he could have a legitimate reason to be looking at them, although I couldn't think of one. It was an unsettling coincidence.

I realized with a start that I might be able to add one piece of information that could either lay my suspicion to rest or confirm my fears. I reached into my desk drawer and pulled out a copy of Nicholas's resume. Latoya was the one who had talked to his references when we were considering hiring him, but I knew that he had been at the Penn library for a couple of years before that. In fact, he was still working there when we'd offered him the job at the Society. I didn't recognize the name of the person who had recommended him, but it wouldn't hurt to talk to her, and I could come up with some pretext for my call.

I punched in the number, and someone picked up on the third ring. I introduced myself, then said, "Nicholas Naylor used to work for you, right?"

"Yes, until you snatched him away. I don't hold it against the Society—he's a smart one, and you were lucky to get him. How's he working out?"

"He's doing great work here. He's made amazing strides in organizing things, even in the few months he's been here. I did have one question, though."

"Yes?"

"He said that when he was working there, he'd given his database management system a test run on one of your smaller collections. Do you recall what that was? I wanted to know how it compares to what he's working on here."

"Oh, sure. We have a nice collection of Edwin Forrest literature and letters, and we thought that was diverse enough yet small enough to make it a good test. You know of Edwin Forrest?"

All too well. I swallowed and tried to sound normal. "Indeed I do. We have a fair collection of our own here. Did he suggest the topic or did you?"

"I really can't recall, but we agreed that it was an appropriate choice. Was there anything else?"

"I'd love to compare notes sometime on our Forrest collections. We're thinking about putting together a small exhibit. Well, that's all I need. Thanks for your help."

"No problem."

We hung up, and I sat staring at nothing, my mind and my stomach churning. *Oh, hell. Oh, flaming bloody hell.* Nicholas had been looking at Forrest materials at Penn. He'd left a good job there to work at the Society, and knew we had a comparable collection of Forrestiana for him to mine. I hadn't known. But why should I have? The Forrest stuff was but one small collection among the Society's many. I had known of the trust only as a line item on the Society's annual budget. I'd never had a reason to look further.

I shouldn't blame myself for my ignorance, although I did. But what was Nicholas doing, hunting down all the Forrest materials? Unfortunately I was beginning to think that I could guess.

I reached for the phone to call James, but the call went straight to his voice mail. I debated about leaving a message, but then I was startled by a rap on my door, and looked up to see Nicholas. "Sorry it took so long," he said, "but I brought the information on the Water Works that you asked for, so you could look it over before this afternoon's meeting."

I marveled that my voice stayed level. "Thank you. Why don't you give me a few minutes to read through this, and then we can figure out how to handle the discussion?" I was torn between wanting to get him out of my sight so I could process what I'd just learned, and fearing that I'd somehow tip him off that I knew more than I should.

"Okay. Let me know when you're ready." He left.

I sat there staring at the pages but not seeing them. My mind was spinning. Nicholas had the Forrest files. Nicholas fit our generic description of our suspect: he was a polite young man, and he knew about the inside workings of a cultural institution. And he knew about the Forrest Trust. But we still had no motive, and it was a long step from that to labeling him a killer.

CHAPTER 25

Before I could go back to stewing, the phone rang. I grabbed it before Eric could, hoping that it would be James, but instead it was Front Desk Bob. "There's someone here to see you—a Jacob Miller?"

In my distracted state, it took me a moment to recognize the name of the baby-faced lawyer. "I'll be right down, Bob." I hurried to the elevator.

In the lobby, I greeted him warmly. "Jacob, I didn't expect to see you again so soon."

"I found something in our files that I thought you might want to see," he said. "Is there someplace we could talk?"

I led him to the first-floor conference room. Once we were seated, he handed me a manila envelope. "You don't have to read it now—I can give you the gist. When I started looking at the files, I realized that a couple of the members of the Forrest Trust had contacted me since their last board meeting and suggested that they'd like to be ready to make a decision about dissolving the trust by the next meeting. They asked me to draft documents for the review of the full board."

"Is that what you're sharing with me?" I asked.

"Yes. Things are moving more quickly than I recalled. And until you told me, I hadn't realized how involved the Society is—you've got a large chunk of the physical collections here, and I thought it appropriate that you should be kept informed. I checked with the trust members whom I could reach and they had no objections to keeping you up to speed."

"I appreciate that. Listen, while you're here, may I ask if anyone else has made inquiries about the status of the trust in the past year or so? Apart from us here and the trustees?"

"Actually, yes. There were some queries in the past few months. I didn't see them originally because they were in a newer file. Someone named Washington, I think, had asked about any pending changes in the trust. It's a matter of public record, but I think he received a polite brush-off letter. You know, thank you for your interest, et cetera."

"Franklin Washington?" I asked, although I was pretty sure I knew the answer.

"That sounds right. You know him?"

"I know of him. Was there anything else?"

"No, that's all. I take it you're too busy to give me that tour you mentioned?"

"Today, yes, but give me a call and we can set something up. I love to show off the Society." True—just not today. "Let me see you out."

I escorted him to the front door and went back to my office. No phone messages, and it was already past three. Nicholas and I would have to leave for the Water Works very soon. I considered briefly pleading illness—and my stomach was certainly tied up in knots—but I was afraid that might arouse his own suspicions. Plus it would be rude to the staff at the Water Works to blow them off at the last minute, and it was never smart to annoy a city official.

Of course Marty chose that moment to show up at my door. She took one look at me and shut the door behind her. "Something's up," she stated flatly, which didn't increase my confidence in my acting abilities.

I ached to tell her what I suspected, to share the burden, but I hadn't even told James yet—and I still wasn't one hundred percent sure I was right. I ducked the question.

"The lawyer who's handling the trust stopped by. He said a couple of the trustees asked him to pick up the pace with the dissolution, so they could consider it at their next board meeting. Rodney thought that would be pretty soon, didn't he?"

"He did. Wonder if our killer knows that?"

I thought briefly before answering. "Maybe. Jacob said that someone named Franklin Washington had been making inquiries about the future status of the trust."

Marty's eyes widened. "Franklin Washington, as in the guy at the rehab center?"

"The same."

"This is not good. Have you told James?"

"Not yet. He's not picking up on either of his phones."

"Maybe he's wrestling with his bosses to get them to take this seriously."

"I hope so!" I said fervently. "Was there anything else? I'm supposed to be prepping for a meeting at the Water Works in about thirty-six minutes."

"Sounds like fun—or more fun than sitting here worrying. Call me if you learn anything new."

"Of course I will, Marty."

After she left, I checked my watch. It was already three fifteen. I grabbed Nicholas's report and started reading.

Nicholas appeared at my door just past three thirty. "Should we head over there now?"

I met his eyes. He didn't look any different to me. Maybe I was way off base. Maybe the overlap between his job at Penn and the one he held now was coincidental. Yeah, right. "Yes, we should. We'll have to take a cab—I didn't drive in today."

"No problem. Let me go get my folders."

When he'd left, I took a deep breath. So far, so good. I sat for a moment to collect myself, then stood and gathered up my bag. I walked out of the office and stopped at Eric's desk. "Nicholas and I are headed off for the Water Works for our meeting, and I don't think I'll be back today. You can go home whenever you're ready." I leaned closer and said quietly, "If Agent Morrison calls, you can tell him to call my cell—I need to talk to him."

"Got it. Thanks, Nell." He stopped to take a look at me. "Are you okay?"

Great, I'd blown my "normal" cover again. "I'm fine, Eric. Anything I need to worry about for tomorrow?"

Eric glanced at the calendar on his desk. "No, ma'am, looks clear. Have a nice evening."

"I'll try, Eric. See you in the morning." I hoped.

Nicholas joined me in the hall, carrying a battered soft

leather case with its strap slung over his shoulder, and together we took the elevator downstairs. Was I imagining things, or did his glance linger on Edwin's statue on the first floor for just a moment? Outside, we walked over to Broad Street to find a cab in front of the hotel there.

The ride across town to the Water Works was a short one, despite the growing late afternoon traffic, and we pulled up in front of the administration building with a few minutes to spare. Once I'd paid the cabbie, we took a moment to orient ourselves. The Schuylkill looked placid today. The ensemble of buildings that stretched out along the waterfront faced west, so they caught full sun at the moment, and if you squinted just a bit, you didn't see the dilapidation caused by a couple hundred years of weathering and neglect; instead, you saw the monumental ensemble as its planners had intended, a series of modern temples. I had to admit I was impressed, and the feeling seemed to have infected Nicholas as well. He came up beside me and said, "It's a handsome place."

"Have you been to the Water Works before, Nicholas?" I asked.

"More than once, but not lately. My school included it in its educational field trips. It's an impressive site, isn't it?"

"It is. I've always been amused at the effort to give the whole thing a classical air while addressing such nasty problems as yellow fever and sludge. Quite incongruous," I said. "Shall we go in?"

We found our way to the administrative offices, where Phebe was waiting for us. She led us down the stairs to the department's small, windowless conference room.

"Good to see both of you again," she said. "I'm really getting excited about the possibilities for this project. So, what luck have you had with finding information for us in your documents?" she asked.

"I'll let Nicholas tell you—he's been doing all the work," I replied, then sat back and gave Nicholas a nod. As he spoke, I had to admit that he'd been thorough, and he presented some creative possibilities that showed surprising insight. All in all, he'd done a good job, and I could tell that Phebe was pleased.

"You know, I see real potential here," she said. "Let me look at our long-range calendar and we can figure out a timeline for the next step—assuming, of course, that the funding comes through, but I'm pretty sure it will. I think with one figurehead company on board, we can approach some of our other industrial donors on this one. Supporting this kind of project will make them look sensitive to environmental issues, which never hurts. Nicholas, would you mind sending me a written summary of your ideas that I can take to my staff and board? It should be shorter than this one, and less detailed. Nell, can you think of any potential funders? That is, if you don't mind sharing? Of course the Society will receive recognition for your participation."

"I think it's a great idea, Phebe. I'll be the first to admit that I've learned something just listening today, and we're happy to help out." With a start I realized that it was after five, closing time for the Water Works. "Good heavens, we should be going. I hadn't realized it was so late."

"No rush," Phebe said cheerfully. "I never seem to leave on time, and while we say the place is closed, it's hard to make sure all the visitors are gone. You know how that goes, right, Nell?"

"I do indeed. And your restaurant is open for dinner, right?"

Phebe nodded in response. "Yes, it's become very popular. Have you tried it?"

"I haven't had a chance, but I've heard good things about it." It comforted me to know that there would be other people on the grounds.

I was surprised when Nicholas interrupted. "Do you mind if I spend a little time looking around? As I told Nell, I visited here on school trips years ago, but not recently. And it's such a treat to see it without tourists."

"Of course, no problem. Nell, would you like a tour?"

"I don't want to put you out, Phebe, and I've probably seen it more recently than Nicholas." I turned to Nicholas. "Nicholas, why don't you go on and take a look at the buildings. There are a couple of administrative issues I wanted to talk to Phebe about. You don't need to wait for me—take a cab and keep the receipt, and I'll make sure you get reimbursed." He'd given me the perfect opening to separate myself from him.

"All right. Phebe, I'll send you my summary early next week, after I run it by Nell, and I'll flesh out some of the details we've talked about. I'll see myself out."

I watched him go, then turned back to Phebe, who said, "What an interesting young man! Has he been with you long?"

"Only a few months. He is indeed interesting." Phebe had no idea just how interesting. We covered a few more details about local funders, which I knew well. Only half my mind was on our discussion: I couldn't see outside the building from where we sat, so I couldn't see where Nicholas had gone. I had no desire to spend any more time with him today; I wanted nothing more than to tell James what I'd learned and let him run with it. After a few minutes, the chitchat with Phebe was driving me crazy. I stood up. "I've taken up too much of your time, but thank you so much. I'm looking forward to working with you."

"As am I, Nell. I'll see you out—I think everyone else is gone." I followed her back upstairs to the reception area. Outside, we could see a staff member or guard, maybe a hundred feet away—the tourist-herder? Phebe waved at him, then pointed at me, and he nodded, which I presumed meant that I was approved to stay a bit longer. We parted ways at the door, after more effusive thanks and promises. Had this been a normal occasion, I would have felt well satisfied, but my mind was elsewhere at the moment.

This was not a normal occasion.

CHAPTER 26

Once outside and in the clear, I pulled out my cell phone, which I had politely shut off during the meeting. James had finally responded, and had left a terse voice mail message. He said he had good news. I was both relieved and dismayed: finally he was ready to make a move, but he still didn't know what I knew. I hit Reply, and he answered immediately.

"Nell, where are you?"

"At the Water Works."

"What's up?"

I took a deep breath. "I think Nicholas Naylor is the killer."

He was silent for a moment. "Your Nicholas? Why?"

"He's been squirreling away the Society's Forrest documents—I stumbled over them in his office today. He used to work with the Forrest materials at Penn. James, he fits. What's your news?"

"We've finally opened an active investigation. I guess I overwhelmed their doubts with the sheer weight of our circumstantial evidence. Where is Nicholas now?"

"Here."

"At the Water Works?"

"Yes. Or at least, he was—we had a meeting here with an administrator. He's not with me, though. He said he wanted to enjoy the building without the tourists."

"I'm on my way," James said grimly. "I'll be there in a couple of minutes. You should leave—now. Stay away from him."

"I'll find a cab."

He hung up before I did. It was sweet of him to try to keep me out of harm's way, but this was a very open, public place. I wanted to see him confront Nicholas, if only to confirm what I suspected. I didn't think Nicholas posed any threat to me. He probably believed he was smart enough to have covered his tracks, and that he could bluff his way out of any trouble. He'd done well so far.

Nicholas was nowhere in sight, although there were parts of the public spaces that I couldn't see from where I was standing. Had he left already? It would take James a few minutes to get here from his FBI office. I didn't want to run into Nicholas, if he was still here, but I thought it would seem natural to stroll around the grounds and admire the view, which was pretty impressive. I decided to start with the gazebo structure at the far end and work my way back toward the drive.

The sinking sun was in my eyes, making it hard to see. I felt painfully exposed, crossing large stretches of pavement, trying to look natural, all the while trying to keep one eye out for Nicholas and the other out for James. But I figured that visibility kept me safe.

I'd reached the last building, a small, round columned temple, which offered a commanding view of the river, the train tracks, and highway across the river—and the rest of the Water Works buildings. I leaned over the railing, admiring the cheerfully decorated buildings of Boathouse Row to the north, before turning around and looking for Nicholas—and I found him. No wonder I hadn't seen him before: he was seated near the bottom of a shallow flight of stone steps, almost like bleachers, which must have been twenty feet below the level of the rest of the buildings. He was alone, staring across the river.

James, where are you?

I hesitated, not sure whether to retreat while I still had the chance. It had been some twenty minutes since Nicholas had left the meeting, so I had to assume he was either lost in contemplation or was waiting for me. At that moment, he looked up and noticed me. Now what? I had no choice but to raise my hand and wave. If I ignored him, that would look suspicious. I figured I'd do better if I tried to act natural (like that was possible). I was just a clueless fundraiser-turned-president who was here to network with my peers and collaborate with local institutions in order to share local history with the public. That was my job, and any other day it would have been true. Today my job included distracting an employee so he'd stay around long enough for the FBI to take him in for questioning in a string of murders. *So* not in my job description. But I was going to do my best, so I should go talk to

Nicholas and pretend it was business as usual. If I could do that with my heart trying to jump out of my chest.

I crossed the pavement and went down the long flight of stairs that reached the level where he was sitting. I plastered on a smile.

"I thought you'd be long gone by now," I called out as I approached.

Nicholas had resumed his contemplation of the slow-moving river, and now he turned slowly to look at me. "I suppose I was caught up in the spirit of the place. It's quite striking, isn't it?"

"Yes, it is." I stopped a safe few feet away from him and sat on the lowest tier of steps.

Nicholas turned to look back at the row of columned buildings behind and above me. "In the decades after it was first built," he began, as if lecturing, "the Water Works became a destination site in its own right. People would come here for recreation, bring a picnic, and make an afternoon of it. Entertainment was much simpler then, don't you think?"

"I agree." At least that was the truth. "And the so-called garden cemeteries like Mount Laurel fall into the same category as the Water Works—entertainment for the masses, unrelated to the underlying purpose. But to look at it another way, I often think that people then had more time to focus in those days, because they weren't constantly inundated with imagery and . . . noise, I guess. Visual noise. Back then they could stop and smell the roses, so to speak." I was babbling, but I couldn't seem to stop myself. Did Nicholas notice? How long would it take James to look down here, out of sight of most of the other buildings? Was he even coming? Had something happened? What was I supposed to do, just go home as though everything was fine?

Nicholas went on, his voice almost dreamy, "Edwin Forrest used to enjoy an evening constitutional along the river, when he was in Philadelphia—good for the breathing, he thought. He'd come this way and profess to be surprised when he was recognized by his fans, but in reality he fed off their adoration. In fact, he once gave an impromptu performance of a bit of *Coriolanus* on the steps here—the setting with all the columns must have felt right. No amplification then, of course, but I imagine his voice would carry regardless. Can't you visualize it?"

Oh, hell. He knew I knew. I felt suddenly cold. He wasn't looking at me, but rather out over the river, gilded by the low sun. I on the other hand was staring at him as though he were a snake poised to strike. Was he toying with me? How much did he know, or guess? Should I bull my way through this absurd conversation? Should I run? Where the hell was James?

Nicholas didn't turn but he said quietly, "You know, don't you? That's why you've been keeping tabs on me."

Well, that answered that question. "I won't bother to say, 'know what?' "

"I'm glad to hear that, Nell. I do respect your intelligence."

"What gave me away?"

"Little things. I know Felicity was checking the call slips—I saw them on her desk. I've seen you poking around in the stacks, and I could tell what you were looking for. My mistake. It never occurred to me that anyone would look at the slips if they went hunting for the documents and didn't find them. After all, nobody's looked for them for years. I didn't want to muddy the provenance of the documents, which is why I never took them out of the building—that would have cast doubt on their authenticity, and that was the last thing I wanted."

Suddenly I was tired of guessing, of trying to piece together fragments that made no sense. I had the primary source sitting in front of me. "Nicholas, what *did* you want? What did those people ever do to you?"

Finally he turned to look at me. If I'd expected to see a monster emerging from behind the facade, I was disappointed: Nicholas looked no more than mildly curious. He ignored my question and said, "What do you know about Edwin Forrest?"

Humor him, Nell. Let him spin out his story until James shows up to save the day. "I've learned a lot about him in the past couple of weeks. Forrest was one of the first American superstars, if I may pin that anachronism on him."

Nicholas nodded thoughtfully. "That he was. Fiercely talented, extremely hardworking, and dedicated to his profession, which, after all, took him from the mean streets of Philadelphia to more places than he could ever have imagined. He changed the face of American theater, almost single-handedly. And he was rewarded for it by the public, in both praise and income."

"He wasn't exactly a saint. His private life was a mess," I said bluntly, which might not have been a good idea. *Not smart to cast aspersions on the idol of a serial killer, Nell.* But I was nervous.

"It was," Nicholas agreed without rancor. "I think he

had little patience for humdrum realities—he thought he was above common judgment. And of course, his wife, Catherine, was a slut."

The term sounded harsh as he said it, although it was probably accurate. "Why does he matter to you?"

"Oh, come on, Nell. I'm sure you've already guessed: you must have read the will by now—it's the basis for the trust. I'm a lineal descendant, although Forrest never publicly acknowledged my ancestor. Times were different then. But I can prove that I'm the last scion of Edwin Forrest."

"I thought it had to be something like that." *Damn, Nell, can't you come up with something better than that?* "So, what? You felt your ancestor—it was a she, right?— she was deprived of what was rightfully hers?"

Nicholas smiled at me. "Very good. Yes, in part. She was too willing to settle for the crumbs he tossed her. I intend to claim what should have been her inheritance, plus interest."

"I'm sure you know others tried and failed."

"You mean that pathetic distant cousin? I have a far stronger claim."

"Nicholas, most people have never heard of Edwin Forrest, even in Philadelphia. How did you come to know so much? About your ancestor? About the man himself?" *Spin it, Nell, just like Scheherazade. Just a little longer.*

"Family history. Tales handed down from generation to generation. Surely you know about that? Your good friend Marty can quote chapter and verse about what Major Jonathan Terwilliger said and did in seventeen whatever. My family had less to work with, but they treasured the small number of stories they had about Edwin. And we had a few artifacts, memorabilia. They've all come to me now.

"My great-great-grandmother—Edwin's bastard daughter, Elizabeth, to be specific—was grateful for whatever scraps he threw to her. She received a tidy little legacy in Edwin's will and professed to be content. I'll concede that perhaps they agreed that if he had acknowl- edged her directly, she would have been dishonored in the eyes of polite society. Of course, anyone with any sense still jumped to the logical conclusion when they heard the terms of the will, but at least the fiction could be maintained."

"Miss Lillie," I said, almost to myself.

I didn't intend for Nicholas to hear me, but apparently he had. "Very good! You have been doing your home- work! As I said, Elizabeth, or Lillie if you prefer, was content with her share—after all, her nominal father was a well-to-do stockbroker, so she was financially secure in any case. But what Edwin left her was a very small portion of what he was worth at the time of his death. Instead of supporting his own flesh and blood, he had to go and endow an absurd place to shelter decayed actors and actresses. He was thinking of his future reputation, feeding his glorious ego. And now the trustees want to give everything away. I was running out of time."

"What is it that you want, Nicholas?" I said again. "Is this really about what's left of the money? How do you think you can get your hands on it? Because the lawyers went through the will when Edwin died, and nobody managed to challenge it successfully. What makes you different?"

His face flushed. "Because nobody back then could ever

prove their case. I can prove mine, far better than that pathetic cousin. I am Edwin Forrest's direct descendant."

"So that's why you started working at Penn? Because you wanted access to its Forrest collection?"

"Yes, so I could go through the library's holdings carefully, without attracting too much attention. And then the position opened up at the Society, which has most of the rest of the materials. That was fortuitous, wasn't it? I knew what I was looking for, and I found it. Combined with what's been handed down to me, there's finally enough to take to court. But then the damned trustees got it into their heads that they should dissolve the trust, and if that happened, it would be too late for me. I had to move quickly or lose my chance."

What he said might make sense, but why resort to murder? "I can see why you would need to do something, but why kill the trustees, if your case is as strong as you say? Why not just take it to court? Or convince them to come to some sort of settlement?"

"I never intended to kill anyone. I approached them one at a time and made my case. Most of them wouldn't even listen to what I had to say, which I thought was rather rude of them. And then I thought that perhaps a newer, younger appointment to the board, someone with a fresh viewpoint, might be more willing to hear me out. More flexible. Only, to install a new trustee I had to create a vacancy, which turned out to be surprisingly easy."

Somehow that didn't quite jibe with the fact that he had gone calling on the trustees armed with a baggie full of pills. Just in case they didn't go along with his agenda? But bringing that up now was *not* a good idea. He didn't have to know how much we had already learned, or guessed.

"But, Nicholas—six people?" I said. "Wasn't it clear that you weren't going to win them over?"

"They wouldn't listen." He said it as though it justified everything. This young man had some serious delusions.

"That's a very interesting story, Mr. Naylor."

James had arrived.

CHAPTER 27

I'd been so focused on watching Nicholas that I hadn't heard James's approach, and apparently neither had Nicholas, so intent had he been on convincing me—just as he claimed he had tried to convince the trustees, six of whom had died at his hands. I wasn't any more convinced than they had been—which, when I stopped to think about it, meant that he would have had to eliminate me too, since obviously I knew too much, and I was in his way toward achieving his goal.

James had spoken from the top of the stairs behind us, and then began to descend at a normal pace. "I'd like to hear more of the details," James said, sounding calm and reasonable. "Say, back at my office?"

Nicholas wasn't fooled. "Nice try, Agent Morrison. I can't say I'm surprised. It was only to be expected that if Nell was concerned about the deaths, you must be involved as well. So you represent the official arm of the law, come to haul me in?"

James glanced briefly at me before answering. "That was the general idea."

Nicholas smiled faintly. "Tell me, what do you think you can charge me with?"

"Right now I only want to hear the rest of your story," James said.

Nicholas continued to look surprisingly untroubled. "You want to take me in for a talk? How do you justify that? You have nothing on me."

"I think you're wrong there," James replied, his voice as level as Nicholas's. He began walking slowly along the walkway on the river side, and I stood up and inched away from Nicholas without taking my eyes off him. Finally Nicholas looked surprised. Had he really believed he could get away with murder, six times over? And then decline the FBI's request for a conversation? I was beginning to believe that Nicholas had a rather shaky grip on reality.

We must have made an odd tableau, the three of us, all in a row, bathed in golden light, focused intently on each other. James was moving carefully toward Nicholas, so I kept moving away, just as cautiously. So engrossed were we that none of us noticed Phebe approaching. She leaned over the railing and called out, "Yoo-hoo. There you are! I was afraid you were still on the grounds. The guard wants to go home. It's well past closing time."

In the time it took her to say that, before she had even begun to absorb what we were doing, our tableau collapsed. Nicholas, the most tightly wound, was startled by Phebe's unexpected appearance, and his hand crept toward his leather bag. He pulled out a surprisingly large knife, and I found myself wondering if he carried that around the streets of the city regularly. James's focus on Nicholas hadn't wavered, so he saw Nicholas's move and said urgently, "Nell, he's armed!" and quickly moved to put himself between us.

Which Nicholas took to be a threat. Almost by reflex, he brought the knife in front of himself. James moved to deflect it and Nicholas held his ground, and the knife was between them. I was behind James so I couldn't see what was happening until James stepped back to avoid Nicholas's lunge, and then he tripped over me and we both fell onto the stone steps, and James's head hit with a *thud* that I could feel in my gut. When we all stopped, James was lying on top of me, pinning me down, but Nicholas was left standing, blood on the knife, on his hand, looking shocked. The whole thing couldn't have taken more than a couple of seconds. And then Phebe started to scream.

James wasn't moving. He outweighed me significantly, so I couldn't move either. "Call 9-1-1!" I yelled at Phebe, with little confidence that she was listening. She was still screaming. God, would the woman never shut up? "Get help—now!" I yelled again. She finally cut off the sound, looked down at us, then turned tail and ran back toward the administration building, where I hoped she had the brains to find a telephone or the guard.

I turned back to the bigger problem. Nicholas still hadn't budged, apparently stunned, but I could see that the import of what had just happened was beginning to sink in. Attacking an FBI agent in front of witnesses was not a good idea, and he looked panicky, which made him unpredictable and therefore even more dangerous. Maybe he had stayed cool during a whole string of murders, each carefully planned and executed; but striking a blow, up close, with a deadly knife, was an entirely different thing, and he clearly hadn't been prepared for it. I had no idea what he was likely to do next. Fleeing seemed like a good option for him, but unfortunately James and I were more or less in his way.

"James," I hissed urgently in his ear. "Move!" No response. This was not good. I pushed against him to try to move him away from me; he slid heavily down one step, and my hand came back covered with blood. That spurred me to scramble and kick my way out from under him, but when I looked at him he was barely conscious. Where was all the blood coming from? He must have thrown his arm up to ward off Nicholas's knife, because his jacket sleeve was slashed and there was blood trickling rapidly down his arm. But his head was bleeding, too, soaking his collar. Altogether there was too damn much blood everywhere.

"James?" I said again, and this time he opened his eyes and managed to focus on me.

"Nell, go," he rasped, and then he looked behind me. At Nicholas, who had finally shaken himself out of whatever paralysis had gripped him and looked ready to . . . what? Slash his way through the both of us?

I leaned over James again, while keeping an eye on Nicholas. "Like hell I'm leaving you here." Then I straightened up partway. "Nicholas, put the knife down," I ordered, trying to keep my voice steady.

"No, it's a family heirloom," he replied, his voice petulant. "Jim Bowie gave it to Edwin. It's part of my proof." He took a step closer, the bloody knife in his hand, gauging the angles. If he got past us, chances were he could disappear in the city easily enough. But we were still in his way, despite the fact that James was not in any shape to stop him.

But maybe I was. I did the only thing I could think of: I reached under James's jacket and pulled out his gun.

Now Nicholas looked confused: he hadn't expected his staid boss to pull a gun on him. I pointed it at Nicholas, holding it with both hands. Which weren't shaking, I was proud to see. "Put the knife down," I said clearly and distinctly.

Nicholas looked at me as though I'd grown a second head. "You can't be serious, Nell."

That offended me. I was holding a loaded weapon and facing a man who had admitted to killing at least six people and who had just stabbed James while I watched, and he really thought I would just let him walk away? "I mean it, Nicholas. Put it down now or I'll shoot you."

He cocked his head at me. "You wouldn't do that."

"Want to bet?"

He took a step closer, shifting his grip on the knife, and I pulled the trigger.

CHAPTER 28

Phebe had gotten it together enough to make a phone call. When the police arrived, they found a scene unlike any the Water Works had ever known: An FBI agent covered in blood, some of which was spreading at a horrifying rate over the marble steps, with the president of the Pennsylvania Antiquarian Society trying to stop the flow bare-handed—unsuccessfully—and another man huddled a few feet away on the walkway, clutching his leg, also bleeding. I hoped fervently that the bullet had shattered a bone, and that Nicholas would have a long and painful recovery—in prison. His precious knife lay a few feet away, well out of his reach, but just in case, I kept the gun nearby while trying to apply enough pressure to stop James's bleeding. I had made the decision to try to deal with his arm, because I was afraid that Nicholas had managed to slash an artery there. I wasn't doing very well. I comforted myself with the thought that if James was bleeding, then he wasn't dead; the bad news was, he was losing more blood than I had ever seen in my life, and if this kept up he would most certainly be gone shortly.

Understandably the police approached our little scene with extreme caution, guns drawn.

"Move away from the gun, ma'am," one of them said.

I looked at him incredulously. "Uh, I don't think so," I told him as I kept trying to maintain pressure on James's arm. When he came nearer, the cop grasped the problem, and he settled for kicking the gun out of reach.

Phebe came up behind the officers. She appeared to be hyperventilating, and I wondered how on earth she'd managed to choke out "gun" to a 9-1-1 operator, but the police presence was proof that she'd communicated the urgency of the situation. The cops let me be, and one of them turned to call for an ambulance.

The other stared down at me, bewildered. "Can you tell me what happened, ma'am?"

I nodded down at James. "This is James Morrison, special agent with the FBI. The gun is his. He was attacked by that man"—I nodded toward Nicholas, who was now all but weeping in pain—"who's under suspicion for multiple murders. I'm Nell Pratt, president of the Pennsylvania Antiquarian Society." Like that explained anything.

"So the agent shot the other guy?" the officer asked.

"No, I did." I didn't elaborate—I was too busy with my pathetic first aid efforts.

The two officers exchanged looks. Then the first one said, "I've requested two ambulances. Are you saying that we should detain him?" He jerked his head toward Nicholas.

"Yes." So much blood. Where was the ambulance?

I heard a siren in the distance—probably stuck in Philadelphia's rush hour traffic. I would be seriously angry if James bled out because of traffic.

The ambulances arrived after what seemed like a year but was probably more like five minutes, first one, then another, only seconds apart. One of the cops went back up the stairs, waved the first EMTs over, and had a quiet word with them, pointing to James, and when the EMT approached I struggled to my feet.

"He hit his head. Hard." Like they couldn't tell.

"Was he conscious?" one of the EMTs asked.

"Just for a minute," I said. Was that bad?

The EMTs added a neck brace to their ministrations. I reluctantly backed away to allow them space to work, giving Nicholas a wide berth. I looked down at myself to see that not only my hands were bloody, but my clothes were as well. The blood was beginning to darken and stiffen. I suddenly felt sick. There was so much of it.

The full view of me must have startled the police officers. The first one said, "Are you all right, ma'am?" as he looked at all the gore.

"I'm not injured. All the blood is his." I nodded toward James, who the EMTs were transferring almost tenderly to a gurney. Once he was strapped in, they hurried to haul him away, taking the steps carefully.

"Where are you taking him?" I called out.

"Jefferson," one called back over his shoulder without stopping. Doors slammed in the distance; the ambulance pulled away, siren blaring. I stood numbly while the second crew appeared and the cops went through the same ritual: a word with the EMT, a nod toward Nicholas. A gurney, a transfer, and he was gone.

"Where are they taking him?" I asked the nearer cop, not that I cared.

He answered, "Penn." I nodded, as though it meant anything to me. "Ma'am, we're going to have to take you to headquarters and get your statement about what happened here. As long as you're all right."

I bit back my first sarcastic response. *Yeah, sure I'm all right, standing here covered in blood. Business as usual.* Instead I finally said, "I want to go to the hospital."

"With who?" one of them asked me.

Did they really not know? "The agent."

"Are you a relative, ma'am?"

No. We were friends, lovers, something with no legal standing. I shook my head.

"Then you'll have to come with us until we get this sorted out. Don't worry, he's in good hands."

I looked at my own hands, covered in blood. Then I looked around. "That's my bag there." I pointed. "And that"—I pointed toward Nicholas's bloody knife—"I know that's evidence, but it's also a historic artifact, so take good care of it."

The cops looked at me as though I was crazy. I didn't care. I was just trying to protect a small piece of local history, which had somehow become evidence of a major crime. I was having trouble holding myself together at the moment. There was too much I didn't dare let myself think about, like how James was doing. Or if he was dead. I stifled an involuntary sob at that thought.

"We'll tell the forensic team. Come along now."

With surprising gentleness one of the young policemen led me up the stairs and across the lawn to a waiting police car parked in the driveway and handed me into the

back, behind the metal grill. They didn't speak to me. I
didn't care. I felt like I was muffled in invisible cotton: I
could see and hear well enough, but everything seemed
so distant. I couldn't process what had just happened. One
minute we'd been having a conversation, the next minute
two men were lying on the pavement, bleeding. Idly, I
flaked away some of the drying blood on my hands. The
officers hadn't offered to let me wash my hands, but why
should they? My bloody hands might be evidence of . . .
something. I couldn't begin to imagine what they must
be thinking right now. The explanation I'd given the cops
was kind of inadequate—and why should they believe
me? I realized I was rubbing my thumb over the back of
my hand, over and over. The blood wasn't coming off.
James's blood.

No, don't think about that. I bit my lip to hold back
tears. Right now I had to focus, had to make sure I had
all my facts lined up. The police knew nothing about the
string of murders; right now they were working on what
had just happened: an inexplicable stabbing and shooting
on the grounds of a department of the city. But the only
way I could explain was to give them the background.
How much was I prepared to say about the murders and
the rest? Would they believe me? Would the FBI confirm
anything? Could I possibly explain what I, a civilian, was
doing in the middle of it all with a gun belonging to
someone else, covered in blood?

The welcome silence continued as the police cruiser
drew up at a door at the back of police headquarters, a
door I'd never been through before in my dealings with
the Philadelphia police. I'd always gone in the front; was
the back door for suspects? I was assisted out of the car

and escorted into the building, up an elevator, down a hall. I attracted only a few curious glances, but I supposed that someone covered with blood was a common sight in this building. One of the officers stopped to confer with a colleague at a desk.

"Where's my bag?" I asked, feeling defenseless without it.

"It's safe, ma'am."

"I need to make a phone call."

"You're not under arrest, ma'am."

"I know that. There's someone I need to speak to."

The officer riffled through my bag to make sure I didn't have any more concealed weapons, then handed it to me and pointed toward an empty chair at a desk. "Help yourself."

I found my cell phone and hit Marty's speed dial number, praying that she would pick up. When she did I said abruptly, "Marty, James is at Thomas Jefferson Hospital. Nicholas stabbed him, and he fell and hit his head. I'm at police headquarters, and I'll have to explain what happened. I'm going to tell them everything we figured out. Can you go to the hospital?"

Bless her, Marty had recognized the crazy woman on the phone as me and she didn't quibble. "Will do. Do you need anything? If I don't hear from you in a couple of hours, I'll come bust you out of there."

"Fine. I just wanted you to know what was going on with James, and where you could find me." I hung up. At least Marty could stay with James. If he was conscious. How hard had he hit his head?

"Thanks," I told the officer.

"No problem," he said. Then he led me down yet

another hall and deposited me in what I guessed was an interrogation room. The officer left me alone in the over-bright, shabby room that looked just like the ones on all those cop shows, even down to the glass wall on one side. The drab paint and the furniture made the blood on my clothes and hands seem all the brighter, shockingly intense even if darker now than at first.

No clock in the room. Deliberate, no doubt. I looked at my watch, which they hadn't taken away from me. Was I a suspect? They hadn't arrested me. But why wouldn't they have let me clean up? Were they trying to preserve evidence? Or just keep me off-balance? Right now it didn't take much to do that. It was approaching seven o'clock outside in the real world. Inside this room it could be any time. I didn't really care, except for James . . .

What was I supposed to do now? Someone would come and interview me. I would answer their questions, simply and honestly. I had nothing to hide. I—we—had had suspicions, but nothing that we could take to the authorities, as wiser and more experienced James had found out. If there was any blame to be spread around, some of it should land squarely on his superiors' heads; they had refused to trust his instincts when he told them that he believed there was something very wrong going on, citing a lack of proof.

What would Nicholas say? Could he come up with an explanation that would sound convincing? What the hell was wrong with him, anyway? He was nursing a grudge that went back well over a hundred years to a woman he had never known, who he decided had been cheated of something. Heck, Nicholas admitted that *she* hadn't believed that, or had chosen not to argue. She'd been content with her settlement, so the grievance was all his. Of course, there was money involved—maybe even a lot of money—which he seemed to think now belonged to him, but I didn't have the legal expertise to know whether anything he could come up with at this late date would have a chance of breaking the trust. But the thing of it was, *he* believed it. And because of that, I was sitting here with bloody hands and a growing lump of fear in the pit of my stomach.

Good God, I'd been working with a serial killer for months without realizing it. Hell of an administrator I made. And a lousy judge of character.

I don't know how much later it was when the door finally opened, and in stepped one of my less favorite people, Detective Meredith Hrivnak. We'd crossed paths before, and not happily, but at least she knew who I was, which saved a lot of explaining.

"Well, well, look at you," she said, grinning. "You've gotten yourself into another mess, huh?"

I indulged myself in a sarcastic reply. "I don't think I'd call identifying a serial killer and holding him for arrest a mess, precisely."

If she'd had antennae, they would have twitched to high alert, but she managed to keep her face impassive. "So you just can't keep out of it, can you?"

"Believe me, that wasn't my idea. Can you tell me how the FBI agent is?" I wasn't sure how much she knew or remembered about my relationship with James, but my need to know overcame my caution.

She regarded me steadily for a moment, probably weighing her options. In the end she said, "I don't know." She pulled out a chair and sat across from me. "So, let's start at the beginning. Who's the guy with the bullet in his leg?"

"His name is Nicholas Naylor, and he works for me." I took a deep breath and started in, beginning with reading Adeline's obituary on the train, to looking at other, similar obituaries and realizing they were connected. Then I backtracked to when I had hired Nicholas, and what he had been doing at Penn, and what he'd apparently been doing (and concealing) at the Society. To how we'd ended up today at the Water Works, when the police got involved, and why James had joined us there. It must have taken over an hour, and by the time I was done I was empty and exhausted.

Detective Hrivnak hadn't interrupted. She didn't speak immediately when I had finished, looking first at her notes, and then at me. Finally she said, "Just for the record, you thought you'd identified a serial killer, and it didn't occur to you to mention it to the police? Us, or the state police? Anyone?"

I no longer had the energy to be indignant. "I only figured out it was Nicholas this morning. Agent Morrison had been trying to get his people at the FBI to take a look at it, and they said there wasn't enough evidence that *any* murders had occurred. We had at least six victims, but all were elderly, and each of them had been officially declared to have died of natural causes. We had no crime scenes. We could connect them only through a very obscure small trust set up more than a century ago. We couldn't prove *anything*. Heck, if I had heard my own story, I would have shown me the door. Just what the hell would you have done differently?"

Detective Hrivnak had the grace to look chagrined.

"I'm not saying I agree with you, but okay, I can understand why you did what you did. But it might have been smart to run it by someone, to cover your own asses."

"We tried!" I shot back. "How is it that a bunch of women in the back office at a cultural institution managed to figure it out, when nobody else could?" I slumped back into my uncomfortable chair, my brief anger spent. "When can I get out of here?"

"Now, I guess. I've got nothing to hold you on—well, maybe illegal use of a handgun, but I think there were extraordinary circumstances. Good shot, by the way. I didn't know you had it in you."

CHAPTER 29

Whatever else she might have said was cut off by the sound of an argument in the hallway, and I was pretty sure I recognized Marty's voice. "You have no right," she was yelling. Someone tried to placate her in a quieter tone, but she was having none of it. "Where are you keeping her?"

They were outside the door now. It was snatched open, and Marty barged in. "Nell, I . . ." She stopped dead when she got a good look at me; I had forgotten that I was still covered with blood. Marty looked stricken, and she said in a gentler tone, "You're coming with me, Nell."

I glanced at Hrivnak, who nodded, then I stood up and followed Marty.

She didn't say anything as we navigated our way through the anonymous grey hallways back to the parking lot, but she kept one hand on my elbow, in case I showed any signs of running into a wall, which was a real possibility. Outside, I was startled to see that it was still light. I stopped and drew in a deep breath, scented with bus exhaust. "How is he?"

Marty didn't answer immediately, as if weighing which answer would hurt the least. I held her gaze until she answered reluctantly, "We don't know. He lost a lot of blood—as I suppose you know. They're worried about cranial bleeding. He's not conscious." She looked at my clothes. "What the hell did Nicholas stick him with, anyway?"

"The Bowie knife that belonged to Edwin Forrest." I swallowed something between a laugh and a sob.

"Damn," Marty said. "A Bowie knife? In that case, Jimmy was lucky. It could have been a lot worse, if Nicholas wasn't such a klutz."

"Can we go to the hospital now?" I asked. There was no way I was going anywhere else.

"All right." Marty led me to her car and settled me in the passenger seat. I wondered briefly if she'd mind some blood on it.

When she got in on the other side, I asked, "How did you plan to bust me out of there if they'd arrested me?"

Marty started the car. "My brother's former prep school roommate is the city attorney. I made a couple of calls."

"I figured it was something like that." I leaned back against the seat. On the ride over I filled her in on the bare bones of my reasons to suspect Nicholas, now amply confirmed. It didn't take long to reach Thomas Jefferson Hospital. Or at least, I thought it didn't—time was doing a weird accordion thing, speeding up and slowing down erratically. This day had been going on forever, but I knew it wasn't over yet.

Marty didn't ask any questions when I was done talking, which was just as well, because I wasn't sure I could answer coherently. I'd spent all my coherence on Hrivnak. Of course the detective was right: we should have handed our suspicions and evidence over to some authority. Except we'd tried—or at least, James had—and the authorities hadn't wanted it. After the messy and very public confrontation at the Water Works, maybe now someone would listen. Kind of late, though, wasn't it?

Marty pulled into a No Parking zone on the street and came around to open my door. Either I had forgotten how a door worked, or I'd completely run out of initiative. "Come on, upsy-daisy." She held out her hand.

"Upsy-daisy?" I said as I managed to stand up on the pavement.

"Follow me," she said. I followed.

Inside, the hospital didn't look much different from the police department, except there were more people and most of them were wearing scrubs or white coats instead of uniforms. But there was too much light and noise, too many hard edges. I stood in the middle of the human stream, unable to decide which way to move, while Marty conferred with someone sitting in front of a computer terminal behind a counter. Then she came back. "He's in the ICU. I think we could bull our way in, but you might want to clean up first."

I looked down at myself and tried to frame a question. "What . . . how?"

"I'll snag you some scrubs. Meet you in the ladies'." She pointed toward the restroom and gave me a small shove in the right direction. I kept going.

Once inside, I stopped in front of the first bank of mirrors and leaned heavily on the counter. Then I looked at my reflection, and the sight of myself unnerved me. I looked like I'd been butchering a steer with an axe. I looked away from my reflection and turned on the water in the sink. One of those damned faucets that gave you thirty seconds of water and turned itself off—at that rate, I'd be clean by next Tuesday. I wadded up a paper towel to stop the drain and leaned on the water faucet until a few inches of water accumulated in the sink. Then I pulled out a handful of paper towels, added a liberal amount of soap from the stingy dispenser, and began scrubbing, starting with my hands.

Marty appeared with an armful of colorful scrubs, which she dumped on the counter. I pulled off my shirt and pants and stuffed them in the trash—no way was I ever going to wear them again. The blood had soaked through to my underwear, but there wasn't a lot I could do about that. I stared at the scrubs, trying to guess what size I wanted, until Marty lost patience, grabbed a shirt from the pile, and handed it to me. I put it on; it hung on me like a curtain. Marty handed me unmatched pants, which were too long, but I rolled up the waistband.

In the middle of the process, some unfortunate woman came in to use the facilities. She took one look at me, half dressed, still covered with blotches of dried blood, and backed away quickly and fled out the door. Marty gave a snort of laughter.

I scrubbed and scrubbed, but there was still blood crusted under my fingernails. "Good enough?" I asked Marty.

"You'll do."

It felt good to be clean again, but it was only a small boost, and I was terrified of what was coming. "Okay, now what?"

"Upstairs."

Thank God she knew where she was going. I followed her through the hall and we stopped at a bank of elevators. I laid a hand on her arm. "Marty, what can I expect?"

She looked at me with eyes as somber as I'd ever seen. "I won't lie to you, it's kind of touch-and-go. They stitched him up—or maybe it's all staples now—and gave him a lot of blood, but he hasn't regained consciousness, which has them worried."

"Okay, got it," I interrupted. I didn't want to hear any more. The elevator arrived and we boarded. No one else got on. Marty pushed a button.

"Will they let me in?"

Marty turned to face me squarely. "I'll take care of the staff if they try to keep you out. All I know is, it would kill Jimmy if he wakes up and you're not there. So if you turn tail and run now, you'd better keep going."

"Marty, that's not what I meant. Bottom line, I'm scared."

"Of what?" Marty demanded.

I swallowed. "Of losing him." Of watching him die. Or not wake up. Or wake up as a vegetable. The possibilities were many, few of them good.

"Nell, he's a strong man—you know that. He'll pull through. You just saved his life, and you had to shoot somebody to do it, which we'll have to talk about later. You think that's not enough to prove your right to be here?

You're going to be there when Jimmy wakes up, because he will want you there. Whatever you work out after he's back on his feet is your business, but you're not going to bail on him now."

"I didn't plan to." If I was honest with myself, I supposed I was trying to protect myself from losing him. I didn't know if I could handle that.

The elevator door finally opened, and Marty steered me down another hallway, to a nurses' station. Machines flashed and blinked from all sides, but there was little human noise. Marty leaned on the counter and asked the nurse, "Any change?"

"Morrison? No. Is this his fiancée?"

She was looking at me. I managed to work out that using that label was probably the only way I'd be allowed into his room, so I nodded silently.

"Only one person at a time. Don't touch anything. And don't get in anyone's way," the nurse said crisply. "Understand?"

I nodded again. "Can I talk to him?"

"He's unconscious."

"I know that. But talking won't mess up your machines?"

"Nope. Go right ahead. Just don't expect him to answer."

"Got it." Marty set off down the hallway, and I followed more slowly.

At one doorway, she stopped and turned to me. "This is him. I'm going to go find some coffee or something." She turned abruptly and marched off without waiting for me to answer.

The door was open, and I walked into the room. James lay on his back, with assorted tubes and wires connected to beeping machines. At least he seemed to be breathing on his own—was that a good sign? Stubble, flecked with grey, stood out against his pale skin. His left arm was wrapped with stained gauze. They'd shaved part of his hair, and a line of . . . staples? arced across the bare patch.

I tiptoed around the bed to his other side and laid my hand on his. No response, but at least it was warm.

Now what? Did I expect that my being here would fix everything, and he'd wake up and smile? Maybe I didn't expect that, but I sure as hell *wanted* that. "James?" I whispered. Nothing. I sighed.

Well, I was here, and I was staying, so I figured I should make myself as comfortable as I could. There was a stiff chair upholstered in plastic in one corner, and a smaller and even less appealing one closer to the door. I pulled the larger chair close to the bed, away from all the wires and beeping blinking machines, then dragged the other chair in front it. I slid down, put my feet up on the second chair, and settled in to wait, watching James's face.

Now I could face the terrors I'd stuffed deep inside me. My mind kept running a silent loop of that stupid, stupid scene: the three of us, locked in confrontation at the Water Works. I didn't think Nicholas would have attacked me. Even James's arrival hadn't spooked him, because he still thought he had everything under his control and that he could walk away. I could see Nicholas calculating his next step when Phebe had startled everybody and set off the cascade of disaster. Even then, Nicholas might have held on to his composure—until James had made a stupid, chivalrous gesture trying to protect me, and Nicholas had read that as a threat and overreacted.

And James had paid for his chivalry. He was here because he had been trying to keep me safe. He could die because of some dumb primitive reaction. I'd hate him for it, but he'd still be dead. And that idea set off some primal howling in me as well. *You can't die! We're not finished!*

CHAPTER 30

Eventually I slept, sort of, out of exhaustion, but it was nearly impossible to sleep in a hospital because there were always nurses coming and going, and monitors making startling noises. Now and then a nurse would glance over at me, her expression giving nothing away, and I was afraid to ask any questions. The chair wasn't exactly ideal for sleeping, either—not only was it lacking in padding, but the plastic was slippery, so I'd nod off and find myself sliding toward the floor.

After a while I gave up trying to sleep. Marty hadn't come back—surprisingly tactful of her—so here I was, alone with my thoughts, until James woke up. The perfect time to face all the issues I'd been dancing around for months. When had I started deluding myself about where he and I were going? How soon after James and I had first connected?

I'd been screwing up a lot lately, hadn't I? Maybe I

should start with when I'd hired Nicholas and work forward from there. Sure, he looked great on paper, and he was good at what he did. But if I was honest, I'd never liked him. He was a cold fish. Okay, hindsight was all well and good, and I'd done everything I could to stifle my dislike. But what I found most troubling about Nicholas was that he had no empathy, no warmth. I knew you couldn't put those requirements in the job description—"Must like other people"?—but a few basic people skills sure made working somewhere a lot more pleasant for everyone. It was small comfort that my instincts had been proved right. Was James supposed to pay the price for my reluctance to go with my gut about Nicholas?

As a distraction, I decided to worry about what I should say to the press. What would do the least damage to the Society? At the rate we were going, it wouldn't be long until some journalist labeled us "Philadelphia's Murder Museum" or something equally tacky. Or maybe pin a title on me. Pistol-Packing President? Nell Pratt, Crime Magnet? Why did I keep finding myself in the middle of crimes? Now I'd graduated to shooting someone—that had to be a first in our cultural community. No doubt the press would eat that up. *Museum administrator shoots suspect.* Or to be more lurid, *Society Prez Blasts Employee.* I wondered if the newspapers had gotten hold of the story yet, and what they'd made of it. Probably too late for today's papers, although the local newscasters might pick it up at eleven, especially since an FBI agent was involved. But no doubt everyone would be all over it tomorrow.

Stop it, Nell, my inner voice said sharply. *You're sitting here watching the man you love struggling to stay alive—maybe you should be thinking about that? How are you going to feel if he dies?* I had to shut my eyes at that. It hurt. A lot. To think that I'd had a hand in it just made it worse.

Please, James, don't die. I wanted to see what we could have; I wanted to make it happen a lot faster than it had so far. He was a good and decent man; he was a smart and competent agent; he was funny and caring, and, yes, I loved him. I wanted more than a casual date when our schedules allowed. I was pretty sure that he did, too, even though he hadn't pushed too hard.

Exhaustion took over. Eventually when I opened my eyes again, the sun seemed to be coming up somewhere outside. I checked my watch and found that it was shortly after six a.m. I looked James over by daylight. Well, he was still breathing, and none of the alarms attached to him had gone off that I was aware of—all good. Any more sleep for me was probably out of the question now, so I scooted my chair closer to the bed and took his hand.

Which moved, this time, sending my heart into over-drive. James's body shifted, and then his grip tightened on my hand when he realized, consciously or uncon-sciously, that it hurt to move. I didn't let go. I was all but holding my breath.

His eyes opened, focused on the ceiling, then his head turned to me. "Nell?" he croaked. "What the hell happened?"

I smiled through sudden tears. "Nicholas attacked you with a knife at the Water Works. Do you remember anything?"

"Kind of. Wait—did you take my gun?"

"I did. I had to stop Nicholas."

His brow wrinkled. "You shot him? Is he dead?"

"Nope. I got him in the leg. The police are holding on to him."

"You never mentioned you knew how to shoot."

"You never asked." That was a conversation for later.

"What's the damage?" His gaze wandered to the machines tracking his every breath and twitch.

"Nicholas came at you with a Bowie knife. It is now in police custody as evidence. He got you in the arm and it bled a lot. Then you kind of tripped over me and hit your head on the steps. How do you feel?"

"Like crap, but at least I'm alive. And so are you. I'm sorry I screwed up."

"*You* screwed up? James, neither of us had any reason to believe that Nicholas would turn violent. We have no evidence that he had ever physically attacked anyone before. So we were both wrong. Look, while the doctors here were sewing you back together last night, I was spilling the whole story to Detective Hrivnak at police headquarters, so the Philadelphia police now know as much as we do."

A nurse I hadn't seen before chose that moment to bustle in, and I retreated to a corner to give her room to work. "Good morning, Mr. Morrison, nice to see you awake." She looked at various readouts and made notes on her clipboard. "How are you feeling?"

"My head hurts. My arm hurts. When can I leave?"

"The doctor will be making rounds later. She'll talk with you then."

I sat down again when the nurse left. "James, you're in no shape to go anywhere."

He didn't look convinced. "So what did Hrivnak say when you talked with her?"

"You might have let the FBI know first," said a tall greying man in a smart suit, standing in the doorway. I didn't recognize him. "I'm Randall Cooper, Special Agent in Charge of the Philadelphia office. You, I take it, are Eleanor Pratt?"

I stood up, but hung on to James's hand. I was done playing nice. "I am. And as I understand it, James brought this case to you and you passed. You're damned lucky that nobody else died. Although James could have."

Cooper eyed me neutrally, but I wasn't about to back down. He glanced briefly at James, who met his glance. Finally Cooper said, "It seems I was wrong. I will be happy to hear what information you have collected, as soon as you are able, Agent Morrison. Ms. Pratt."

My God, was that actually an apology? "Who has custody of Nicholas Naylor?" I asked.

"I understand that the Philadelphia police are holding him based on yesterday's incident at the Water Works. We'll decide who gets to claim him once we've gone over your information." He held my eyes for a few seconds, then looked at James. "Morrison, I'm sorry. The doctors tell me you'll be fine, but don't push yourself. Tell me when you're ready to talk. Naylor will stay in custody. Nice to meet you, Ms. Pratt." He left as quietly as he had come.

I looked at James. "What was that about?"

He had a faint smile on his face. "You heard him—he actually apologized. I think it's a department first. We were right, and he just admitted it. I'd celebrate, but since my head feels ready to explode I think we'll have to postpone that."

"Whenever you're ready."

CHAPTER 31

Nurses came and went, poking and prodding James, and removing several attachments. I stayed, although I kept out of their way, sitting quietly in a corner. This was James: being with him now trumped my queasiness about blood and stitches and all that stuff. One nurse even cranked up the head of his bed just a bit, so it wasn't so difficult for him to look at me, although I could tell that moving his head at all hurt him. James kept drifting in and out of awareness, and I didn't know if I should worry about that or not.

It was afternoon when Marty finally reappeared. She stopped in the doorway to check out the scene. Her face lit up. "Hey, you're awake, Jimmy! That's certainly an improvement."

"I think so, although maybe you should check with me when the painkillers wear off," James said.

"The docs have anything new to say?" Marty's glance shifted back and forth between James and me.

"The nurses seemed to be pleased by his progress," I told her.

"Good to hear," Marty said. Another white-coated person came in, a woman who looked to be about my age. I deduced that she must be a doctor, based largely on the name stitched on the front of the coat, which was followed by M.D. She glanced briefly at Marty and me, then turned to James. "Mr. Morrison?"

"Agent Morrison," James corrected her.

"Ah. Right. How're you feeling?"

"My head hurts—what do you think? When can I get out of here?"

The doctor studied him. "We want to keep you another day or two, to make sure there's no cranial bleeding or swelling. Let's see how you feel tomorrow, and we'll think about releasing you then." She turned to Marty and me. "Would you mind waiting in the hall? I have to check a few things."

Marty and I dutifully trooped out into the hall. "You want a ride home?" Marty asked.

"Am I leaving?"

"I think you should. Jimmy's awake and in good hands, and you look like you need some food, a shower, and time to collect yourself. He'll understand if you take off for a while."

"All right. Thank you. But I have to tell James I'm leaving first."

"No problem. I'm not in a hurry."

"Are you going to talk to Louisa? And Rodney?"

Marty's brow wrinkled. "Oh, shoot, you're right, I

should. When this story hits the press, somebody is bound to track them down. I'd better warn them, although I doubt they'd talk to anybody. Still, they should know."

An irrelevant thought popped into my head. "You realize that Edwin gets yet another moment in the spotlight? I hope he's enjoying it, wherever he is."

The doctor emerged from James's room, scribbling on her clipboard. I intercepted her. "How is he, really?"

"And you are?"

"His, uh, fiancée," I said, at the same time Marty said, "She's the woman who saved his life."

The two-pronged attack seemed to rattle the doctor. "Well, there's no permanent damage. The knife wound in the arm caught an artery, which was why there was so much blood, but we took care of that. What was the weapon?"

"An antique Bowie knife."

"You're kidding? The real thing?" When I nodded, she went on, "Well, the best I can say is that it was clean and sharp. Good thing we gave him a tetanus shot anyway."

"And the concussion?"

"We're keeping him just to be on the safe side. Head injuries can be tricky, and problems don't always show up immediately. If there are no further problems, his recovery should be typical."

"What's typical?"

"He'll probably have headaches, maybe blurred vision. Balance problems. He could be irritable or have trouble concentrating. You going to be able to take care of him?"

What? Oh, God, she must be assuming we lived together and that I'd be there when he got out. I wasn't about to argue now. "Uh, sure. How long before he'll be able to return to work?" I asked. I had a feeling that if he couldn't, or even if he had to sit out for a long time, he might go crazy.

"Hard to say. A month, maybe? Depends on how quickly he recovers—there's a lot of variability, so I won't try to guess. You should make sure he doesn't try to do too much too soon."

"I'll do my best. Can I go back in now?"

"Sure. I've given him something to keep him comfortable for a bit longer, but we have to keep him awake. He might be a bit loopy."

I glanced at Marty and then went back into the room. "Hey, Nell, you look good." He grinned at me. Must be a great painkiller.

I took his hand again. "Hey yourself. Your doctor says you'll be fine, and they might let you out tomorrow, or the day after."

"That's good. What happened to my gun?"

"I think the police have it. It's evidence."

"Oh, right. I want it back."

"James, you don't need it right now."

"I guess not. Maybe tomorrow."

"James, I'm going to go home for a little while now, but I'll be back tomorrow." I wasn't sure he understood what I was saying, or if he'd remember in three minutes.

So I was surprised when he said, "Nell?"

"Yes, James?"

"You sure you're all right? You weren't hurt?"

"I'm fine, James. You kept me safe."

"Good. I'll see you later."

I rejoined Marty in the hallway. "I'm ready to go. Which way?"

We found an elevator that led to the main lobby. No newshounds in sight, and nobody seemed to recognize me. Once outside, Marty led me to her car, parked nearby, and now festooned with a couple of parking tickets. She removed them and pitched them into the backseat. "Next stop, Bryn Mawr."

CHAPTER 32

I think I fell asleep as soon as I was belted in. I didn't wake up until she shook my shoulder. When I opened my eyes I realized we were in front of my house. "That was fast. Thanks, Marty."

"Don't thank me just yet. I'm coming in with you. There are some things we need to talk about."

That didn't sound promising. I fished my keys out of my bag and managed to get my front door open. Marty brushed past me as I was trying to extricate my key from the lock.

"You got anything to eat here?" Marty said, making a beeline for my tiny kitchen.

"Uh, I don't know?" It seemed like days since I'd been home. Or eaten a meal.

Marty was muttering to herself as she rummaged through my cabinets. "Olive oil, pasta, garlic, cheese— okay, I think I've got it." She turned to me and spoke up. "How about anything to drink?"

"Wine in the fridge, hard stuff in the cabinet next to the dining table." Should I be concerned that I knew I had alcohol but wasn't sure about food?

"Right," Marty called out. "Go take a shower. Food'll be ready by the time you come back."

I followed her orders, marveling at how Marty had taken over my house, and why. Nonetheless, the shower felt wonderful, and I let the water run until it turned cold. Maybe I couldn't scrub off the last twenty-four hours, but at least I'd be clean enough to face what was coming. I toweled off and pulled on cotton shorts and a tee shirt.

When I came down the stairs, Marty handed me a filled wineglass and told me to sit at my table. Arguing would take too much energy, so I sat. Three minutes later, she emerged from my kitchen with two large steaming bowls that smelled wonderful. She set one in front of me, then set the other at the end of the table and sat down in front of it. "Eat," she said. I ate.

After I'd consumed most of the bowl of food, Marty took a critical look at me and said, "Okay, you look half-way human again. Like I said, there are things we have to talk about."

Ominous start to any conversation. I took a swallow of wine and said, "Like what?"

"Like Jimmy."

Of course. "Marty, I thought you agreed not to meddle."

"I changed my mind. I've been watching you two, and I think you both need a swift kick. What do you think you're doing?"

"We're taking it slowly."

"Yeah, right, like a glacier. Heck, even the glaciers

move faster these days. Look, yesterday he almost died. You spent the night next to him holding his hand and hoping he'd wake up, which, let me tell you, wasn't a sure thing. Doesn't that mean anything to you?"

"Of course it does!" I protested, trying to stifle the memory of James's blood running warm through my fingers. "So?"

Marty cocked her head and looked at me with something like pity. "Nell, you are in such deep denial. Didn't I hear somewhere that you'd been married before?"

I really was having trouble following her train of thought. "What's that got to do with anything? Marty, why are we talking about this?"

"Because I care about you, and I care about Jimmy, and I have to wonder what your problem is."

I shrugged. "I was married, it didn't work out, end of story. He didn't beat me or cheat on me, if that's what you're wondering. Things just didn't turn out the way we'd expected. No hard feelings on either side."

Marty slapped the table, hard, and I jumped. "That's the point! Doesn't that bother you that you could let it end so easily? That your husband mattered so little to you? Nell, don't you see that you're taking the easy route—no risks? And that's not going to work for much longer. You've got to *give* more. What the hell are you so scared of?"

Ah, well, that was the question, wasn't it? Here we sat in my careful crafted little home, which had room for only one person. My hidey-hole, built to suit me and only me. Not even a cat, for God's sake. And that was the way I had wanted it.

And, damn her, she was right about my emotional life,

too: I'd made safe, boring choices, unwilling to get hurt again.

Until James had come along. He knew my relationship history. He was willing to take his time, or let me take mine. Did I want more with him? I had begun to think the answer was yes, but I had no clue how to make that happen. And then the disaster at the Water Works had happened.

Marty was still watching, silently, letting me work through this. Now she said softly, "How did you feel when he went down?"

I shut my eyes and something inside me tore. I opened my eyes in tears. "I was terrified. Not for myself—somehow it never occurred to me that I might die there. But I realized that if I didn't do anything, then James would die, and I couldn't let that happen. He told me to leave, and I couldn't. I had to do something, so I shot Nicholas."

Marty sat back in her chair. "Interesting answer. I think you're getting closer to the truth. Were you worried that somebody was going to blame you for screwing up? Or is there more? Come on, Nell—you can say it."

"I didn't want to lose him," I whispered, almost to myself. "I love him."

Marty didn't answer, but she raised her glass to me.

CHAPTER 33

The evening wound down shortly after that. Marty had squeezed from me the answer she wanted to hear, and now I felt empty. She announced that she was spending the night on my couch because it was late and it had been a long day and she didn't feel like driving back to the city. Reading between the lines, I wondered if she thought she'd been too hard on me and was afraid to leave me alone. I didn't argue—I was glad for her company—and too tired to argue. I headed for the stairs, but stopped on the first step and turned to face her.

"Marty? Thank you." Then I went up the stairs to my bedroom, fell into bed, and was out like a light.

I woke up with the sun and lay in bed, trying to piece together my life. Today was Saturday, or at least I thought it was. I would have to deal with the press today, so I couldn't just hide out here wearing my jammies and eating ice cream. Not that I would anyway: I was going back to see James. I was going to spend as much time with James as he and the hospital would let me. And after he was out of the hospital.

Marty had been brutal the night before, but she hadn't been wrong. When had I slid into taking the easy way out? Did I really think that little of myself?

Apparently the answer was yes, and Marty had recognized that. What was I waiting for to commit? James was a terrific guy. He cared about me, and he'd shown it. And when he lay bleeding under my hands, something had changed—I just hadn't allowed myself the time to think about it until Marty had all but rubbed my nose in it. If he had died, I would have been devastated.

But I had a second chance, and if I didn't take advantage of it, I didn't deserve any sympathy—or James. I was scared to death of screwing this up, but I wouldn't be able to live with myself if I didn't try.

Practical considerations: the hospital would release him, today or tomorrow, and all he had to look forward to was his rather spartan apartment in Philadelphia. No matter how much he might protest, he wouldn't be in any shape to take care of himself for at least a few days, and he needed somebody to watch for problems. So what was I going to do about it?

I was taking charge of the situation. I just needed to work out how. Bring him here? But then if I went to work, he'd be stuck out here. Therefore I'd have to stay at his place, which would enable me to spend time at work but still get to him quickly if he needed something.

The press was going to start digging into the Nicholas story. There was no way to stop it. What a shame no one had gotten pictures of our deadly tableau on the banks of the Schuylkill. I had to figure out how to spin the story to the Society's advantage. Daring Heroine Saves the Day? (or at least Saves the Life of FBI Agent?) *Nell Pratt, president of the Pennsylvania Antiquarian Society, fought off an armed killer to save the life of FBI Special Agent James Morrison in a deadly confrontation at the Philadelphia Water Works.* Part of me cringed at the idea of being the focus of that kind of attention (and I was pretty sure that James would hate it, too), but the president side of me said it was what was best for the Society. My shy side would just have to suck it up.

I heard thumps from downstairs and deduced Marty was stirring. Time to get moving. I found my shorts and tee, slipped on flip-flops, and went down the stairs.

"Coffee?" I asked to the lump on the couch that was Marty.

"Please. Pretty please. Why are you so bloody cheerful this early?"

"Because you finally explained to me what was wrong with my life, and today I am going to start fixing it."

"Wonderful," Marty muttered, then untangled herself from the blanket and stumbled toward the bathroom.

I went to the kitchen, where I made coffee. By the time the French press had done its thing, Marty was back, looking more alert.

"Seriously? You're not mad at me?" Marty said. "Because I was pretty blunt with you. And I was scared, too, about Jimmy. That was too close for comfort."

"Marty, I know you're right and I needed to hear it. And I know you have my best interests at heart. And James's."

"You mean you'd tell me if you thought I was wrong?"

I nodded. "You want food?"

"Of course. I think I saw some English muffins hiding in there."

When we had all the components of breakfast, we sat at the table. I decided to start the ball rolling. "Marty, we have to get ahead of the press story. Do you have a relative at the *Inquirer*? Or the local news stations?"

"You have to ask?"

"Then call him or her or them and let's see if we can promise them a full story for the Sunday edition for the paper, and maybe the Sunday morning news shows. Tell me where to be and I'll show up and spin my heart out. Just make sure they clear the facts with the FBI."

"I love it. Is that all?"

"No. Whenever the hospital lets James go, he's going to need some help. I assume he's not going to go back to Mom and Dad's and let them baby him?"

Marty swallowed a laugh. "I think he'd eat glass before he did that. What's your idea?"

"I'll take care of him. It doesn't make sense to park him out here, but I can stay at his place for as long as he needs me. Think he'll object?"

"Unlikely. Or it will be once he tries to stand up and realizes how helpless he is. You okay with changing bandages and that yucky stuff?"

"I'd better be. If not, I'll find a visiting nurse or someone like that to take care of that part of things, and let the FBI foot the bills. But I'll be there."

Marty sat back in her chair and contemplated me with a smile. "Wow! When you decide to change things, you don't mess around. Okay, you've gotta know the news was all over this, but so far nobody at the Society has said anything publicly. I alerted the Society board that it was coming, so they weren't caught by surprise, but we all agreed that you should be the sole spokesperson. So you've got to get out there and do it—fast. And you'll tell it so you look like you saved the day, right?"

"Of course. If I'm going to keep stumbling into crimes, I might as well make it work for me, and for the Society. Go ahead and set up the interviews for later this afternoon, will you? We can meet at the Society. I think I should talk to the interviewers in the reading room, because it looks less snobby than my office, but it's still impressive—shows off the Society well."

Marty straightened her back and saluted. "Yes, ma'am! Right away, ma'am!"

I fixed her with an eagle eye and she relaxed. "Okay, I'll do it. You'll be seeing Jimmy before that?"

"Yes. I'll find out when they're letting him go and plan from there."

I drank my coffee and listened with half an ear while Marty made arrangements over the phone to meet a journalist and a photographer later in the afternoon, in time to make the deadline for the Sunday local news section, and then she talked to various people at the local network affiliates. I dressed smartly because I needed to look like someone who was in charge. And who could shoot. In a way I hated to go public with that, but if it made it a better story . . .

CHAPTER 34

Marty left for the city before I did, since she still had to change clothes—no way was she going to miss my big interview. Before I went out the door to my car, I took a look around at my home, most of which I could see from where I was standing. It was so small. If it was the extent of my personal universe, it was kind of sad. But I had a feeling that would be changing.

In the city, I parked in the lot across from the Society and walked the few blocks over to Jefferson Hospital. Without knocking I walked into James's room and shut the door behind me.

He was half sitting, trying to read a battered paperback that some pitying soul must have handed him, with a pair of reading glasses perched on his nose. I found it both sweet and funny that he had never revealed to me that he needed glasses. He must have had them in his pocket all along. Still pale, but he looked better—so much better.

He looked up when I entered and did what was nearly a double take, as far as his aching head permitted. "Nell? Why so dressed up?"

"You've seen me cleaned up before."

"Of course I have. I guess I expected you to look, I don't know, a bit more casual."

I approached the bed. "May I?"

"Sit? Of course." He scooted over a bit, but not without wincing, I noted.

"It won't hurt you?"

"I'll survive. Sit, please."

I sat. "The reason for the fancy duds is that Marty has set up an interview with a reporter from the *Inquirer*, and a couple of others. I thought it was important to get my side of the story out before the press twists it beyond recognition. I doubt that I'll be able to keep you out of it, but I'll make sure your boss knows what's happening. But the focus of this piece is the Society and its take-charge leader—me."

"I don't need the publicity, but I can see that it's a good strategy for you."

"We'll see." I wondered if I would need to define our relationship for the population of the greater Philadelphia area. Was there a code word for "significant relationship?" I guess I was going to wing it. "How are you feeling?"

"Stiff. Some bruises that I didn't notice before. My arm hurts, but not half as much as my head. The last nurse promised me I could walk to the bathroom later today, if I was a good boy."

"Sounds promising. When will they turn you loose?"

"Tomorrow morning, it looks like. They want to be very, very sure that my head will not fall off."

A sense of humor was a good sign, wasn't it? "I'm coming home with you," I said in a tone that I hoped brooked no argument.

"What?"

"You shouldn't be alone for the next couple of days. I'll stay at your place." His eyes searched my face, and I held his gaze. "James, I want to do this," I said softly. "Please."

He finally nodded, and his mouth twitched. "I won't promise it will be pretty. I've already discovered I'm a lousy patient."

"You never knew that?"

He shook his head. "I've never been a patient in a hospital before. No childhood crises, no broken bones, no bullets. Obviously it was just a matter of time, although the Bowie knife thing kind of surprised me. That should up my reputation at the Agency." He studied my face again. "You're sure?"

"I am."

We kind of smiled stupidly at each other for a few moments, until James asked, "Is there more?"

"Kind of. Nothing awful," I rushed to add, "but Marty took me home last night and pointed out some basic truths. They weren't nice to hear, but she was right. What it comes down to is that I've been coasting along, getting by on 'good enough' but not really trying."

I plunged on. "I've been deluding myself about my relationships—about us. What I thought was being cool and in control was mainly a way to protect myself. If I didn't invest myself fully in a relationship, it wouldn't hurt as much when it didn't work out. I was expecting them to fail from the start, so of course they did." I stopped and swallowed; I was getting to the difficult part. "I don't want that with you, James. That became very clear at the Water Works. I didn't want you to die until we'd figured out what we have. I wasn't going to let Nicholas or anyone else make that decision for me. If this doesn't work out, I want it to be because one of us says so, not because we didn't try."

"I wondered when you'd figure it out," James said, with a half smile.

"What, you were waiting for me to do the work? You might have given me a shove, you know."

"As far as I know—and I'll admit I'm no expert— that's not how it works. If I told you what to do, you might have walked away. You have to want it as much as I do."

"Oh," I whispered. "I don't deserve you." I swallowed the large lump in my throat. "Well, the old me doesn't deserve you, but maybe the new me will." I leaned over, careful to avoid the bandages and miscellaneous attachments, and kissed him gently. Then I pulled back an inch or two and we smiled at each other.

At which moment, a nurse bustled in and didn't look the least embarrassed by our behavior. "Sorry, gotta take the vitals, you know."

"You go right ahead," I said, standing up and glancing at my watch. "I've got to get back to the Society. You think I should call your boss and give him a heads-up about the article?"

"Let me do it. He owes me, so now's the best time to cash in on that. You go and give one hell of an interview."

I smiled. "I plan to. And let me know if you come up

with a good nickname for me, if I'm going to be Philadelphia's new protector of the arts. 'History-Woman'
doesn't have much of a ring to it. Will you be my side-
kick? Because I think we make a good team."

"We do."

CHAPTER 35

I was walking back toward the Society when my cell phone rang. It was an unfamiliar number. I answered anyway and was mildly shocked to hear Agent Cooper's voice.

"I understand from Agent Morrison that you are planning to speak to the press today?"

"Yes, I am." I thought about adding something defensive and then stopped myself. He had called me. What did he want?

"I'll assume I can't dissuade you, but may I ask you to be discreet?"

"You mean, not make the FBI look like a bunch of idiots for missing this? I wouldn't do that. I will tell the press that this case was solved through the joint efforts of Agent Morrison and myself. I don't need to go into details—like the fact that your office refused to get involved until the last minute. My main goal is to cast the

Society in the most positive light possible. Do you have a problem with that?"

I thought I heard him sigh. "Thank you. I appreciate your tact. I was wondering if you'd like to be present when we interview Nicholas Naylor?"

Would I! I controlled the excitement in my voice when I said, "When will this take place?"

"Momentarily. He's still in the hospital at Penn but he's been medically cleared for this interview."

I thought quickly. Marty had set up the *Inquirer* interview for four, and we couldn't push it any later or we'd risk missing the deadline for the Sunday edition. But it was important to me to hear what Nicholas had to say, and I might even be able to help out with the right questions. Of course, maybe Agent Cooper was hoping to delay me long enough to miss my own interview. But what the hell—I could make it to Penn by cab, and then be back in time for the interview. "I'm on my way."

I hung up, then immediately hit Marty's number. When she answered, I said quickly, "Small change in plans. The FBI, apparently in exchange for not skewering them in the press, has invited me to sit in when they interview Nicholas, any minute now. I can leave there in time to get back for the interview at the Society."

"You damn well better not leave me holding the bag. I'll come pick you up. Good luck with the FBI bigwigs. How's James doing?"

"Surprisingly well, and he didn't even argue with me about coming home with him."

"Amazing—you've turned him to mush. Or maybe it's the drugs. I might drop by the hospital and say hello to him."

"You do that. I've got to go. See you later!" I hung

up, then picked up my pace toward Broad Street, where I knew there would be taxis. A taxi would definitely be faster than extracting my car and driving over, and now I had a ride back.

At the hospital, I had to jump through a few hoops to gain access to the floor where Nicholas was being held. I was relieved when I emerged from the elevator and saw Agent Cooper waiting for me.

"Ms. Pratt? Let me explain how this is going to work." We began a slow stroll down the hall while he talked. At the end of the hall there was a man standing outside one of the doors. It was all too easy to identify him as an FBI agent, both by the suit and by the way he snapped to attention when he saw Cooper. "We have not spoken to Mr. Naylor at any length yet. We are assured that his wound is not life-threatening, and that the pain relief he has received has not impaired his judgment. Since you know him, you may be able to confirm his mental state."

"Are you going to let me talk to him?"

Agent Cooper cleared his throat. "That would be, uh, highly unusual. I can't allow you to interview a suspect in the FBI's custody, but I'll confess that there are aspects of this case that lie outside our expertise. For example, can you explain who this Edwin Forrest is?"

I sighed. Poor Edwin. "How long do you have, and how much do you need to know?"

"Perhaps we could get a cup of coffee and you could give me an outline?"

"Fair enough."

Agent Cooper signaled to another agent who was trying to blend into the woodwork and failing, and asked him to find coffee for us. Then he escorted me to a small waiting room on the same floor. "What do I need to know about this Forrest, and why is he so important to Naylor?"

I launched into a brief history of Edwin Forrest, his Philadelphia origins, his role in theater of the nineteenth century, and his will and the subsequent creation of the trust. Agent Cooper didn't interrupt but made notes on a small notebook. When I reached the point at which I had entered this story, I said, "I hired Nicholas about three months ago to replace an employee who died unexpectedly. Nicholas had been working at Penn, and he came highly recommended. What I hadn't realized then was that Penn has an extensive collection of Forrest correspondence and memorabilia, as does the Society. I understand now that Nicholas was mining our collections for evidence to support his claim to whatever is left of the Forrest Trust's assets."

"Does he have any legitimate claim?"

"I'm not a lawyer so I can't say, but he claims he's descended from a woman who was Forrest's, uh, love child"—that sounded so much better than bastard—"and who was mentioned in his will. In any case, he believes he has a claim and in his mind that justified his actions."

"Which were?"

"According to what he told me when we were at the Water Works, seeking out members of the Forrest Trust and asking them to support his claim. And when they turned him down, he killed them, hoping that their replacements might be more agreeable."

"I see. How did the conflict at the Water Works come about?"

"Nicholas and I went there on Society business, to speak to one of the administrators about an unrelated project I had asked him to do some research for. I called James to tell him that Nicholas was at the Water Works with me."

Cooper nodded once. "Thank you. In sum, you're telling me that Naylor is obsessed with this supposed connection to Forrest, whether it's true or not, and I take it that there is a substantial financial reward if he can prove it. Correct?"

"Yes," I said, "and the trustees he killed were standing in his way, or so he thought."

"I am not a profiler, but I'd guess that he's suffering from some kind of delusional disorder, and he believes that he has the right to do whatever it takes to achieve his goals. The trustees who turned him down were no more than inconveniences, in his eyes."

"May I talk to him?" I asked again.

"I suppose you've earned that right. I'll give you a few minutes with him, off the record, and then we'll proceed with the official interview, which will, of course, be recorded. You may observe that if you choose. And I'd like to ask if we may call on you for clarification of any points that come up, such as the Forrest information."

"I will be happy to do that." I hesitated a moment, but figured I'd never have a better chance to satisfy my curiosity. "Why didn't you pursue this investigation sooner? You could have saved a couple of lives."

"I regret that. When Agent Morrison brought the matter to my attention, I thought the evidence was thin to nonexistent, and I couldn't afford to allocate any of our resources to it. It was a poor decision on my part, in hindsight. In no way does this reflect poorly on Agent

Morrison's abilities, if that's your concern. I'm willing to put that in his record. He's a good agent, and a good man."

And that was probably the best we could hope for from the FBI. "I agree. Can I see Nicholas now?"

"Of course." He led the way back down the hall and I followed. I wasn't sure what I was hoping for, or why I'd even asked. Maybe I wanted closure. Maybe I wanted one last look at Nicholas, to see if there was any outward evidence of the evil inside him. He could have killed me, and he had nearly succeeded with James.

Outside the door, Agent Cooper stopped and gestured me toward the room. I took a deep breath and walked in.

Nicholas was seated in a hospital bed, its top half slanted up. Even though his leg was swathed with bandages, there was a handcuff attached to one of his wrists and to the side rail of the bed. He looked surprised to see me. "Nell? What are you doing here?"

"I've been filling in the FBI about Edwin Forrest. And you."

"Oh. Of course. I'm sorry about what happened. I didn't mean to hurt that agent, but I was startled, and I guess I overreacted. Is he all right?"

"He will be." I perched on a chair. "Nicholas, why was this so important to you? Is it the money?"

He looked at me with no expression. "The money was part of it. But there was a matter of honor. Elizabeth Welsh bore an illegitimate child, at a time when that meant something. She may well have loved Edwin Forrest, and she may have been content with what little he chose to give her. But the man had a monstrous ego. He wanted to be remembered, and that's why he funded the Edwin Forrest Home rather than leaving his estate to his only child. I was trying to right that wrong. And I think I put together a good case. I was ready to go to the courts, and I think I would have won. And then I learned that the trustees wanted to dissolve the trust, and I knew I had to act quickly."

"Nicholas, you murdered six people," I whispered.

His expression didn't change. I looked at the moderately handsome, demonstrably intelligent man in front of me. He should have had a rich life ahead of him. Instead, out of a warped sense of entitlement, he had killed several innocent people. Worse, he didn't see anything wrong with that. There was no way he could ever explain that to me. I stood up again. "Good-bye, Nicholas." I turned and walked out, and he didn't call out after me.

"I'm done here," I told Agent Cooper.

"Give James my best wishes," he called out after my retreating back. I kept going.

I called Marty on my way down the elevator. She said she was already circling the block and she would meet me at the main entrance.

"That was fast. How'd it go?" she asked, as she pulled out of the hospital driveway.

"As well as I could hope, I guess. I talked to Nicholas."

"Really? And?"

"He makes me sad. All that ability and potential, wasted because of an obsession. And he still doesn't understand why what he did was wrong. There's something missing inside him."

CHAPTER 36

The interview with the *Inquirer* went well, or at least I thought so, and I'd taped a couple of short segments for the news broadcasts. I had been as open as I could be, given the constraints on what I could say. I hadn't ducked talking about any of the Society's recent messes—there was no point anyway, since they'd gotten plenty of media attention. I was upbeat, positive, and forward-looking. I said in every possible way that the Society had hit a few bumps in the road lately, but we'd survived over a hundred years and we were aiming for at least a hundred more. I came away feeling like I had aced the big exam. Marty and I had a quick dinner, and I went home and crashed.

Of course, the proof was in the pudding, or the printing, or something like that, so I waited with bated breath until my Sunday paper arrived at dawn, hitting my front door with a solid *thunk*. I picked it up, but before I could bring myself to strip off the plastic bag and look at it, I sent up a silent prayer. We deserved a break, didn't we? At least I thought so.

Inside, I moved with silent deliberation to pour myself a second cup of coffee. I sat down at the table, awash in bright sunshine, and carefully laid out the paper, section by section. I finally pulled out the local news section, smoothing it with my hand.

Yes, there was the article, front page below the fold, four columns wide, with a picture of me, as well as one of the facade of the Society, with a large headline "Museum Administrator Caught in Gun Battle." I read the article slowly, word by word, and at the end I sighed with relief. It was accurate, on point, and fair. Nobody had been slandered or misrepresented, or even sensationalized. I came across as serious and responsible, and I sounded reasonably intelligent. James's role and that of the FBI were mentioned only in passing. It was all I could have asked for, all things considered.

Of course the phone rang the minute I finished reading. Marty. When I picked up, she said without preamble, "What did you think?"

"I thought it was well done. I should send that relative of yours a box of candy or flowers or something."

"Already did. In case you're wondering, it's not a close relative, and we've had our differences in the past. So you're the one who pulled this off. I was just the go-between. You should feel proud."

"I do. And grateful."

"What's the plan for today?"

"I'm going to go sit with James until they discharge him, and then I'm taking him home."

"Need any help?"

I didn't need to think about that. "Thanks for offering, but I'm doing this by myself."

"You do know he's going to be pretty wiped out? Even if he doesn't realize that?"

"I do. Don't worry, Marty—I know this may be difficult. But if you . . . care about somebody, that shouldn't change just because they're sick or cranky, or both." *Still ducking the L word, eh, Nell?*

Marty chuckled. "I think you're catching on. How about this: I'll stock his refrigerator so you won't have to go out again, once you get there. He may sleep a lot, so take a book along."

I had trouble picturing Marty nurturing anybody, but her heart was in the right place. "The food is a good idea, and thank you. You have a key?"

"I do—I'll leave mine there for you. I won't be needing it anymore."

"Thanks for everything, Marty." Starting with introducing me to James.

"You'll be at work tomorrow?"

"All things willing, yes."

"So I'll see you then. Don't rush—I'll alert Eric to what's going on, if he hasn't already figured it out, and I'll tell him to set up a staff meeting."

"Great. I've got to get going now."

"Give my love to Jimmy, and tell him to follow doctor's orders. And yours. Bye!"

Showered and dressed, I started throwing clothes and other necessary items into a bag to take along. For how long? It wasn't as though I was leaving my house forever, just long enough to get James back on his feet. After that? That was still open to negotiation, for both of us.

I drove into the city and parked near the hospital, easy to do on a Sunday. As I walked toward the entrance, I had to admit I was a little jittery. I'd put on a brave face with Marty, but I had little experience with nursing or caregiving. I couldn't even keep a plant alive, because I couldn't remember to water it. I was blessed with a strong constitution, so I rarely got sick, and when I did I usually recovered quickly; like James, I had no experience with afflictions that required hospitals. Now I'd volunteered to take care of a man who had been stabbed and had nearly split his head open, who was being released by the hospital into my care. I wasn't sure that was a smart thing for the hospital to do.

But I'd promised, and I kept my promises. I walked into the hospital, took the elevator upstairs, and approached James's door, my pace slowing the closer I came. The door was wedged partway open, for ventilation—or had he asked, so he could watch for me? Why was my heart pounding?

I got as far as the doorway and then stopped. There he was, still on the bed but at least more or less dressed, like he was waiting. For me. Marty must have brought him some clothes to replace the blood-soaked ones, because the sweats he was wearing looked familiar. James turned as soon as he heard me, and our eyes locked for an endless minute.

"You came."

"Of course I did. Did you expect me to change my mind?"

"I would have understood if you did. This won't be easy."

"I know. I don't expect it to be easy."

I crossed the distance between the door and the bed in two strides. I would have flung myself into his arms, except I didn't think that was a good idea given the number of stitches he'd received, so I stopped at the bed. But he wouldn't accept that, and pulled me into his arms—gingerly. I realized I was crying when I saw tears splashing on his sweatshirt. I pulled away and scrubbed at my face.

"I don't know why I'm crying."

"It's okay."

I fumbled in my bag for a tissue, not to blot tears but because I really needed to blow my nose. We were off to a great start.

"Did you see the article in the paper?" I asked.

"I made some unlucky orderly track down a copy as soon as I woke up. It really puts you in a good light."

"Thank you. I was channeling some strong and wise woman who wasn't me. But I agree—no complaints. Are they still going to let you go this morning?"

"They're willing to discharge me as long as there's someone around to look after me. That would be you, for the record. They are going to hand you a stack of instructions and prescriptions and I have no idea what else and make you swear you will do what they tell you to do or they'll wash their hands of any responsibility. And I will complain and moan every step of the way and do it anyway. I hurt. I'm hungry and thirsty and I want a shave. But we will get through this."

I believed him.

We started the long and convoluted process of discharge, signing documents left and right, and after what seemed like a week later we were ready to go. The hospital insisted that James leave in a wheelchair, and he was looking kind of strained anyway, and I had to go get my car. The attendant promised to wait with him on the sidewalk while I pulled around the building, and then when I arrived he helped James into the front seat and went back inside with the wheelchair. James was lying back against the headrest, his eyes closed.

"James," I said carefully, "how many steps are there up to your apartment?"

"Shit," was his only answer. I remembered at least two flights. "Just go, will you?"

I drove carefully to University City, where he lived, avoiding potholes—no easy task in Center City. At least there was a parking space in front of his building.

Somehow we made it up the stairs. It took fifteen minutes, and by the time we reached his apartment James's face was grey and he was sweating. I think my face was red, and I was sweating, too. His balance was definitely not all that it should be, but at least he hadn't fallen down the stairs.

"Keys?" I said.

"Left pocket," he said, making no move to retrieve them. He leaned against the wall while I fished in his pocket, then opened the door.

He made it a few feet in from the door, then stopped and stood swaying, like a tree ready to fall. I slipped under his uninjured arm. "You're doing fine." We made it to the bedroom, and he toppled on the bed. As far as I was concerned, that was more than enough exertion for one day, so I told him to rest, then pulled his shoes off, and threw a light blanket over him. He was asleep before

I tiptoed out of the room, pulling the door partway closed behind me.

I was exhausted myself, and I couldn't begin to imagine how he felt. I had no idea what to do next. I supposed I should check to see if Marty had delivered the promised food: a quick peek in the refrigerator confirmed that. I should go retrieve my own bag from the car, but it wasn't exactly urgent. I should read through all the hospital materials in a more leisurely and focused manner—but I'd left them in the car, too. In the end I said the hell with all of it, and lay down and took a nap.

It was late afternoon when I woke up with a start and immediately felt guilty. Fine caregiver I made. I listened, but didn't hear any sound coming from James's room. Or rather, no unusual sound; a light snoring let me know he was alive. I should jump up now and make chicken soup or something. Was he supposed to eat lightly, or had he already passed that stage of things? I needed the hospital's instructions. With a resigned sigh, I looked for the keys that Marty had said she would leave for me. They were in plain sight on the kitchen counter, but they were holding down an envelope with my name on it. A sticky note, in Marty's handwriting, read, "Louisa sent this over this morning." Somehow I didn't think it was a get-well card. I opened the envelope—nice, heavyweight stock—and pulled out the single page inside, written in a strong, slanting hand. I read it, and then I reread it, since I had trouble taking it in.

Martha has conveyed to me the difficulties you encountered on behalf of members of the Forrest Trust. I believe I can speak for the remaining trustees

when I offer you the most sincere thanks for what you
have done.

    As you have reason to know, the trustees have
decided that the time has come to dissolve the trust
and distribute its assets, since it no longer serves
Edwin Forrest's original intentions. We have already
drafted a tentative list of proposed recipients, but I
believe that it would be appropriate, under the
circumstances, to offer the Society the items for which
it is already custodian, including the monumental
statue of Edwin in the role of Coriolanus, along with
sufficient funds to catalog and maintain the collection.
If this gift taxes your resources, you may feel free to
decline the offer. In any event, please accept our
heartfelt appreciation.

It was signed Louisa Babcock.

Oh, my. I stared at the note in my hand, reread it, and
began to laugh. When I'd been fending off Nicholas's
attack and fighting to save James, collections acquisition
had been the furthest thing from my mind, yet here was
the result. The world definitely moved in mysterious ways.
And I'd get to keep Edwin's statue at the Society, which
pleased me ridiculously.

Still laughing, I picked up the keys, went down to my
car, and retrieved everything I hadn't brought upstairs
already. I let myself in, but apparently not quietly enough,
because James called out, "Nell?"

I dropped my bags and papers and hurried to the bedroom. "Are you all right?"

"I thought you'd gone." He was only half awake, and
he sounded like a little boy. It broke my heart. I crossed

to the bed and carefully lay down on his uninjured side. "I'm here, James. I'm not going anywhere."

He wrapped one arm around me and went back to sleep.

I laid my hand on his chest, over his heart. Strong and regular.

This might actually work.